D0389700

...my dear..., for ... ...

...for you, dear son ...

...ance brave ...

...you are the immortal her...

...to some as Tsepesh; to...

...f the Devil. Let me sta...

...it is there this record b...

...e Stefan, taken from me...

...taken from me the sam...

...ortal heir of an immortal m...

...e Impaler; known to others ...

...tact, then, with the mom...

...l best begins. I write this f...

...me the same day as your...

...day as my life. For you are...

...: Vlad, known to some as...

...racul, son of the Devil. L...

...death, for it is there this...

...son, dear Stefan, taken f...

...ther, taken from me the...

CHILDREN OF THE
VAMPIRE

CHILDREN OF THE VAMPIRE

THE DIARIES OF THE FAMILY DRACUL

JEANNE KALOGRIDIS

Delacorte Press

Published by
Delacorte Press
Bantam Doubleday Dell Publishing Group, Inc.
1540 Broadway
New York, New York 10036

Copyright © 1995 by Jeanne Kalogridis

All rights reserved. No part of this book may be reproduced or
transmitted in any form or by any means, electronic or mechanical,
including photocopying, recording, or by any information storage and
retrieval system, without the written permission of the Publisher,
except where permitted by law.

The trademark Delacorte Press® is registered in the U.S. Patent
and Trademark Office.

Library of Congress Cataloging in Publication Data

Kalogridis, Jeanne.
Children of the vampire / by Jeanne Kalogridis.
p.   cm.
ISBN 0-385-31412-4
I. Title.
PS3561.A41675C48   1995
813'.54—dc20   95-16602
CIP

Designed by Nancy B. Field

Manufactured in the United States of America
Published simultaneously in Canada

October 1995

10 9 8 7 6 5 4 3 2 1

BVG

For S.

ACKNOWLEDGMENTS

This book would not appear in its current incarnation without the help of the following people:

My beloved consort, George, who gently holds my hand through every obnoxious phase of the creative process and provides right-brained solutions to all my left-brained plot problems. Without his intelligence, patience, steadfast love, and annoying fucking sense of humor, life wouldn't be anywhere near as fun.

My cousin, Laeta, a nova-brilliant writer whose first drafts I am not worthy to lick. Laeta, thank you so, so much for your swift insights on the book, and for the inspired ending. I couldn't have finished this without you.

My dear friend, Kathy O'Malley. Thanks, Kath, for your constant love, encouragement, and wise suggestions.

My editor, Kristin Kiser. Kristin, thanks for putting up with me; I know it hasn't been easy. Thanks, too, for your cheerful patience and enormous hard work. I *promise* the next one won't be this late.

My erstwhile editor, Jeanne Cavelos. Thanks, O Evil and Debauched Twin, for the comments and inspiration.

My agent, Russell Galen. Thank you, Russ, for always being there, always being the consummate professional, and always bringing me gently back to my senses no matter how wildly I rant and rave.

Friend and facilitator, Renee Martinez. Thanks, Renee, for all those long, gruesome discussions, and for those ideas you cheerfully offered and I cheerfully stole. . . .

Friend and laughing yogini, Suza Francina, who provided information about Holland and the Dutch language—and the yoga lessons that brought amazing relief from pain after hours scrunched over the computer.

Radu Florescu and Raymond T. McNally, whose work *Dracula: Prince of Many Faces* has served as an extremely useful reference in the creation of the *Family Dracul* novels.

But the greatest debt of gratitude is due my beautiful mother, whose patience, graciousness, love, and faith in the midst of suffering has served as a beacon for us all.

DRACUL FAMILY TREE

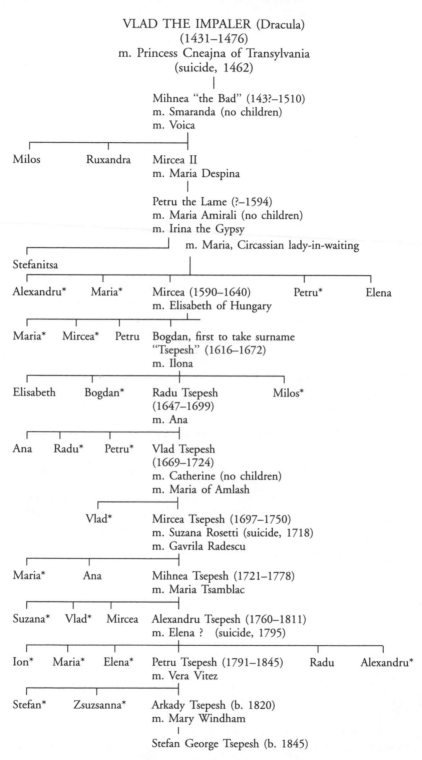

VLAD THE IMPALER (Dracula)
(1431–1476)
m. Princess Cneajna of Transylvania
(suicide, 1462)

Mihnea "the Bad" (143?–1510)
m. Smaranda (no children)
m. Voica

Milos   Ruxandra   Mircea II
m. Maria Despina

Petru the Lame (?–1594)
m. Maria Amirali (no children)
m. Irina the Gypsy
m. Maria, Circassian lady-in-waiting

Stefanitsa

Alexandru*   Maria*   Mircea (1590–1640)   Petru*   Elena
m. Elisabeth of Hungary

Maria*   Mircea*   Petru   Bogdan, first to take surname
"Tsepesh" (1616–1672)
m. Ilona

Elisabeth   Bogdan*   Radu Tsepesh   Milos*
(1647–1699)
m. Ana

Ana   Radu*   Petru*   Vlad Tsepesh
(1669–1724)
m. Catherine (no children)
m. Maria of Amlash

Vlad*   Mircea Tsepesh (1697–1750)
m. Suzana Rosetti (suicide, 1718)
m. Gavrila Radescu

Maria*   Ana   Mihnea Tsepesh (1721–1778)
m. Maria Tsamblac

Suzana*   Vlad*   Mircea   Alexandru Tsepesh (1760–1811)
m. Elena ? (suicide, 1795)

Ion*   Maria*   Elena*   Petru Tsepesh (1791–1845)   Radu   Alexandru*
m. Vera Vitez

Stefan*   Zsuzsanna*   Arkady Tsepesh (b. 1820)
m. Mary Windham

Stefan George Tsepesh (b. 1845)

*Died in childhood or born afflicted w/ physical or mental deformity

Loosely adapted from Radu R. Florescu & Raymond T. McNally, *Dracula: Prince of Many Faces,* (Boston: Little, Brown, 1989).

May your own blood rise against you.
—ancient Wexford curse

The Testament of Dunya Moroz

Excerpted from the
Journal of Mary Windham Tsepesh

17 April 1845. I then asked her to explain more fully the covenant, the *Schwur* of which she had spoken. She would not do so until I took her to my bedroom and locked the door; and even then, she kept glancing nervously at the window. Her tale was so simple yet eerily elegant that I made her stop and speak slowly, that I might record it here, in her own words:

> This is the story of the covenant with the *strigoi*, which my mother told to me, just as her mother told her, and her mother before her.
>
> More than three hundred years ago, now almost four, the *strigoi* was a living man, Vlad the Third, known to most as Vlad Tsepesh, the Impaler, *voievod* of Valahia, to the south. He was greatly feared by all for his great ambition and his bloodthirstiness, and for his crimes he came to be known as Dracula, the Son of the Devil.

There are many stories of his terrible cruelty, especially to those guilty of betrayal or deceit. Adulteresses would have their womanly parts cut out, then were skinned like rabbits, and their skins and bodies hung from separate poles where all in the village could see. Sometimes a stake would be driven between their legs until it emerged from their mouths. Those who politically opposed Dracula died horribly as well, skinned alive or impaled. Sometimes he impaled guilty mothers through the breasts and speared their unfortunate babes onto them.

Despite his cruelty, Dracula was respected by his people, because during his reign no one dared be dishonest, or to steal, or to cheat one another, because all knew recompense would be swift. It was said one could leave all one's gold in the village square and never fear it would be stolen. Dracula was admired, as well, for his fair attitude towards the peasants and his courageous fight against the Turks. He was a skilled and brave warrior.

But the day came when, in the midst of a campaign, one of his own servants, in truth a Turkish spy, betrayed and slew him.

His men believed him dead. But the truth was that Dracula saw his coming defeat, for the Hungarian and Moldavian forces had recently departed, leaving him vulnerable to the Turks. It is said that at that time he was so hungry for blood and power, he made a pact with the Devil to become immortal through blood-drinking so that he might rule forever, and that he anticipated his own death, knowing he would soon rise thereafter.

Once undead and immortal, the *strigoi* brought his family north from Valahia to the safety of Transylvania, where the Turks were not such a threat and where he was less likely to be recognised. He claimed to be his own brother, but the truth of his identity came to be whispered on the people's lips.

He soon set himself up as *domnul* of a small village. He

was fearsomely cruel to those *rumini* who disobeyed but generous to those who served faithfully. But soon times became difficult for the villagers. Many died from the *strigoi's* bite, and those in nearby towns were terrorised as well. Soon the population dwindled, and the survivors discovered how to keep the *strigoi* at bay. Some brave souls even tried to destroy him, and the *strigoi* became frightened his evil existence would soon come to an end. It became difficult, too, to keep secret all that was going on at the castle. He might control the mind of one man, or two, or even more, at the same time; but he could not control the actions and thoughts of an entire village. And so he could no longer keep secrecy about what was happening at the castle. The tales spread all over Roumania, and soon he was in danger of starving.

So he went to the village elders and made the covenant: He would not feed upon any in the village, and would support them more generously than any *domnul* in all the land, and make certain the wolves did not attack the livestock, if they in turn would protect him, help him to feed upon outsiders, strangers, and keep silent regarding the covenant.

The villagers agreed, and the town prospered; no one was killed except those few foolish souls who disobeyed. A generation ago, when the world was torn apart and starving because of Napoleon's wars, we were safe and well fed. Because of the *strigoi*, we have never gone hungry in a land that knows hunger. Cattle and horses no longer died when wolves attacked in winter, and the *rumini* lived well—so well that it became the custom to offer voluntarily those babies born too sickly or crippled to survive, of which there are many now, for few outsiders settle in the village because word of the covenant has spread throughout the countryside.

He also agreed: no *strigoi* but him, for the good of all. He pierces their bodies with stakes, then decapitates them, so they will not rise as undead.

For all the good he has brought us, we villagers fear him; for there are many stories of the terrible punishments he inflicts on those who break the pact, who try to harm him or warn those chosen as his victims. No one who ever tried to destroy the *strigoi* has survived. Many villagers grumble and wish him harm; they grumble, and grow fat off the proceeds of the *strigoi*'s fields.

They say, too, that he has a similar covenant with his own family, an agreement that he will harm none of his own, and that the rest of the members may live in happy ignorance of the truth and be free to leave the castle forever—in return for the assistance of the eldest surviving son of each generation.

I stared at her in horror, knowing in my heart what she would reply even as I demanded, "What do you mean, *assistance* of the eldest son?"

She turned her face away, unable to meet my stricken gaze. "His help, *doamna*. To see that the *strigoi* is fed. For the good of the family, the village, the country. . . ."

⊹⊹ ⊹⊹ ⊹⊹

Excerpt from
the Diary of Arkady Tsepesh

21 APRIL 1845: "Oh no," said she, in a whisper so harsh it cut through the air between us, cut through my heart as easily as V.'s dagger cut through a child's tender skin. "Then you know nothing of his true covenant—with the Devil.

"Your soul, Kasha. Yours, and that of your father, and his father before him. The soul of the eldest surviving son of each Tsepesh generation: that is the gold with which he purchases his immortality."

⊰ XIV ⊱

CHILDREN OF THE
VAMPIRE

Roumania

OCTOBER · 1845

⊰ PROLOGUE ⊱

The Diary of Arkady Dracul

UNDATED ADDENDUM ON SEPARATE PARCHMENT. Let me start, then, with the moment of my death, for it is there this record best begins.

I write this for you, dear son, dear Stefan, taken from me the day after your birth, taken from me the same day as your brave mother, taken from me the same day as my life. I will spare you no detail of evil; best you know the full truth of your heritage, that horror might compel you to escape it. I write this in full faith that it will someday find you—before *he* does.

For you are the mortal heir of an immortal monster: Vlad, known to some as Tsepesh, the Impaler; known to others as Dracula, son of the Devil. I, your father, am tied to him by blood and fate; when his evil soul perishes, so shall mine. He aims now to bind you to him, that your soul might purchase his continued immortality. And when you sire a child, he shall seek to corrupt that fresh innocent's soul and buy himself yet another generation of existence.

As for my demise: I perished in the grey light of pre-dawn, in the land beyond the forest, in the monster's arms while you and your mother made your separate escapes. I came within a single expiring breath of destroying him, for I was as yet uncorrupted; but at the instant of my death, he made me as he is—a vampire, trapping my spirit between Heaven and earth and thus staying his execution.

I am now, like him, a monster. But I know not what has become of you, or of your beloved mother. I only know that I exist for the day I see him destroyed, and you freed from the family curse. . . .

❈ 1 ❈

The Diary of Arkady Dracul

30 OCTOBER 1845. The dragon wakes.

So say the *rumini,* the peasants, when the thunder rolls over Lake Hermanstadt and drums against the surrounding mountains. In its crescendo they hear the voice of *drac,* the great dragon: the Devil himself, roaring a warning to those souls foolish enough not to flee his wrath, foolish enough to linger on the banks of the wind-tossed lake in the face of the rising storm. Dozens die each year, struck down in a blazing mortal moment by lightning.

The sun is recently set, and I, like the tempest, am recently wakened. I remain, fearless, seated upon the cold earth beneath the shelter of a towering pine, and stare yearning up at the dazzling bolts that fleetingly illuminate the threatening clouds, out at the black, depthless water that has lured many a suicide. I long for death; but that sweet oblivion is not to be mine. Not until my work is done. . . .

The air smells electric; the brilliant, jagged streaks dazzle me to blindness. They pain me, as once it pained me to stare full into the sun. Even without their light, on this forbidding moonless eve, I see clearly enough to wield my pen, to perceive the colours of all surrounding me, as though it were day: the deep evergreen of trees and mountains, the indigo water, the browns and greys of dying grass upon the shore.

Renewed thunder, cascading from the sky and echoing again and again and again as it hammers the mountains encircling the lake, so fearsomely that it is easy to understand why the uneducated *rumini* attribute it to the Evil One.

To my ears, it is no warning but an invitation to the school of darkness: the Scholomance, where the Devil's own acquire the black arts—and lose their souls.

Mine is already lost, along with my mortal life, months before. Yet I remain here, hesitant—not quite willing to ally myself with Evil in order to fight it.

Here is the truth: To save my wife, my child, all the coming generations of my family, I am a monster. So shall I remain until I am powerful enough to destroy *him*, the greatest of all monsters: Vlad, my ancestor and nemesis.

For months since my transformation, I had been unable to continue my diary, unable to chronicle my infinite despair at the bloodthirsty creature I have become. Now I see the need to leave a record, in the event—God forbid!—of my failure, and Vlad's continuance.

For I have tried to destroy him; oh yes, I have tried. In my naïveté, I went to his castle again the second night after my horrific rebirth, armed with a dagger and stake beneath my cloak.

I found him that night, sitting in his drawing-room as was his habit in the halcyon days before all the servants had fled, while I was still an ignorant mortal. For once, I made my way through the echoing, unlit halls of the castle without trepidation, for I could see easily in the darkness—see every mote of dust, every spider, every delicate web—and I could hear with preternatural accuracy every scurrying rat, every whisper of the night breeze outside the walls. I could even hear the faint murmur of my sister's sweet voice in the far wing of the castle—and the faint reply of a stranger's voice, a man.

Perhaps I might have gone to rescue him—but I knew if I succeeded in my mission, he and countless others like him would be saved. I could see, too, the portraits of my ancestors, hung upon the castle walls, beginning with that of the Impaler, with his severe hawkish features, his long black curls, his drooping mustache. He was surrounded by a dozen others, all from different generations, all with faces and features that were variations upon his. . . .

All with souls that were tied to his service, by a pact as ancient and evil as their blood.

And I—I resembled him more than any other. Indeed, I have become, like him, a monster; but I am a monster bound to destroy him . . . and myself.

My prey was silent, but I knew his custom; and so I glided soundlessly down the corridors until at last I arrived at a closed door, its lower edge beribboned with a strip of flickering light.

I moved to fling it open with my hand. To my surprise, even before my fingers touched the brass knob, tarnished by four centuries of my ancestors' hands, the door slammed open, struck by no more than the force of my will.

V. sat in his chair, staring into the fire, which illumined his marble-white features with a warm orange glow and caused a thousand tiny flames to be reflected in the cut-crystal decanter of slivovitz at his elbow. Dressed all in black, he sat regally, his palms atop the armrests, his demeanour that of an aged royal patriarch—but his visage was that of a younger man, middle-aged, with a long iron-grey mustache and hair that flowed onto his shoulders.

He looked like my father, before V. had entirely broken his spirit; but there was a cruelty around his lips, his dark green eyes, in place of Father's kindness.

At the unsettlingly loud slam of the door, he did not move but remained planted like a rock, his hands still gripping the armrests, his gaze still on the fire. All that moved were his lips, very slightly, into a faint mocking smile.

"Arkady," he said softly. "What a welcome surprise. And how are your dear wife and son?"

The question tore at my heart, as he knew it would; I could only pray he was as ignorant of the answer as I. When no reply was forthcoming, he slowly swivelled his head towards me.

Immediately, I put my hand upon the stake at my belt.

At the sight, his smile broadened to a grin; then he threw back his head and laughed, so heartily and so loud that the sound rang echoing off the ancient stone walls. He continued some time, while I stood, feeling both furious and foolish.

At last he drew a gasping breath and wiped the tears from his eyes. "Forgive me," he said, grinning, his eyes agleam with unholy mirth. "Forgive me, dear nephew. After so many years, one becomes . . . jaded. One forgets the thought processes of the neophyte. Arkady"—he nodded towards the sharp wooden stake in my hand, at the shining dagger still sheathed at my belt—"do you really think to use those things?"

"I will," I said, my voice low with hate. To think that I had once innocently loved him! "I am younger and stronger than you, dear, dear uncle—"

"Younger, yes. . . . But you will find that, in undeath,

it is age and experience that confer strength." He sighed as he rose and turned to face me. "Very well. Let us dispense with this before it interrupts my plans for my houseguest."

What followed took place with inhuman swiftness, faster than any mortal eye could perceive.

I leapt at him with the stake, aiming to plunge it deep into his chest. As I did so, he stepped aside with supernatural speed and grace—and caught the hand that held the stake, with such might that my arm was pulled from its socket.

I howled, tried to wrest free, but his strength out-matched mine tenfold; with a brutal yank, he tore the arm from me, leaving my shoulder a stump that spewed my latest victim's blood. As I watched, stunned, he tossed it—the fingers still clutching the stake—with casual grace into the fire.

But I too was no longer mortal; so, neither, was my wound. The pain blinded for one brief brilliant instant, then transformed into pure energizing rage. Again I charged—this time knocking V. into the flames.

As he struggled to rise, hair and waistcoat ablaze, I retrieved my severed limb—only to realise, with amazement, that another had instantaneously and completely regrown to take its place. I snatched the charred stake from my erstwhile fingers and, oblivious to its blistering heat, rushed with it at V.

To my surprise, he spread his arms in welcome, a smouldering, willing target that wore the Devil's own grin. I struck out with every shred of my newfound immortal strength, determined to drive the stake clear through his cold heart; struck out again. Again. Again.

The stake would not pierce him.

Like a madman, I flailed at him with it—but it was as though the very air itself formed an impenetrable cushion above his chest. I hammered away until the wood itself began to splinter. All the while, he laughed, soft and low, with the condescension of an adult watching a helplessly furious child; but then his amusement faded and turned to murderous fury.

"Fool!" he spat. "Do you really think you are better than all the others—that you can destroy me, when all have failed? You and your son cannot escape. Yield, Arkady! Yield to destiny!"

"Never," I whispered, and read in his eyes my destruction; I knew then I should have to flee or meet the fate I had intended for him. I turned and flew through the air—barely in time. As I burst from the room, the violence of my exit causing the door to slam shut behind me, he hurled the stake after—with such force that it split the wood and remained stuck in the thick door, quivering like an arrow.

I fled to escape certain destruction.

The experience filled me with horror—not at the thought of my demise but at the thought that true death would not come soon enough, that I should have to continue as I was—a monster, drinking blood from victim after innocent victim until at last I succeeded in destroying V.

My choices were few: I could persist in attacking V. as I was—clearly unskilled in the ways of the undead and most likely to be the loser in another struggle. I could surrender and allow myself to be destroyed—yielding to Evil and passing the curse on to my poor unwitting son, just as all my forefathers had passed it on to me.

Or I could try to find my little son, and Mary—Mary, my darling! My last glimpse of her is emblazoned forever in my mind: she standing in the caleche, golden hair dishevelled, the blue ocean of her constant eyes filled with such infinite love, such infinite pain above the pistol clutched in her white trembling hand. . . . I return to the moment of my death and recall the sounds: the screams of horses, the thunder of hoofbeats, the rumble of the caleche wheels. And I am haunted by the image of Mary, white-lipped and stricken while the frightened horses bolt and run wild with her. Her heart is the strongest I have ever known; but her body was weak, drained of blood after a difficult birth. Is it possible she has survived?

But in finding them, I risked leading V. to them. That I could never allow. I determined that I would first have to teach myself how to best use my newfound powers, so that I might become a better match for V. But to do so, I needed safety.

So it was I left my native Transylvania for Vienna—a place with which I was familiar—in hopes of losing myself in that populous city and thus buying time to ponder my strategy. It was there I first learnt of the Scholomance, and the truth V. had withheld.

⁺⁺ ⁺⁺ ⁺⁺

The night I learned of the Scholomance was also the night of my greatest depravity, the night I learned how far I had fallen from human grace; by no coincidence, it was the night my sister came to me. So recent, so shamefully fresh in my memory; shall I write it down? Bear witness to my own capacity for evil?

Forgive me, Stefan . . .

It began with hunger waking me. I rose and paced restlessly from room to room in the small house I had procured, fighting the need that gnawed my vitals like the Spartan boy's fox, knowing that sooner or later I would have to indulge it and go out into the glittering city to seek a victim. (Going out into the city is acutely painful, in a way; I loved Vienna when I was alive, for its food and music and shops.

But I can enjoy none of those things now—except music, and then I must limit myself, for to sit hungering in a fragrant crowd—to smell the scent of blood on the air, to hear their soft, seductive heartbeats—without being able to hunt is too maddening, too distracting. I have tried and was never able to pay the performance a second's attention unless I had previously fed.) I would much prefer starvation . . . and indeed, there have been times when I have, out of pure self-loathing, come close to it. In the end, duty—until Vlad is destroyed, I must survive—and desire always win.

So I was again riven by that interior war, debating whether to forgo sustenance that night or to kill—knowing that I was close to losing all strength, all power—when a knock at the door interrupted.

I knew at once who it was; hunger hones the senses to exquisite sharpness. Standing next to the heavy wooden door that opened onto stone steps and the city streets, my fingertips resting on its carved panels, I sensed animal heat and heard breathing—the distinctive rasping breath of the man I knew only as Weiss.

With abrupt, furious abandon, I flung open the door. I had a score to settle with Herr Weiss, and the painful craving for nourishment served to fuel my anger, to give it a bitter, dangerous edge.

The door slammed against the interior wall. Huddled upon the top step, Weiss flinched—only slightly, and then only because he thought the darkness outside hid him from clear sight.

Not from mine. I could see him, of course, as though he stood in a shaft of daylight: a small, unimposing, and shabbily dressed man with thinning red-grey hair beneath a frayed cap, his upper spine so stooped from a life of physical labour that he seemed perpetually on the verge of bowing forward. Beyond him lay the glittering streets of the city, and a night ripe for hunting.

At my appearance, Weiss reflexively removed his cap, clutching it in two dirty hands in a lower-class gesture of courtesy; but his expression remained hard, defiant in the face of my obvious anger. For a scant second, he squinted beyond me, trying to see inside my house—as he always did, I suppose to see whether anything worth nicking lay inside. As always, he failed, for its interior, lit by a single taper, was scarcely brighter than the night outside.

"I have come, Herr Rumler, to—" he began, but I cut him off with an imperious sweep of my hand. Normally I would have made him step just inside and held our sensitive conversation there; but at the moment, anger and hunger overwhelmed me, leaving me unconcerned about appearances.

It was a cold autumn night. Weiss' words hung as mist in the air; my own left no trace.

"Herr Weiss," I hissed, my voice a soft, furious whisper, "I do not suppose you are in the habit of reading the papers?"

In his look of illiterate confusion, I found my answer. "Of course not," I replied for him. "Then let me tell you the latest news that has all Vienna astir. It seems there is a murderer afoot in the city—a most vicious lot. He decapitated a poor victim, then drove a stake through his heart. And then," I continued, my pitch rising with anger, though still I spoke too softly for others to hear, "the fool left the body lying in a cemetery, where the local authorities could easily find it!"

Weiss' eyes widened, then narrowed, at this revelation; the stubborn hardness returned to his features. "Good Herr, I can explain—"

"I will not hear it!" I shouted, my hunger and temper and carelessness all rising. "I pay you not for explanations but for performance! You have a good deal of impertinence, sir, if you have come here expecting payment!"

Light glinted off the fine sheen of oil covering Weiss' pockmarked cheeks as he lowered his head and kneaded his cap in his hands; not in a show of remorse, of which I believed him incapable, but in an effort to summon a suitable rebuttal.

In that instant of silence, a gust of wind wafted through the doorway—carrying with it Weiss' scent. It was the sweat-laden, pungent odour of an unwashed human, a smell from which I would have turned my head only months before. Yet now I could detect the muted, bittersweet smell of his blood, hear the soft, insistent drumming of his heart. His radiant warmth drew me like a frostbitten man to a fire.

I could have killed him in that moment—swiftly, brazenly, in the shadows of my own doorway, drinking until I felt that very last heartbeat.

But such indulgence would have led to other problems: disposal of the corpse, the very reason I had need of Weiss' services. For reasons unfathomable, I find myself unable to complete the necessary grisly chores to prevent my victims from becoming as I am. It had taken great effort and much discreet enquiry to find someone who would perform such a task without question. Weiss not only did so, he took unwholesome delight in it.

Yet could I trust him now, after this startling failure? And if I must choose a victim, would it not be better to rid the world of his likes than an innocent stranger?

In the fleeting second that Weiss stood silent and I contemplated this dilemma, the sound of hoofbeats against cobblestone stayed my hand. I watched as a beautifully appointed carriage, drawn by two black geldings, approached down the street. By that time, my hunger had become an all-consuming flame; I had made my decision to damn the consequences and pull Weiss inside the doorway, where I could drink my fill. I had only to wait 'til the carriage rolled past—

But as it neared, it also slowed. I watched in anguished frustration as the driver reined the horses to a stop in front of the house. The police? Had my hired idiot led them here?

But this was too fine a carriage for the local gendarmes. Herr Weiss turned, peering anxiously at the sight as the driver dismounted and opened the lacquered door. And then my accomplice released a whispered curse of awe at the vision that extended a gleaming white hand to the driver as she stepped out, with the graceful flash of a dainty slipper beneath long skirts.

I froze in the shadowed doorway, my hand on the doorknob, and assumed the interior stillness that usually rendered me invisible to mortals. For this vision was my own sister, Zsuzsanna.

My poor sweet Zsuzsa, born lame, with twisted leg and spine, doomed because of them to remain forever a spinster. I still recall with sad fondness the sound of her uneven footfall echoing through Father's house. She was a sickly, fragile creature with milk-pale skin, eyes the colour of night, and raven hair that conspired with her sharp features to evoke a severeness that could not even kindly be called beauty. How Father and I loved her, protected her, doted on her because of her frailty, her unloveliness, her innocent need for us. . . . Her loneliness and desire had driven her to the brink of a sweet, harmless madness.

But the woman who stood before me—straight and whole and utterly comely, dressed in a flowing black cape— was Venus herself. Against the midnight velvet of her wrap, her skin shone like the splendid full moon against the backdrop of night. She paused in the street to gaze in our direction, then lowered her hood to reveal a face shaped like a heart beneath a dramatic widow's peak—a face of dazzling loveliness: eyes sparkling like stars, skin pale and glowing and possessed of that strange fiery opalescence I saw each night in my own flesh.

And lips red as blood. My attempt at invisibility failed. At the sight of me, those full, tender lips parted to curve upward in a crescent, revealing brittle, deadly white beneath.

I took an indecisive step backwards, wondering whether to flee for my immortal life, for I heard men's voices in the carriage. If Vlad accompanied her—

She stepped forward and raised a hand in a beseeching gesture. "Arkady!" she called, in a voice as innocent and true as the Zsuzsa I had once known—and as sweetly seductive as a siren's. "Dear Kasha, you must trust me! I could no longer bear to be with him. And so I have searched for you. . . ."

I remained motionless, my hand still on the doorknob as she approached, reducing Weiss to speechless, slavering ecstasy as his narrow dark eyes with their jaundiced whites caught sight of her.

"Kasha—" At his frankly lecherous gaze, Zsuzsa shyly lowered hers and adopted a confidential tone. "Dear brother, I must speak to you alone."

I turned towards him, amazed to find that my protective brotherly instincts were undimmed despite our transformations, despite the fact that he was in far worse peril from my sister than she from him. "Leave us."

He did so with supreme reluctance, despite my mental efforts to compel him; Zsuzsa's beauty, it seemed, was more mesmerising.

And then I warily faced my sister, permitting myself no

reaction, no familial response as she reached out to clasp my hand. The flesh of mortals is warm, so warm; but her gloved grip was cool as my own.

For an instant, then, her glamour wavered, and I caught a glimpse of the sister I had known. She looked up at me with brown eyes burnished with magnificent immortal gold, but in them I saw the gentle, loving gaze of my Zsuzsa. The sight tugged at my pulseless heart.

"You must believe me," she said in a tone both humbled and anguished, too soft for human ears to perceive. "He is not with me; I would never lead him to you, never endanger you, no matter what I have become. Did I not tell you all I knew about the covenant? Did I not warn you to flee with the child?"

"Yes," I said softly. It was the truth; Zsuzsanna had warned me when I was still blessedly mortal, had done all she could to spare me and my family pain—but at the same time, she could not endure the thought of Vlad, her benefactor and seducer, her murderer, destroyed. "But if you come to me, you must know—"

Her features slackened with soft simple pain. "I know," she whispered. "You live to destroy him. And I"—she glanced away, and when she looked back and began to speak, her voice rose with sudden passion—"I can bear him no longer. Kasha, I can never raise a hand to slay him, but I cannot stay with him and be witness to the cruelty!"

"Is he unkind to you?" I asked swiftly, before I could repress a renewed surge of fraternal protectiveness.

She shook her head; a jet ringlet agleam with indigo highlights fell across a forehead that caught the moonlight and glinted pale blue, rose, silvery white, like the finest mother of pearl. "To the visitors. To me he is only . . . mocking of my innocence, my unwillingness to torment others." She paused, then with renewed desperation, cried, "Let me stay with you! Please—I cannot go back to him!"

I remained standing stiffly, my cold hands still unresponsive in hers, my expression implacable—but the truth was that I had been swayed utterly from the moment we touched. These past months after my unfortunate separation from my wife and newborn child, I had been heartsick and alone, more utterly alone than I had ever thought possible in my past human life; so much so that I had come to understand, if not approve, Vlad's reasons for making Zsuzsanna as she was now. I wanted desperately to believe my sister; and looking into her lustrous eyes, eyes that gleamed as though molten gold had been stirred into their natal brown, I saw there no deceit, only love and longing.

Now there could be someone else to share the horror my existence had become; someone else who would understand and not turn away in disgust.

I drew an arm's length back to scrutinise her solemnly —a difficult feat, maintaining sternness in the face of such magnificence—and said: "Understand that you can never again communicate with him. And swear that you will never under any circumstances inform him of my whereabouts or plans against him."

"Even if it means his destruction," she agreed, her expression somber. "I swear it." And at the first flicker of acquiescence in my expression, she reached forward with typical Zsuzsa impulsiveness and embraced me. "Oh, Kasha, dear brother! I have missed you so horribly!"

I could restrain myself no longer but returned the embrace, leaning down to kiss the top of her head as I had so often done in life. Her jet hair was finer now, and softer than a child's, imbued with a glossy radiance that seemed to emanate a faint bluish halo. It was also perfumed—something it had never been in Zsuzsa's sheltered existence. The over-whelmingness of it offended my predatory senses, but the spicy fragrance could not hide, for me, the scent of one un-dead: a non-odour, born of absences—the absence of warmth, of the strong animal smell of the living, tinged with the faintest trace of cooled, bitter blood. Beneath my hands, her spine was straight, perfect and uncurved, as it had never been in life; but the flesh covering it was cold.

I released her at last and said, in a tone still tentative, still faintly challenging, "But there are others in the carriage."

She flashed a dimpled smile and leaned forward on tip-toe to whisper in my ear with girlish delight: "But I could not come without a gift. A present for you!" She lowered herself, lifted gloved fingers to my cheek, and stroked it fondly. "You have grown thin, brother—look at you! You are hungry. I could see it from the carriage. If I am responsible for interrupting your supper—then I must make amends."

Before I could respond, she turned and gestured to-wards the coachman, who again swung open the lacquered door. Two grinning young men climbed out, each gripping in one hand a bottle of champagne as he steadied himself against the carriage. The first to emerge was medium height, golden-haired and a bit too well fed, his plump neck bulging over a tight starched collar that showed above a well-worn opera cape. He gazed over at my sister, then nudged his companion and whispered something sly, thinking it could not be heard by those of us at the entry. The language and accent marked him at once as a Londoner.

Dibs on the princess. You take the serving-girl . . .

He let go a coarse, piercing laugh. That, along with a distinct air of arrogance, made me despise him at once.

His companion was taller, dressed in newer clothing,

with an athlete's build and a crown of brown curls that emphasised his youthfulness. He appeared slightly less inebriated than his friend—or perhaps he simply made a more reserved drunk. He smiled distractedly at his partner's crude remark, but his rapt attention never wavered for an instant from Zsuzsa. He was a man smitten.

I had lived many years in England; my beloved wife is a native of London, and in my former life I would have been grateful to meet anyone from that thriving city and share conversation. I admit, I still felt a certain gladness at the prospect—but how could I be so cold-blooded (which, literally, I am) as to enjoy a chat with these visitors, only to dispatch them?

"Gentlemen!" my sister called gaily in English, gesturing for them to join us. "Come and meet my brother! He is our host to-night!"

They made their way, smiling and swaying, towards us; the blond man stumbled on the stone stairs and was caught by his companion. Taken aback by the suddenness of it all, I composed my expression but could not bring myself to mirror my sister's welcoming smile. These men were, after all, staggering to their doom, not the party they anticipated— though had I not known Zsuzsanna, I would have been utterly convinced. Her enthusiasm and gaiety were unfeigned.

For an instant I debated turning them all away. Watching them walk, unwitting, into a trap seemed too cruel, too calculated. My conscience could scarcely tolerate swift, silent preying on the dregs of Viennese society: streetwalkers, burglars, pickpockets eager to prey on an apparently naive gentleman.

But the wind had already carried their scent to me; and I stood as transfixed by it as they were by Zsuzsanna. She glanced at them, then up at me. I saw the glint of craving in her eyes, and knew it was outmatched by that in my own. Her smile widened again with satisfaction, for she recognised that the hunger left me powerless to protest.

And as the man with the dark, curling hair bent down to retrieve his companion, I saw beyond them something white: a small, wiry girl in a modest dress and shawl climbing from the carriage and hurrying to stand shyly behind the approaching group. She was anaemically pale, with the same black hair as myself and my sister, but altogether human— yet I fancied I caught the faint fragrance of bitterness along with mortal warmth. I did not realise it then, but now I know: it was the smell of the Changing, of one still living but doomed to undeath.

I stared at her with the shock of recognition. This was Dunya, who had served me and my wife as chamber-maid in Transylvania; who had helped to deliver our child; who had been bitten by Vlad and used as his unwitting spy to betray us. As unfeeling as I had become, through necessity, over the past months, the sight of Dunya filled me with pity. She could have been no more than sixteen or seventeen, the purest and kindest of souls; yet her loyalty to us had brought her to this undeserved, terrible fate. She looked up at me, her eyes owlish with surprise and faint terror. I tried to imagine how I appeared now to those who had known me before my Change; mirrors are of no use to me now. Was I as frighteningly handsome as Zsuzsanna?

"Dunya," I said softly, acknowledging her presence with a nod. She gave a small curtsey, then dropped her gaze. I wanted to tell her that I was glad to see her again—but in truth, I was not. I could only feel sorry that she had fallen in with such company as my sister and myself. For we were no longer the kindly masters she had served so well in life, but murderers—capable of harming her and anyone else we fancied. I knew that Dunya served my sister now not out of loyalty, or love, but because her mind was no longer hers to control. She had been bitten by Vlad, which made her his pawn; and apparently also by Zsuzsanna, who clearly had a mental hold on her.

What had my sweet sister become—my Zsuzsa, who as a soft-hearted girl had wept inconsolably over the bodies of small creatures and birds when Father and I returned from hunting? Worse, what had *I* become, to welcome her into my home?

Along with pity, I felt a surge of distrust, and turned to my sister, speaking in a tone too low for our drunken guests' ears. "How could you bring her? She is Vlad's eyes, Vlad's ears. . . ."

Zsuzsa's gaze was steady, untroubled by guilt at the notion of violating Dunya's free will. "She is mine alone now. We will be quite safe." And at my expression of curiosity, added: "There are many things you have yet to learn, Kasha. You are still such an unschooled innocent. . . ."

She turned towards the two men, who now stood before us. "Gentlemen. May I present to you my brother, Arkady . . ." She paused here to search my face with a swift uncertain glance. ". . . Tsepesh."

"Dracul," I corrected her. In life, I had insisted upon being addressed as Tsepesh—the surname borne by my human family for generations. I had found the name Dracul odious because of the connotations the peasants had given it over the centuries; they claimed it derived not from the dragon on my forebears' crest—but from the Devil.

And we were the sons of the Devil.

Zsuzsanna accepted the correction with amused grace. "Dracul. And these gentlemen are on holiday from London." She gestured at the portly blond man first, then the other. "Mister Reginald Lyons, Mister Anthony LeBeau."

LeBeau, his eyes sparkling, his cheeks faintly flushed with liquor but his speech and movement quite unaffected, bowed politely. "I can't tell you what a relief it is to speak English—even more so to be able to enjoy the company of such a charming and beautiful young lady who speaks it!"

His companion, however, leaned heavily against his friend, and in a voice loud enough to rouse the neighborhood, asked, "So is it true, as your sister says? Are you a prince?"

"Yes, of course," I replied in a tone barely civil. Conversation was nigh unbearable; I wished only to see these men inside and their blood quickly inside my own veins. "We are descended from royal blood, from a prince who ruled—"

"Roumania, wasn't it?" LeBeau inquired conversationally, looking askance at Zsuzsanna.

"Yes. The southern part known as Wallachia. Our bloodline dates back to the thirteen hundreds." Unwilling to delay relief any further, I turned without apology and made my way back inside.

Zsuzsanna and her chamber-maid followed. The men made it as far as the entryway and hesitated; in my distractedness, I had forgotten that the rooms were unlit save for a single flickering taper, which threw ghoulish shadows upon the ceiling, and left all but a small area of the room shrouded in darkness.

"Sorry," I apologized curtly, and set myself to lighting candles and lamps. The light revealed my rather Spartan surroundings to their feeble mortal eyes: a large, unused dining-table, covered with dust and silver candelabra, a long sofa, and two worn chairs. Not what one would expect of royalty, but far more than I felt deserving of.

Dunya helped her mistress off with her cape; beneath, Zsuzsanna wore a fine gown of pewter satin and watered silk with a startling décolletage that caused me to avert my eyes and Lyons and LeBeau to widen theirs.

While the shy little chamber-maid took our guests' cloaks, I prepared to strike. Apparently my sister read my intent expression, for still wearing the hostess' smile, she sidled over and whispered into my ear:

"Not now. Do you trust me, Kasha?"

It was a question I could not answer; moreover, the hunger had evoked in me a state of frantic desperation. I could forgo appeasement no longer. Yet, looking deep into her fathomless dark eyes, I found I could deny her nothing.

Her smile grew smug. "Trust me, and be dismayed by nothing. Only do as I instruct you. . . ."

Lyons wandered over and stood swaying before us, a crooked drunken grin beneath an astonishingly ruddy nose. "No servants, then? Rather an unusual for a prince, wouldn't you say?"

Zsuzsa held my arm affectionately as I replied, my tone cool, "I send them all away at night. I value my privacy."

If the man felt the none-too-subtle barb in my words, he gave no sign. Instead, he turned gleefully towards Dunya, who was scurrying to put the wraps away. "Time for a little celebration! Bring the champagne, would you? There's a good girl."

I translated into Roumanian for her. She complied as best she could, though she was unused to such sophisticated tasks—I had to open the bottle for her. Standing beside her, breathing in her scent, the gnawing ache in my vitals nearly overtook me. She glanced up to see me contemplating her with a hunter's deadly intensity; clearly she knew my thoughts, for she took the champagne and retreated quickly.

And when glasses were found and filled, and the bottle left beside Lyons at his request, she fled to a distant shadowy corner, as far from me as possible.

Inflamed by bloodlust, I determined to ignore my sister's request and feed at once. But something about her arresting gaze held me back.

Instead, transfixed by desire, I stood watching Zsuzsanna. She sat between the two men on the sofa, continually pouring them champagne as she made coquettish conversation. Soon Lyons was sagging against her; his head began to loll a bit, and I could see her glancing at the man's plump, ruddy neck.

"My dear Mister Lyons," she said with a crystalline laugh. "That collar must be abominably tight. It is late, and you are in relaxed company. Perhaps you should be more comfortable. . . ."

Smiling, Lyons raised a thick hand and waved her away. "No, no, I'm quite used to it." But she persisted and, after a bit of flirtatious coaxing, helped him off with the collar—and boldly planted a kiss on his neck.

This thrilled me like a voyeur—an ecstatic warmth coursed through me, not unlike sexual titillation—but to my profound disappointment, Zsuzsa did not sink her teeth into Lyons' neck, merely brushed her lips across the tender skin there. It was as though she was teasing Lyons, teasing herself. Teasing me.

Lyons was clearly too drunk to do much about it; at the last moment managing to slam his glass down on the sidetable, narrowly avoiding disaster, he fell heavily into her lap. As he did, he reached for her bosom, managing to free one incandescent white breast from the grey satin.

To my shock, my sister did not replace the breast but brazenly let it remain exposed as she began to unfasten Lyons' shirt. He fumbled, somehow managing to catch the breast in his palm; but inebriation rendered him apparently incapable of doing more.

His younger, soberer companion was quite undone by the scene. Mesmerised, he too disposed of his glass and leaned over to kiss Zsuzsanna full on the mouth.

I tensed, anguished; how could she bear it—feeling those warm, blood-filled lips against hers without biting into them, tasting them?

Yet LeBeau pressed them against her harder, harder, until I saw that he shook with emerging passion. Delicately, tentatively, he put a great hand round my sister's waist; and when she did not resist, he slid it upwards, gradually, until at last he arrived at her other breast and freed it, too.

Overwhelmed with disgust and hunger, I watched, dismayed at what my innocent sister had become, eager to pounce upon our distracted victims.

Zsuzsa sat, wanton and unashamed, as LeBeau leaned forward, ignoring his fallen companion, and put his lips to one of her uncovered breasts. She looked over at me then, her eyelids half-lowered, and graced me with a seductive and reassuring smile. Deftly, she unfastened the collar of the now-frenzied LeBeau and threw it aside.

He raised his face for air, to quickly shed his waistcoat; she kissed him, undid his shirt. Then, as if remembering for the first time, he glanced over at me and moaned, "Your brother . . ."

Still there was no glimmer of shame in her impossibly beautiful face; instead, she looked slyly over at me again while asking her suitor in a low, throaty voice: "Do you want him?"

LeBeau recoiled in shock and embarrassment—yet after

a pause, that shock transformed into a gleam of shy intrigue, curiosity.

Zsuzsa lifted a finger and beckoned me to come.

I was repelled, disgusted beyond words. I was so on fire with hunger, fuelled by her teasing refusal to feed at once, that I was half mad. Yet I found myself like the visitors—compelled by her beauty, by her ecstatic appreciation of the circumstance, to do her bidding. Dare I say it? I am not living, but I am still a man, aroused by beauty—even if it be my own sister's, God forbid—still capable of sexual lust. But that lust, I have found, most often transmutes itself into a desire for blood instead of body; many a time I have fallen prey to the beauty of a lone prostitute on a dark corner—only to have her then fall prey to me.

But I have never permitted myself to fall victim to a woman's sexual charms; dead I may be, but I have a living wife, whom I most desperately love and long for.

I resisted. But the hunger drew me; Zsuzsa's gaze drew me even more. I could feel the pull of her magnetic eyes and knew I was being manipulated, just as the hapless guests were being manipulated, yet the craving was so great, I no longer cared what happened to me—no longer cared if Vlad himself appeared and destroyed me, so long as I was first allowed the opportunity to appease myself, to feed.

I went and stood in front of the couch where Lyons lay with his head in Zsuzsanna's lap, breathing stertorously, his hands engaged in a frantic effort to unfasten his trousers, his small glassy eyes, hidden in folds of plump flesh, focussed on the pearlescent breasts that his partner fondled.

LeBeau looked over at me, then turned to Zsuzsa and with embarrassment stammered: "N-no, no . . ."

"As you wish," she said. "Shall he watch for now?"

The question enflamed and emboldened him. He struggled free of his trousers, scooped her out from under Lyons, lifted her up onto the arm of the couch, threw back her dress, and freed her.

She laughed softly—my sister, my sweet, innocent sister laughed. I was stricken to silence, to helplessness, by shock as much as by hunger; but there along with them both came a strange dreamy feel, a sensation much akin to overindulgence in laudanum. I opened my mouth to protest, tried to move to intervene, and found I could do nothing save watch horrified. Yet the horror itself began to fade, dulled by a strangely pleasurable languour.

I watched as he lifted her onto the back of the sofa and took her: she still laughing with delight, her legs clutching him like a harlot's, the satin skirt spilling over the back of the sofa like a quicksilver waterfall, brushing against the inebriated Lyons' face. Despite his drunken stupour, he registered at last what was happening and slurred belligerently: "See here now, LeBeau! It was agreed—"

So he struggled upwards and came to his knees on the cushions.

"Lift me," Zsuzsa murmured, and her lover lifted her, holding her, so tiny, so apparently fragile in his great arms. Lyons crawled towards them until he reached my sister's back, then reared up and—

Dear God, how it shames me to think I was so swayed by her, in such a stupour myself that I could do nothing to stop them! Instead I watched like one drugged while my sister, with a muted cry of pain and pleasure, took two lovers in my presence; and all I could think of was my own mounting excitement—inspired not by the depravity I witnessed but by the knowledge that my hunger would soon be appeased.

With a look and a subtle tilt of her head, Zsuzsa signalled me to approach. By this time, LeBeau was moaning at the imminence of ecstasy, his eyes closed, his head thrown back, his pale face draped in shadow as sweat trickled down from his dark curls. His chest was pressed to Zsuzsa's; Lyons' chest was against her back, so that she was effectively pinned.

LeBeau gave a gasp and began to arch away from her.

"Now?" Zsuzsanna whispered languidly. "Do you want my brother now?"

"Yes," he hissed, his face contorting; he squeezed his eyes shut, then abruptly opened them wide, ablaze with fire. "Yes!"

With predatory swiftness, I moved behind him so that the young man was caught between his soon-to-be murderers, even as my sister was trapped between our two victims.

As LeBeau emitted a moan of disappointment and anticipation, Zsuzsa disengaged herself from him with a slight, subtle movement; her stare was fixed keenly upon me.

"Help him," she said, too softly to be heard by any without the keen senses of the unliving—any but me.

Great was my revulsion; greater still was the power her gaze, her words, her presence had on me. I felt hypnotically compelled, as helpless and passive as one trapped in a dream. An excuse? Perhaps.

Perhaps not, for I remember desiring to struggle, and a faint spark of outrage that my own sister should manipulate me so. Clearly, her attempts to convince me that she was still, at heart, the sister I had known in life were cruel lies; at the worst, she had learnt powers I did not yet possess (for I tried to mesmerise her in turn and could not) and intended to use them in order to destroy me, at Vlad's bidding. At the very best, she had sunk into the mire of utter decadence.

God forgive me; I obeyed her, still standing behind Le-Beau and reaching round his waist to assist him in his pleasure. I touched him, felt in my palm his thunderous pulse. I rested my cheek against his neck (for he was taller than I) and felt there, too, the pounding of his heart; the enveloping fragrance of warm human flesh, warm human blood, provoked me to a frenzy. I opened my mouth like a serpent to strike—

Not yet, Zsuzsa said, though I could see her face in the flickering candlelight, could see that her lips had not moved. Yet the word echoed silently in my mind; I found myself frozen to inaction, trapped in a purgatory of perpetual desire.

And then LeBeau's moans grew louder. When at last he cried out in release, arching against me, Zsuzsanna leaned forward—awkward because of Lyons' persistent, clumsy thrusts—and savagely sank her teeth into LeBeau's neck.

The grip on my mind eased; with a burst of fury that evoked a short scream of pain from my victim, I did the same.

And drank and drank and drank . . .

The blood tasted, as it always does, ambrosial, pulsing with power and strength, with life. But at that moment it tasted of something more: I thought at first it was the champagne that made me giddy, but soon I came to realise that it was LeBeau's final ecstasy, so intense, so all-consuming that I shuddered, swaying, near swooning. Feeding has always been for me an enormously sensual experience; but this—this was beyond anything I had known, almost too pleasurable to bear.

Beneath the river of ecstasy ran an undercurrent of memory and emotion: dimming impression of a girl with a plain sweet face, and a silver-haired woman and man, all mixed with a sense of shame.

I might have lingered there in his thoughts, but the closeness of those who are dying has always distressed me; I prefer to kill quickly, neatly, to stay separate from such personal sensations. At that moment, I wanted to feel nothing but the ecstasy.

It was accomplished without difficulty; for in the end, the memories always fade, and my victims, mercifully mesmerised, die still and pliant in dreamy bliss.

LeBeau himself, transported by both our caresses and our fatal kisses, fainted. With animal fierceness, my sister and I pressed harder against him, still suckling, holding his limp body upright with our own.

Drinking, Zsuzsa peered up at me from under half-closed eyelids, her gaze intoxicated, sensual. We shared a look of utter satisfaction; then she raised her face, lips and teeth dark with LeBeau's blood, and whispered:

"Better, yes? The taste . . . ?"

Yes. But like a virgin corrupted, I was shamed by her question, unable to reply. I closed my eyes, sucked harder on the wound I had inflicted, and thought of nothing but what unalloyed joy it was to drink and drink. . . .

And such blood! Young and strong, intoxicated by rapture and champagne . . .

I almost drank too much. The flow of blood lessened, though I drew harder; LeBeau's heartbeat grew fainter, fainter, until at last it stilled.

He was dead. Even so, I continued drinking, not caring what evil might come of it. Zsuzsa pushed me away with immortal force; a growl, deep and menacing and utterly inhuman, escaped my throat as LeBeau dropped to the floor between us.

Not enough! It was not enough! Stricken, I looked at Zsuzsa, who still fought to steady herself against the oblivious Lyons' grunting efforts.

"The next is all yours, brother," she murmured, dimpling.

I moved behind Lyons, my step slightly uncertain; LeBeau's blood had, to my amusement, induced a degree of intoxication. But my senses were heightened; I felt stronger, keener, more capable of the kill, and filled with a sense of savage pleasure at the prospect. It was as though Zsuzsanna's decadence had freed me, allowed me for the first time in my immortal existence to revel in the hunt—something I had never before permitted myself.

I paused behind my victim. Beyond Lyons' thick, huddled form I could see the incandescent pearl of Zsuzsa's neck and the single dark serpent of hair, fallen from the careful arrangement of curls atop her head and coiling its way down her white shoulder.

LeBeau's blood had relieved the painful craving enough to allow me to savour the hunt; but as I slowly pressed towards Lyons, the smells awakened my appetite again. There came the smell of copulation, of a dead man's body cooling, of a living man's heated sweat and skin and blood.

I placed my hands, feather-light, atop his shoulders. As he did not face me, there would be no chance to mesmerise —but in my newfound decadence, I had no concern for my victim's comfort.

With swift brutal force I bared my teeth and pierced the skin of Lyons' neck, felt the astringent sting of brine against my tongue.

He flailed backwards, screaming in pain and drunken terror. Zsuzsanna disengaged herself and turned towards us to watch the spectacle, breasts and legs still exposed as she settled comfortably against the velvet cushions to watch with sensual approval.

God help me, I took vicious pleasure in his struggles. I

held him fast as he thrashed against me, biting into his neck again, again, again as he fought, until the skin was slashed and hanging, until at last a great vein was pierced and began to spray blood.

It spattered Zsuzsanna's face and breasts. Laughing, she opened her mouth to catch the gushing blood with the innocent delight of a child trying to capture a snowflake on her tongue. But I soon pressed my mouth over the life-giving stream, pulling fiercely against it, drinking until Lyons grew weak and ceased his struggles. He sagged against me, his heart beating like a trapped sparrow's.

I drank quickly, letting him drop heavily when at last he was dead. Suddenly dizzied, I staggered to the couch and fell against it, letting my head loll against the cushions; the man's drunkenness made my thoughts reel.

I closed my eyes and fell into a dream. I was no longer a miserable murderer trapped in the Viennese night, but an innocently mortal man bound from Vienna to Buda-Pesth, lying on the rocking train berth beside my wife and soon-to-be-born child. Had I known what had awaited me at home, in Transylvania, I would never have returned, would have fled the continent with them both. Mary, my Mary! Unwittingly I brought you into a den of unguessable evil, and now I can only pray that you and our son are well, and safe from V. . . .

In my drowsy vision, I reached towards my sleeping wife. She stirred, and the shining golden lashes that fringed her pale eyelids fluttered. At last, her eyes opened, revealing that calm glassy sea of blue, and I wept at the comfort, the love offered there. I reached . . .

. . . and found us both trapped in that timeless moment when, amid the screams of horses and snarls of wolves, against V.'s arrogant laughter that soon turned to a cry of dismay, she raised my father's pistol to my chest and stared deep into my eyes.

I gazed back into hers and saw terrible love and pain.

Explosion. The acrid sting of sulphur. Pain that pierced my heart.

This time, I did not die but reached—and, in my desperate dream, caught her white shining arms and sobbed as they reached for me in turn. She was real, solid in my arms, and as I held her, my face pressed to her sweet golden hair, wet with my cold tears, I was consumed by a passion greater than any I had known as a living man. Even death could not still my desire for her.

I yielded to her caresses, her coaxing, and took her—or was it she who took me? My ardour was veiled by a strange, sweet languour. And at the moment of my release, her beautiful image wavered and became that of the serving-girl, Dunya.

My cry of pleasure became one of alarm. But the languour overtook me once more; there came darkness for a time, then again I fell into another strange dream of passion. Again I reached for my wife; again, I took her, only later to remember that her face was smeared with fresh blood.

Again, I cried out to discover that the woman was not Mary. This second time, to my utter horror, it was my own sister.

My horror grew as the sense of languour evaporated and I realised that, indeed, Zsuzsanna's body was pressed against mine. I pulled away from her in unspeakable revulsion to find that we lay upon the couch; on the floor beside us— oblivious to the stiffening corpses nearby—Dunya lay snoring, her own clothing in disarray.

Zsuzsa sat up and casually began fastening her own dress, but her air of coquettish revelry had vanished; her expression was now solemn, as if for the first time that evening she had committed an act of consequence.

"You," I choked, my voice trembling with shame and fury as I covered myself, "you intentionally mesmerised me. You have done this—but *why?*"

The candles had all burned down; the darkness had eased to the soft grey of approaching dawn. Zsuzsa's preternaturally brilliant beauty was fading with the night. She was still lovely, fetching, but the flashes of electric indigo in her hair, the moonglow incandescence of her skin, the burnished gold in her eyes—all had dimmed so that her beauty, her radiance seemed merely mortal.

After a cautious glance at her sleeping servant, she looked back at me and replied softly, "To save you. To save us all, Kasha." And at my questioning gaze, she sighed. "You are only recently dead; V. says that, for a brief time, you might still be able to produce heirs. A child, Kasha. It is only a child—"

Only a child. I groaned with disgust that my own sister could so casually speak of sacrificing her own child—*our* child. Did she think that, because it was the product of incest, it was any less human, that I should love it any less? Find it any easier to condemn it to a horrific fate?

At my aghast reaction, her tone grew heated, defensive. "I was denied many things in my short life; do not deny me this. Or would you rather he tracked down your only son?"

I looked away, too overwhelmed with self-loathing to answer.

"He would have you killed," she continued quietly. "He has paid your own man to come after sunrise and destroy you, just as you paid him to destroy your victims."

"And why not you?" I asked bitterly. "Why did you not simply kill me as you lay with me, when I was helpless?"

Hurt marred her lovely features, but another emotion soon eclipsed it: surprise. "Then you do not know . . ."

"Know what?"

"He cannot destroy you, Kasha, nor you him. The pact forbids it; we may die only by a human hand."

I marvelled at this in silence, until at last she said urgently, "There is no time. You must leave—"

"With you?" I wheeled on her with sudden fury. "And what fresh deception shall I expect now?"

"No." She lowered her lovely face, and for the first time, bitterness crept into her tone. "No, I am not asking that you come with me, or tell me where you are going. But I will tell you this, because whatever you may think of me, the truth is that I still love you." She looked up again. "You are too easily swayed, Kasha, too easily controlled. He has found you once, and he will find you again; he is too wily, too accomplished, too strong for you."

"If that is true," I said, "why did he not come for me himself? Why would he send you—a woman?"

"It is the price he paid for making you a vampire: He is trapped now for the span of a generation, perhaps more, on the family property in Transylvania. Nevertheless, you must prepare yourself; for even in this short time, he has taught me tricks that have allowed me to do as I will with you."

She paused, and a strange light that looked incongruous with her confidence, her beauty, came into her eye; it was only later that I identified it as fear. "You have heard of the Scholomance?"

"I have heard."

"It is no myth, Kasha. It is all true. You must go there; he would kill me if he knew I have told you. Go there. Learn, and become as strong as he is, or he will destroy you."

"If I go," I said, my face and tone hard, "I will become

stronger than he. And I will see us all destroyed and sent to Hell."

Uncertainty and fear flickered over her features once more; she turned away from me and said only: "Go."

I left her then, she kneeling over sleeping Dunya to wake her; left my sister with the lonely rooms and the blood-ied corpses and boarded the first train for Buda-Pesth that would take me, ultimately, to another train bound further east, for the lands beyond the forest: to Roumania, and Lake Hermanstadt, where the Devil dwells.

Listen: The thunder roars. The dragon himself calls, and I go. . . .

❧ 2 ❧

Zsuzsanna Dracul's Diary

4 NOVEMBER 1845. I came into this world a cripple, with a hunched spine and a twisted leg. Even now in memory I hear the sound that haunted every step I took: the scuffling thump of my uneven footfall as I staggered graceless over the hard stone floors of the family estate.

As a child I knew my mother's tender love—yet knew early that the affection she bore me differed from that borne for my brothers. After she died young, I knew my father's and brother's. They adored me; oh yes, adored the pathetic doe-eyed shuffling creature, with a love tainted by pity.

Pity, that I should be homely; pity, that I would never know any other's love: surely not that of a lover, a husband, a babe of my own. So lonely did I grow that I went slightly mad and in my mind created lovers; created an imaginary companion—my dead brother Stefan, who in reality had been killed as a little boy. But in my mind, he was still alive —and not my brother, but my own child—following me faithfully from room to lonely room as I read aloud to him from books of the life beyond those walls.

For though my body was ungainly and frail, my mind

was swift and robust. Thus my life was limited to academic pursuits, to letters and literature. It was uncommon for Tsepesh women to be permitted an education, but my mother was a strong woman of modern ideas, and a poetess. She taught me my letters early; by the age of eight, a few years after her death, I had mastered not only Roumanian but French and German, and Father had begun my instruction in Latin. As we grew older, Arkady and I amused ourselves with word games and conversed with each other in foreign tongues. To hide my diary from prying eyes, I began keeping it in English. And I dreamt and dreamt of the foreign lands I would never see.

How I despised mirrors then! They always revealed a girl sickly pale from never having seen the sun, never having ventured into the world beyond her stone prison. Unlovely —with features aquiline, severe, and large, longing brown eyes. And beneath that desperate face, a crooked body, the hump of one deformed shoulder rising higher than its mate.

I despise mirrors still: for now they refuse to bear witness to my transformation, showing only a void, an emptiness, in the place where I now stand. How I yearn to see my own face, my own form in my stylish new gowns, to admire myself as others do. I am perfect now—with a body straight and whole—and quite beautiful, possibly the most beautiful woman in the world. I need no mirror to confirm it: The answer is all too clearly writ in men's eyes.

Who turned the duckling into a swan?

Vlad, who during my naïve human life I thought of as my father's uncle. He was sworn not to Change any of his family into immortals such as he—but he broke that promise for love of me. Love because I openly adored him; love, perhaps, because he saw the spirit entrapped within the body.

He woke me to this new life with a kiss; and paid a

price for breaking the covenant—the loss of control over my brother's mind. This put him in jeopardy, for once Arkady became impossible to manipulate, he tried to flee—and Vlad's very existence was threatened.

But Vlad willingly paid the price and became my lover. He wooed me, sought me, led me gently over the precipice of death into a life more brilliant than I could ever have imagined.

I am immortal now; because of him, there is no fear of death, no aging, no suffering (except the hunger), no crippled limbs. There is only beauty, the sensual thrill of the seduction and the kill, the reality that I am admired, adored, lusted after, loved.

And when I learnt that, during my first Changed year, there was a chance I could become with child, I took as many human lovers as I could. But I fear I am already barren. . . . Even so, I shall take men as often as I wish. I will be denied no pleasure; not the caress of a lover, and someday, too, I shall find a way to have my child.

It is Vlad who ended the anguish that was my human life and gave me this new and shining sensual existence. I cannot deny him my love or my gratitude—even if he were to turn on me one day in hatred. I shall always owe him that.

And he denies me nothing. He delights in buying me finery, in spoiling me, delights daily in my beauty. Only one conflict lies between us: my brother Arkady, known to me as Kasha.

Because of what he has done for me, I love Vlad; because of what he has done to my brother and father, I hate him. For Vlad's survival depends upon the damnation of my brother's soul—as it depended on the damnation of my father, my grandfather, and all first-born Tsepesh males before him. Each generation's corruption purchases him an extension of life and power.

But the covenant forbade him to make vampires of those of his family. Just as he paid a price to make me as I am, so he has paid a heavier toll for making Kasha an immortal: Vlad is trapped now on his ancestral land and cannot leave it for the span of roughly twenty-five years.

At the same time, he says he now has only that same amount of time: *one* generation in which to dispatch poor Kasha, thus delivering his corrupted soul—or we will both lose our immortality, our power, our beauty . . . and perish. Since Vlad cannot leave Transylvania, he must rely on me and others to achieve his goal.

Only a generation . . . But my brother was my dearest friend; how shall I allow harm to come to him?

The recourse is to indulge myself for that time and hope that, when that generation is past, I can gracefully surrender this sparkling life along with him who gave it to me. Of course, the danger is that Arkady will grow too strong before then and destroy Vlad, my saviour and first lover—a love that, unlike Kasha's, was never darkened by pity.

And if I do permit Vlad's destruction (after all, I have given my brother the means to become a worthy adversary) —what shall become of me? Vlad is my creator; will the death of my god bring my own? Or does he lie when he says his demise means mine?

The only solution is to protect them both for as long as I can.

Even so, I fear Vlad will have me destroyed if he discovers the truth of what happened in Vienna. He cannot harm me himself, but he can always instruct a hired mortal. Of course, he has failed to find anyone of suitable mental strength and skill willing to risk life and afterlife to destroy a vampire; but someday he will find such a one, if my brother does not discover that strong soul first.

But I shall never tell him how much I revealed to my brother; and Kasha surely will not, and Dunya knows nothing, poor thing.

I wept upon my return to Transylvania. Vienna was paradise: such beauty and riches and opulence as I had never seen in my brief sheltered existence. As a mortal woman I was always too sickly to travel, had never been beyond the walls of the family estate. Vienna was only a dream, a fairy tale recounted by my father and brother.

But now I have seen for myself the bustling streets, the fine apparel, the pastries as decorative as tiny jewels, the grand opera houses. And the people that attended them—ah, the people! Warm and clean and fragrant, attired in satins and silks and diamonds like royalty, prettier than the pastries and far more toothsome. To sit in the opera as one of them, to inhale their scent—the scent of young strong blood flavoured with rich cuisine, the finest wines—and feel the presence of all those warm beating hearts was pure intoxication for me.

And the men—the men! Every male eye in every crowd looked on me with longing. I had my pick of them, thinking all the while, *Surely this is life!*

And if I could experience it only as one dead and damned—well then, dead and damned let me remain.

But this castle is so dull and dark and silent by contrast, especially now that the servants have all gone. The entire village surrounding us lies deserted, empty because Vlad dared break the covenant by transforming me into an immortal. In their foolishness, the peasants feared he would break his agreement with *them* and begin to prey on them.

So they all fled, and we are alone, forced to rely on our

own wits to survive. And the castle grows more desolate and in need of repair each day. I find myself staring out its windows towards the Borgo Pass, praying to catch sight of a carriage filled with warm blood and beating hearts. . . . But soon the snow will render it impassable. There will be only one more visitor until the spring.

One more visitor. In the meantime, the underground cellar lies empty. Had my brother fulfilled his role in the family's covenant with Vlad, the cellar's prison would now be filled with visitors, ensuring an adequate supply over the coldest, bleakest months.

As it is, it seems we will starve . . . and grow weak— and hideous.

Writing this makes me want to take the horses and flee back to the city, makes me wish (guiltily) that I had never warned poor Kasha, for my generosity towards him may be my undoing. How shall I bear losing my beauty now?

I understand all too well Vlad's desire to go to London. Transylvania seems less hospitable every day; travellers grow fewer, despite continuing good weather. To be back in a large city again, with streets full of warm, unwitting people . . .

We should have gone to England long ago—yet Kasha's very existence makes it impossible for us to leave. Vlad will remain trapped in Transylvania until his agents manage to destroy my brother—or until he perishes at the end of twenty years' time.

Perhaps I could have freed Vlad by doing as he wished in Vienna, by sending in the mercenary mortals to kill Kasha. But they, too, were badly trained, of small minds that could focus on nothing but the gold that awaited them once the task was complete.

Shall I be the tool that destroys my own brother?

No. Not yet, at least . . . not yet. At the same time, I am not ready to give up this exquisite new existence; so I am bound to protect Vlad as well. I will harm none of my kin.

I arrived at the castle to-night full of sadness and exhilaration—and hunger. It had been an arduous journey home, much of it by wagon. Our driver refused to take us farther than the Borgo Pass and from there departed for Bucovina, whilst Dunya and Jean and I were left with a wagon and horses (provided for us by Vlad) to fend for ourselves.

Dunya is sturdy but small and haggard after the long trip; and Jean was spent after all our arduous nights together and my surreptitious sips from his strong, sweet throat. So when night fell, I rose to take the reins while the two mortals slept heavily. The horses' fright of me served to make our pace swifter, and soon we were home. I roused Dunya, then carried sleeping Jean to the guest quarters.

I should have kept him near me; leaving him unguarded was a grievous mistake. But I was drowsy after my journey, for I had taken every opportunity to drink my fill of blood. I had done so that evening as well, upon the Bistritz coach, from an elderly Hungarian man (though the poor driver certainly never realised, I am sure, until after he arrived in Bucovina, that his one remaining passenger was stone dead!)

So replete and eager for rest was I that I took my latest mortal paramour not to the upstairs chambers but to one rarely used on the ground floor. (And in truth, I hoped that this would serve to delay Vlad's discovery of him until I had risen.) I, rather than go to the innermost chamber to sleep in my coffin alongside Vlad's, staggered to the nearest casket—down in the cellar.

There I slept until the following night; then I rose—late, some time after sunset—and found, to my dismay, Jean missing from his room. I knew at once I had failed to protect him from Vlad's predilection for torture; nevertheless, I roused Dunya and insisted she accompany me to the throne room. She was reluctant, fearful to do so, but I knew Vlad would insist upon it.

He was in his inner chamber, as I knew he would be, seated upon his throne.

When Arkady left us, Vlad had been as young and beautiful as Kasha. Now he is still strikingly handsome, still possessed of a haunting resemblance to my brother with his pale hawkish features, his coal-black brows, his large upward-slanting eyes. But there the resemblance ends, for the past months have seen him ill-nourished and aging: his once jet-coloured hair is heavily streaked now with iron, and the lines are returning to his face. (I fear so: How soon shall the same happen to me over the long, barren winter?)

There are more differences than mere age between my ancestor and brother. Vlad's lips are thinner, crueller, and more sensual, and his eyes are unlike any others I have seen: the deep evergreen of the forest, heavy-lidded and thickly lashed.

To-night they were full of that peculiar, predatory light I have so come to despise.

As I swung open the great door that separates his chambers from the rest of the castle, with Dunya clutching my skirts like a frightened child, he called out.

"Ah, Zsuzsanna! You are in time to enjoy the entertainment our guest has provided—thanks to your thoughtfulness!"

He was quite right in understanding that I had brought him a gift from Vienna—how could I not, after his generosity to me? But I had hoped to indulge myself with poor Jean once more before Vlad had his way. . . .

I entered swiftly, holding Dunya on my right to shield her from the distressing sight to the left: the black velvet curtains were parted, to reveal the occupied theatre of death with its black iron manacles, its chains, strappado, rack, stakes.

We crossed to where he sat, in full view of that grisly theatre, upon a platform of dark, polished wood, inlaid in gold with the words JUSTUS ET PIUS, just and faithful. Above, upon the wall, hung a centuries-old shield, crumbling with age, adorned with a barely discernible winged dragon: the symbol of the Impaler.

I ascended the three steps leading up to the throne and presented my cheek for his cold kiss.

"My darling!" he murmured, taking my hand to study me with honest appreciation from arm's length—the appreciation of both a doting patriarch and a passionate lover—and for an instant I remembered why I loved him. "Look how ravishing you are!"

I smiled, knowing that his compliment was sincere; I had fed so well in Vienna that without the aid of mirrors I could sense my own beauty, my magnetism, increase. For the first time in many months, I saw an appetite for me, and me alone, in his eyes.

But our passion for each other has faded since my Change. We have made cold love, yes, when the thrill of the hunt and the kill has enflamed us and our human prey has crossed the great abyss. (I am a vampire, but not a fetishist; I take no pleasure in loving the dead.) But his need is to dominate, to rule, to enslave, to strike fear, not to pleasure. And my desire is sparked by the presence of warmth and the scent of blood, my greatest excitement found in the link among hunger and lust and death. And when I have taken from my lover his very essence, all his warmth, all his life—then my love cools as rapidly as his flesh.

Still I smiled at Vlad, twirling to better show off my new dress of silvery silk and satin, the handicraft of a Viennese dressmaker. He admired it but an instant, then gazed beyond me at the poor mortal suspended, naked, from the manacles. "Monsieur Belmonde," he cried aloud in French, "I believe you are already quite familiar with my niece—and consort—Zsuzsanna. Is she not lovely?"

Reluctantly I turned and faced the piteous, terrified visage of our guest. My poor Jean, hung spread-eagled and trembling against the bloodstained stone! He had been such a dandy, a gigolo, an aspiring man looking for his fortune, hoping it would come easily once he wed the wealthy princess I claimed to be—and in fact am. Under pretense of an impending marriage, I lured him here to meet the family—but in a way quite different from that he envisioned. And in Vienna on carriages, across eastern Europe upon trains, in wagons-lits and rocking compartments and even upon the diligence from Bistritz, I partook without shame of his lean well-muscled body and his blood: now they were revealed for the others to admire as well.

Chained to the grey stone wall, he hung from his wrists, head lolling, ribcage protruding like a crucified Christ: such a handsome young man, fair-haired, fair-skinned, with pale eyes wild with horror and that beautiful body that never failed to spark my hunger and desire. But his ribs were striped red; he had been lashed. The game had already begun; ominously, his ankles, too, had been manacled so that his legs were spread wide apart.

"Beloved!" he cried, straining against his fetters to reveal even more muscle, to reveal white, even teeth inside the full, shell-pink lips I longed to kiss again. The manacles clattered against the stone. "My Zsuzsanna! For the love of God, help me! Help me!"

Beneath him, quietly working in the black shadows, stood his tormentor, only recently of our employ—Vanya, a redheaded ogre with a hunched back and twisted legs, a creature who bore the same afflictions I had in my pathetic mortal life. But I had no sympathy for Vanya, with his ruddy skin that stank perpetually of drink, for a fevered excitement blazed in his bloodshot eyes as he smeared oil upon the blunted tip of a long, pointed stake.

I knew what this portended and, panicked, turned back swiftly to Vlad. Jean Belmonde surely adored me solely for my appearance and my wealth and would have proven an unfaithful mate. And though I bore no real love for him, I could not bear the thought of his suffering.

Vlad's lips thinned in a faint amused smile, but there was a hardness in his eyes that commanded me to steel myself, to be strong.

"Not yet," I said softly—too softly for my unfortunate Jean's ears. I tried to hide my revulsion as I reached forth to stroke Vlad's arm coquettishly. "Let me have him first. Uncle, please . . ."

Yes, I am dead, and consider myself beyond the reproach of the living; already damned, and beyond the judgement of any God. But damned or not, I am still capable of compassion for my own victims. If I must kill, then let them die sweetly in my arms; and if I must sin, let it bring pleasure, not pain.

The blood, at least, tastes sweeter.

"Perhaps," he said, smiling. "But you have, it seems, already had your fill of him. First I must know. What of Arkady? Did it all go as arranged? You found him? Went to him?"

"I did."

He moved eagerly to the edge of the throne, lowering his voice. "And you contacted the human agent there as I directed—"

"Yes," I answered shortly. I had thought myself incapable of shame, but a pang of it assailed me at the memory. I had in fact seduced the man Vlad directed me to, and drunk from him, and left him for dead.

Vlad's smile widened to reveal deadly teeth. "Good. Good. . . . Now—tell me—" Here he reached forth to catch my wrist with painfully intense strength and pulled me towards him to the throne. "Tell me you saw Arkady destroyed. Properly."

I lowered my gaze, unable to meet the scrutiny of those merciless green orbs. I might have lied then to spare myself, but I knew the penalty would be far, far worse to dissemble now and be later discovered. And so I said, "I have no doubt he was. I instructed the man carefully myself and paid him well. But I drank too much of drunken blood and had to leave to sleep before the day broke—"

He jerked to his feet, hurling me down the steps with a single imperious sweep of an arm. *"Liar!"* he shrieked, his eyes glowing inhuman red with rage, as though the green forest therein had been abruptly consumed by flame. "You swore to me that you would see it done! You have failed in the one most important thing! Are you too much a fool to realise that we have little time, that we can afford to miss no more opportunities? By sparing your brother, you condemn us! How can you claim to love me?"

I am no longer human; the blow caused me no harm. I landed lightly on my feet beside cringing Dunya and pulled myself to my full height, my most dazzling beauty. "I am no liar!" I shouted, provoked to anger myself. I could not be frightened; perhaps Vlad could have me destroyed if he wished, as he sometimes threatens, but I suspected he was unsure as I of the consequence of harming me. "But he is still my brother, and my blood does not yet flow as cold as yours. How can *you* ask me to witness such a gruesome fate for one I love?"

His face hardened, as though it had been hewn from white marble, and his eyes narrowed even as they pierced me. I knew he was considering the assumption I wanted him to make: that I could not report on Arkady's demise merely because I had left early out of a faint heart.

For a moment, we glared at each other in furious silence, and then he said slowly, "How am I to trust anything you tell me, then? How am I to know you tell the truth?"

He cannot, of course; when he broke the covenant to make me as he is, he surrendered his ability to know my thoughts, and my brother's.

So it was his gaze fell on Dunya.

She moaned in despair as he lifted a single finger to beckon her; for an instant, she clutched my skirts like a frightened child before yielding reluctantly to the magnetic pull of those evergreen eyes. Overwhelmed with pity, I patted her hand before she turned to him, and saw the tears in her eyes.

She ascended the platform with slow, reluctant grace and, with the deliberate, exaggerated movements of a sleepwalker, lifted the dark coil of hair from her neck and offered it to him as he sat. She was not at quite the proper angle for him, and so he put a single finger beneath her chin and, tilting it upwards, moved her head to one side and pulled her back until she leaned heavily against him.

He leaned his head low, his iron-grey hair spilling down over her shoulder, and drank. The girl gave a slight shuddering cry as his teeth pierced her skin again (as they have so many times before). And as he supped, her eyes went dull, then fluttered until at last they closed in that sweet, dreamy languour brought by his kiss.

"Not long," I warned him, for Dunya's sake. "She is tired, and I often made use of her on my way to Vienna."

He obeyed, drinking of her blood and thoughts only a short time, then raising his face, teeth, and lips painted red. Poor Jean no doubt saw in this a preview of his own fate, for behind me came an astonished gasp.

Dunya's ignorance was my salvation. I could read acceptance in Vlad's expression.

"So," he said. "It is true, at least, that you visited him and mesmerised him quite thoroughly. But what is this incorrigible harlotry, my dear, that you pressed yourself and your maid upon your own brother? Most interesting. For if either of you were to bear him a male heir—"

He did not complete the thought, but I finished it for him in my own mind: *Then perhaps there would be no need to find Arkady or his son.*

"Take my child," I replied swiftly, "and Dunya's, into your service. One for Arkady's generation, the other for his son's."

He tilted his head, thoughtful, alabaster lids lowering briefly over emerald eyes. And then his gaze became direct, pointed. "I doubt such substitutions possible. But even if they were . . . you are naïve, Zsuzsanna, to think these two acts might immediately produce children. The chances are that neither of you will conceive. And if you do not?"

For this I had no answer.

"I see. So you thought to find a way to save both your brother and me." He paused, and I saw a brilliant flare of anger in his eyes. As strong as I am, as immortal, the sight still filled me with fear. For though he would raise no hand against me, I knew that my poor Monsieur Belmonde would be spared no pain, no indignity.

With a softness more terrifying than the most earth-rattling thunder, he said, "Do you relish your life now, Zsuzsanna?"

"Yes," I whispered.

"Yet you love your brother."

"Yes. . . ."

"Decide, my dear. For the one precludes the other. A mortal's lifetime, Zsuzsanna. A single lifetime—that is all we have left, before the covenant lapses and we two are destroyed. If Arkady's son dies unbound to us, uncorrupted—so will we die. And if we fail to destroy Arkady during that lifetime, we will also die. You have just cost me an opportunity! How many more will come to us in the next fifty, sixty years? It is not so long a time—a mere nod of the head, the wink of an eye, to us! I fear you still think like a mortal.

"Answer me: Do you wish to die in this castle a hag? Shrivelled, starved, ugly beyond any man's desire, a more pitiful creature than you were as a mortal?"

"No," I whispered. "No."

"That is what you condemn yourself to, Zsuzsanna, with your weakness. With your foolish love."

He fingered the chalice that rested near his hand—the chalice stained with Kasha's blood, and our father's, and our father's father's, and his before him—then lifted it and swore: "With your help or without, I will see Arkady destroyed. And I will drink of his son's blood, and he of mine; a new generation will be bound to my service!"

On the surface, his tone sounded utterly confident—but my perceptions are keen now; I could hear the fear beneath it, the terror, the rage.

To know him fearful frightened me more deeply than I had ever thought possible. I would have felt safer in the presence of a wounded raging lion.

He looked beyond the raised chalice, narrowing his eyes at me. "Your brother is a fool to think himself a match for me! And you, my darling Zsuzsa . . . know that I love you. But my love can turn rapidly to hatred should I be deceived. *Justus et pius.*"

He lowered the chalice then and turned to Vanya. "It is time."

With a grunt, Vanya hoisted the man-long stake in both freckled sinewy arms and, scrabbling sidewise like a strong little crab, dragged it to the end of the rack, where a special groove had been carved for it into the wood.

It was an unwieldy task for one man, much less one bent and crippled, but Vanya managed with much grunting and determination—born, no doubt, of the same desire that brought the bright unholy gleam to his eyes. With a loud thump, the stake fell into the groove, which extended the length of Jean's leg down the center of the rack, and ended, most ominously, just above his lower spine.

The unfortunate man began to scream.

"No!" I cried. "Uncle, please—"

But I knew when Vlad turned his imperious, distrustful gaze on me that my words were in vain; the time had come for my punishment. Jean would suffer now because I had dared disobey. His voice was stern, unyielding, but not without an undercurrent of tenderness. "You have failed me, Zsuzsanna; you, whom I have most loved. Have I ever failed you? Ever denied you anything?"

He straightened regally, and his visage and voice took on a richness, a glamour, a leonine magnificence that had surely been seen four centuries before by those who had attended his court. He became indeed the *voievod,* the warrior-prince who had saved his people from death at Turkish hands: Vlad, he who was called by some *Tsepesh,* the Impaler; by others *Dracula,* son of the dragon. The words beneath him, *justus et pius,* just and faithful, no longer seemed parody; no, he shone, radiant from within, like a beatified saint. An angel—fallen, but no less glorious to behold. For a swift instant—the flicker of a candle, no more—even I, trained by him in the art of mesmerisation, was swayed by his beauty, his greatness, and forgot my pity for my intended, Monsieur Jean Belmonde.

"I am harsh but just, am I not?" he asked me softly as Vanya slid the stake higher, higher, until the point came to rest just at the opening of the chained man's bowels.

Jean's cries grew even more hysterical.

Vlad rose, his movements lordly, as elegant as any work of art I ever saw in Vienna, and took one step, two, towards the bound man. "A madman, am I, monsieur? Do you realise who it is you insult?"

Belmonde began to weep openly, tears streaming down his face, his bloodied chest heaving from paroxysmal sobs. "No. No. I beg pardon, monsieur; tell me what it is you wish, and I will see it done. Anything. Anything! Only do not harm me—"

"I am prince of these lands," Vlad said, his face gleaming from such bright inner fire that he seemed an apparition sent from God rather than the Devil. At the sight, I remembered how it was that I became smitten with love for him. "I bought them with my flesh, my blood, my tears. Did you hear what I told Zsuzsanna?"

Carefully, deliberately, red eyes wide and intent on his victim, Vanya moved the stake higher: a half-inch, no more. Belmonde jerked and cried out, then began to babble tearfully. "Forgive me, Prince, forgive me . . . I am a foolish man, I did not know. . . ."

"I said: Did you hear what I told her?"

Jean fumbled, wild-eyed, for the words. "I am not sure. . . . I— You are—you are—harsh but just?"

Vlad smiled. "Very good, Monsieur Belmonde. And what I have said is true. I ask you now: Is it just to punish an insult?"

The trapped man's lips trembled as he struggled to formulate a reply that might save him. A bead of sweat trickled its way down from his damp golden curls; from a distance I savoured its pungent aroma as my fondness and compassion warred with my growing hunger. "It . . . it is more Christian, perhaps, to forgive it—" His voice broke. "For love of God, I beg you, monsieur, to forgive—"

I might have asked again for mercy to our unfortunate guest, but Vlad despises weakness; my pleas would have served only to provoke more suffering for Jean. So I held my tongue as Dunya, awakened now from her trance, stumbled down to my side and sank, weakened, to her knees. As she clasped my waist and hid her face in my skirt, I put my arms around her and stroked her hair in a useless gesture of comfort. Meanwhile, Vlad interrupted his prisoner.

"So now I am un-Christian," he thundered, "an infidel, like the Turks I defeated so many centuries ago? Two insults! I advise you, sir: Beg for mercy. Beg for your very life!"

Poor Belmonde begged, in an incoherent rush of sobbed syllables. I have quite a facility for French; Jean and I used it almost exclusively to communicate. But this time I understood not a word; not until Vlad at last climbed the scaffolding beside my trembling naked lover and bent low beside him.

Of a sudden, his expression softened, and in a low, gentle voice he whispered to Jean, "Enough. Enough. You shall be released from your chains."

The young man let go a deep, shuddering sigh, then wept softly as he whispered, "God bless you, monsieur; may God eternally bless you."

Vlad stroked Belmonde's glistening forehead, smoothing back the golden curls with paternal tenderness. And then he turned his face just enough to glance down at the foot of the rack, where Vanya stood ready, one shoulder against the base of the shining oiled stake.

The Impaler signalled with a nod.

Vanya gave a mighty thrust. I am immortal, yes; and even if my life extends through all eternity, I pray never again to hear such a sound. (The horror is, I have heard it before—and certainly shall again.) Jean screamed—a scream to pierce the very gates of Heaven. I caught but a glimpse of his body arched in spasm as the stake ascended, piercing his bowels; more than that I could not bear to witness but instead closed my eyes and covered with my palms the ears of poor Dunya, who added her own cry of anguish to his. We clung to each other in our misery.

At last silence fell. I looked up to find that the young man had, in his agony, fainted; now Vanya, atremble with excitement, struggled feverishly to raise the stake.

So he did, with some assistance from Vlad, and erected it in the midst of the theatre of death, upon the scaffolding constructed expressly for the purpose. And Vlad, his own eyes ablaze like the sun, stepped back to admire his grisly handiwork: Belmonde impaled, his head hung to one side, his arms swinging limp as a marionette's, the weight of his own body drawing him downwards so that the stake travelled slowly, inexorably up through his vitals.

By dawn, if Vanya had performed his task precisely, the blunted tip would peek through the corpse's gaping lips.

"Wake him!" Vlad ordered, and Vanya scurried to procure a pole from which hung suspended a rag. This he doused liberally with slivovitz, then raised it to Jean's lips, a cruel parody of the centurion offering Christ bitter gall.

The dying man groaned as he returned to consciousness —beyond speech now, beyond all but pain. I knew what would follow now and dreaded it, yet my own hunger had grown painfully and demanded appeasement. I had grown accustomed, in Vienna, to dining nightly, and the spectre of famine made me desperate to feed while I could. Dunya was too weak, too pale to offer sustenance; I dared not even sip lightly, much less drink to my satisfaction. Jean was entirely lost. From him, I could drink my fill. . . .

I watched, disgusted at my own desire as Vlad took the suffering man's chin in his hand, turning Jean's face towards his.

"Yes, wake," he hissed. "Wake and know who it is that torments you."

And with a savagery that, to my shame, delighted and aroused me, he thrust his teeth into Belmonde's neck. The man cried out again—a weak whisper, now. Shock and pain had sapped him; there would not be much time to drink before death, when the blood began to cool.

I forgot my humanity. I pushed Dunya aside and hurried to the scaffolding, ascending it in a smooth, easy leap invisible to mortal eyes.

I stood beside Vlad, waiting anxiously as he fed, forgetting my distaste for blood tainted by terror, fearing only that there should not be enough for us both. And as Vlad drank, Belmonde's piteous moans ceased. After a time, he fainted once more, and even Vanya's persistent ministrations could not rouse him.

At that, Vlad moved aside, his eyes brilliant, green, triumphant as he watched me press my lips to the bloody wound he had opened.

I drank, angered at my own helplessness to refuse, at my own weakness. Yes, I drank, but it was bitter, bitter, bitter blood . . .

AMSTERDAM

NOVEMBER · 1871
Twenty-six Years Later

⊰ 3 ⊱

Telegramme from Guy de la Mer, Amsterdam, to V. Dracula, c/o Golden Krone Hotel, Bistritz, 12 November 1871

Subject located at last. Itinerary and arrival time to follow.

⊹ ⊹ ⊹

The Journal of
Mary Tsepesh Van Helsing

19 NOVEMBER 1871. My husband is dead.

My husband is dead.

Twice I have written these words; twice it has happened. To-day we buried Jan, who more than two decades ago rescued my child from unspeakable danger.

Did I love him? Yes. But ours was a cool love, more a friendship born of gratitude and respect, not passion—at least, not mine. Even so, my heart aches at the loss, and writing this, I weep stinging tears. I have lost my truest friend; or so, before to-night, I had believed.

But only one man has ever truly had my heart: my beloved Arkady—dead some twenty-six years. This I know as a fact, for it was I who served as his executioner, I who aimed the bullet that tore through his heart.

Would that it had been mine; the pain would have been less. I have treasured the gun all this time; not a night has gone by that I did not caress it in secret, did not press its cold steel to my lips and whisper lovingly to the ghost of him who still haunts me.

But a ghost he is no more. No; far, far worse than that . . .

He came to me to-night. Not as a phantom of imagination or ill-formed spectre from a dream but in the flesh—the cold, cold flesh.

I was sitting upstairs in my room, beside the bed that Jan and I had shared, indulging in sleeplessness and private grief after a long day of funereal ceremony and public condolences. The rest of the family was downstairs asleep, while I sat staring into the fire, recalling the first time Jan and I had met. A prisoner in Vlad's terrible castle, I was labouring to give birth to Arkady's child when Jan appeared, calling himself by a fictitious name. He delivered my son and rescued him from Vlad's clutches; and later, when I escaped and found them both, he comforted me in my boundless sorrow over Arkady's death. For he was himself an unhappy widower; and we two provided each other with a measure of solace.

Now the impossible has happened: My late first husband has appeared to comfort me over the death of my second.

As I sat in total darkness save for the glowing embers in the fireplace, my gaze falling upon the window and the clouded starless night beyond, yet seeing nothing but the memories contained in my mind's eye, something thrummed gently against the pane. The sound continued for some time, I think, before at last I became aware of it; I thought at first it was a misguided bird. Indeed, a large black shape—the size of a great raven—hovered there.

Mild curiosity threaded its way through my grief. As I continued to peer at the dark form, I perceived a flash of white—quite radiant, as though lit from within like a glowing gas lamp. And then the whiteness slowly coalesced into a face: the face of my dear Arkady.

I rose, stricken, a hand to my heart, though I felt quite certain that this apparition was the product of sleeplessness and sorrow. Even so, I could not resist it; I stepped over to the window, thinking that this would surely reveal the vision as a trompe l'oeil, a play of light and shadow, no more.

But no: The closer I drew, the clearer his features became. And how handsome! I had fled Transylvania for my life, without time even to carry with me a portrait of my beloved to keep his face fresh in my memory, but time has blurred not a single detail—the thick fierce brows above a hawkish nose, the large, slightly upward-slanting eyes with long, almost feminine lashes, the high forehead culminating in a widow's peak. Yet his features seemed more even, more perfect and beautiful than ever I remembered: his coal-black hair long, curling, aglitter with sparks of indigo, his pale skin glowing so that it lit up the darkness around him.

And his eyes . . . they were the loving eyes of the husband I had lost so long ago, and at the sight of me they filled with the same pain and longing that tugged at my own heart.

Impulsively, I pulled up the sash, letting in the cold and damp. . . .

Letting in my past. He entered with a gust of wind,

slamming the window shut behind him, and in an impossible instant there before me stood my darling, cloaked in black, strong and handsome and young, untouched by the passage of twenty-six years. No, more than handsome: beautiful. Gloriously beautiful.

And there stood I, an old woman, my hair streaked with silver, my face and body, once as smooth and firm as his, now sagging, wrinkled.

"Arkady?" I whispered, thinking that the strain of recent events had somehow driven me mad. "Is it . . . possible?"

He let out a long sigh—or perhaps it was merely the soft, distant howling of the wind—and on it was carried a single word: "Mary."

I began again to weep, this time with tears of gladness, and reached a hand to his cheek. He smiled palely as I did so; my fingertips brushed not warm, living skin, but the cold flesh of the dead.

I let go a low, horrified wail. For at that moment I understood that this was no phantom evoked by madness, no dream, and I understood what had transpired those twenty-six years ago. My husband had indeed died at my own hand. But instead of going to his rest as I had intended, he had been transformed by Vlad into the lovely, soulless monster that now stood before me.

I pressed my trembling fingers to my lips. My face must have revealed my horror, for the sight of it caused pain to flicker across his.

"Mary . . ." It was the most piteous of groans, uttered in a voice inhumanly melodic and compelling; at the same time, it was unmistakably the voice of my Arkady, tormented by love and regret. He spoke in English, the language we had shared, the language I had abandoned over a quarter-century before, when I abandoned my other life. "Oh, my dear, perhaps I should not have come. . . . Perhaps now was too cruel."

I could not fear him. I was too drained by grief and shock to have concern for my own safety. And whatever he had become, whatever monstrosities he had committed, he still bore the face of my beloved. If he had reached out to kill me then, I should not have resisted.

But the realisation of what had become of my first husband caused me to stagger backwards and collapse into the chair behind me. Arkady followed with movements so utterly silent that his steps made no sound against the wooden floor, and descended to one knee at my side.

"Forgive me," he said, looking sombrely into my eyes; the fire behind him painted one side of his gleaming face with its brilliant orange glow. "Perhaps I should not have come to-night, of all nights, when your sorrow is so fresh. But I did not wish to trouble you while your husband"—he faltered at the word and lowered his eyes, lest I see the pain and jealousy in them—"while Jan lived. But recent events have convinced me of the urgent need to speak with you. And to-day came a development I could not ignore."

"Then Vlad still lives," I realised aloud. All these years I had lived in uncertainty, hoping that Arkady's death had purchased Vlad's destruction, that my child was safe from his family's curse—but never knowing if past horrors would return to haunt us. The night beyond my small window suddenly seemed unspeakably darker, more evil; in that terrible instant I knew my worst fears were indeed true.

"Vlad still lives," Arkady repeated. "At the instant I died, he trapped my soul between heaven and earth. He made me as he is, knowing that I would have to become corrupt—"

I turned my face from the thought that the one I so loved had become a murderer.

He finished, his tone and expression grown hard. "I have no choice, Mary. My destruction would purchase Vlad's continuance. My survival allows protection for you and my son."

"And all those lives you have taken over the past twenty-six years?"

My words evoked fresh pain in his voice, face, eyes. "Each of them will buy a hundred, a thousand, an infinite number more lives. For I swear on each of them that I will see them avenged and Vlad destroyed.

"And the day he dies, so I will choose to die, too. Will you see our children, and our children's children, damned throughout eternity? Let the curse end with me, Mary. Let it end with me."

"Dear God," I whispered. "I would rather have died than see you as this. It is I who have done this to you." And I began to weep.

The sight plainly unsettled him. I am not easily given to tears or fainting; indeed, I killed my husband with my own hand to spare him from service to Vlad, and I somehow managed to survive the following years of the greatest pain any woman, any man could ever know. Suffice it say that had there been but one bullet more left in the revolver that evil morn, I should not be writing these words to-day.

My hand clutched the armrest. Gently, he laid his own atop mine. I tensed at its coldness but did not pull away.

"You were always stronger than I," he said. "Darling Mary, I had feared you dead. How did you ever survive?"

I told him then of my escape twenty-six years before. I had been weak after childbirth, indeed near death; but the moment I fired the fatal shot at my husband, the horses had bolted. I took advantage of their excitement and drove them hard to the north, to Moldovitsa, where I knew the doctor who called himself Kohl would have taken my child. I wanted then only to keep driving until I myself died, but the thought of my baby kept me alive. My memory of what followed is unclear. I know I collapsed then with fever and a kind innkeeper took care of me. My ravings had alerted him to my search for a doctor and infant. Such a pair had stopped by that very inn, though the man had called himself Van Helsing, not Kohl, in search of milk for the baby. They were next headed to the town of Putna.

I knew in my heart this was the same man. When I came to myself, I sent a telegramme to Doctor Van Helsing at Putna, informing him that I had escaped, but my poor husband, who had been fatally wounded, had not.

Within days, I was reunited with my little son. I knew not where to go; I had no cause to return to England and was too dazed by grief to care where I went. Jan Van Helsing convinced me to return with him to his native Amsterdam. So there I raised my child and, after a year and a half of rejecting Jan's proposals of marriage, finally accepted them, so that my boy might have a father. Soon we adopted another child, a little boy. We lived far from the taint of the name Dracul and took the name Van Helsing as our own.

I have two sons now; both believe themselves brothers, though one is adopted. Neither knows anything of the dark past. There seemed no cause to dim their happiness with such tales.

Arkady listened to all this in intent silence; and then he said, "For more than two decades, I have struggled to keep Vlad from finding you. At every turn I thwarted his efforts. . . . At every opportunity, I sent mortals to end his existence. But all of them failed; some fled as cowards and disappeared, some went mad, and others destroyed themselves or were themselves destroyed. I found no heart steady enough, true enough, to complete the task. And try as I might, I could not eternally prevent him from following the path you trod so long ago, for he sent one agent after another—each one shrewder and more determined than the last."

I collapsed into my chair, struck down by the weight of his words, and raised my hand to my heart. "He is here? In Amsterdam?"

Pity crossed his face. "No; he is trapped in Transylvania —recompense for violating the covenant and making one of his own blood a vampire. You need not fear encountering him here, for he has never travelled easily, as he must sleep surrounded by his native soil. I am spared this, perhaps because my blood is not so pure. But he has sent his agent. Here is the proof." He slipped a hand into his waistcoat pocket and withdrew something gold, shining, bright.

A small coin. He proffered, and I rose to take it, holding it at arm's length to better see the imprint in the dim firelight.

I recognised it at once and gave a low cry.

It was the image of a winged dragon, with forked tongue and tail, and a double cross emerging from its back. I did not need to inspect the underside to know the words stamped there: JUSTUS ET PIUS.

I handed it back at once, for the very feel of it against my fingertips was cold, evil, odious. I wanted nothing better than to hurry to the basin to wash my hands, but I knew that not even an ocean could ever wash the taint away. My love for the man who stood before me—nay, the man this creature had once been—had stained me forever.

"Used to purchase lodging," Arkady said softly as he replaced the coin after a second grim glance. "I have been watching you and your family some time, as protection; but daylight limits my abilities, and I cannot go without a period of rest. Like him, I must at times rely on human assistance. But I have never left you unguarded. Even so—"

"What must we do?" I interrupted, struggling to keep my voice a whisper, lest I wake the others.

"You must warn them. Warn our son—"

"He will not believe," I protested.

"He must. Vlad will stop at nothing to find him, to force him to undergo the blood ritual—and then his mind will be Vlad's to control. We must prevent that at all costs."

My pulse quickened with dread. "But how?"

"You have always been the stronger," he repeated. "Dear Mary, can you be strong again?"

I replied nothing, only fixed my gaze upon him and thought of my two innocent sons.

When I came to this quaint country more than a quarter century ago, I considered myself reborn. It is far different from Transylvania or my native England: the temperate winters, the flat, marshy sweeps of land, the creak of windmills, the wide sky with its gilt-edged, swift clouds so favoured by artists, the clean bustling cities filled with smiling industrious people who care not a whit for class—all were entirely alien to me. There is a sense of goodness here, a sweet freshness in the air that blows in from the ever-present sea. Beside it, Transylvania seems anciently evil, decadent, corrupt as a mouldering corpse.

Grateful for the change, I put the terror of the past behind me. I embraced the Dutch people to the extent that I spoke nothing but their language, forgetting my native tongue. For more than twenty-five years, I had been so far removed from danger that I began to believe I and my children were safe.

Now, to find this long-dead fear resurrected . . .

"I cannot," I said, withdrawing my hand from beneath his. "Please . . . do not ask for my help. I cannot bear even to think of putting my children at risk—"

"They are already at risk." He rose abruptly and, with a move swifter than my eyes could perceive, turned from me to face the fire. "I have had twenty-six years to deliberate on what I would do when I decided to approach you and Stefan. I could continue to keep a protective eye on you and remain silent—as I have been doing for the past several months since I found you. But I am barely a match for Vlad. I am almost as wily as he now—but he has had centuries of experience beyond mine. I have attempted several times to destroy him; several times he has learnt of my plan in time and escaped. Many times he has come close to destroying me." He whirled abruptly and faced me. "I could have kept you unawares of the threat and spared you this pain—but your ignorance would only increase the danger." He paused, holding my gaze with soft, desperate eyes, brown eyes flecked with green, eyes I thought I should never look into again, so beautiful and tortured that I fought not to weep. "And you are the only one I can entrust with the most solemn of tasks. I need your promise."

I hesitated.

"Mary," he murmured "you killed me once before, my darling; when the time comes and Vlad is destroyed—if I do not die, can you be strong enough, can I trust you, to do it again?"

I covered my face with my hands, overwhelmed, and felt cold lips brush the top of my head. I remained thus for some time, unable to speak, unable to think, able only to sit shivering at the sense of encroaching evil, at the realisation

that my agonising act of mercy had purchased for my beloved not relief but the most hideous of purgatories.

When at last I looked up, an expression of such pure
sincerity and anguish passed over his features that I rose,
pierced through the soul at the sight of his pain. I had buried
one husband that morning, only to find now another, long
thought dead; my heart welled with such love and sadness at
the cruelty of his predicament that I reached to console him.

"Oh, Arkady . . ."

Sobbing, we embraced at last. For a blessed moment, I
did not notice the coldness of the arms that enfolded me, of
the lips that brushed my forehead, of the tears that rained
upon my hair; nor did I perceive the odd stillness in the
chest where once had beaten a warm living heart. I held him
fast, thinking only that I was reunited with him I loved
most.

And he held me, with all the sweet fierce tenderness of
the husband I had known. Oh, how he held me. . . .

How long we remained in that blissful pose I cannot
say. But the time came when I, swept up in an outpouring of
affection, pressed my lips to his silent breast, the shoulder of
his cloak, his neck—and then his mouth.

He drew away, but not before I caught the unmistakable scent and taste of death and iron. I pulled back—and
saw on his parted lips, upon his collar, dark stains.

Dark in the fireglow, because of the night; but I had no
doubt that were I to light the lamp, those stains would be
bright, fresh, crimson.

I recoiled with a sharp cry.

He released me at once. I brushed fingertips against my
own lips and drew them away, bloodied. He saw the object
of my dismay, and his expression transformed itself into one
of fathomless shame.

"Go!" I demanded as I lowered my gaze, unable to look further at him, to see anything but my own spread fingers, covered with an unknown victim's blood. "Go, please! I cannot—I cannot bear even to think—"

His voice was calm and soft but carried an undercurrent of steel resolve. "You must. Just as I had to return. It was too much for me to have come tonight, too soon after your loss. Forgive me. But consider all I have said."

I turned, mouth open to reply—and saw that I stood alone. Or did I? For it seemed that, from the corner of my eye, I espied a dark moving shadow scrabbling towards the window.

A sudden gust of cold wind made me shiver; I hurried to the window, now open, and pulled down the sash. Beyond, in the moonless dark, I could see nothing—nothing but the silent black shapes of houses across the street, aglitter from a light rain.

I started at a sharp rapping at my bedroom door; the sound seemed startling normal, incongruous with the dreamlike unreality of what I had just experienced. Had it not come, I would perchance have convinced myself that Arkady's appearance *had* been naught but a dream. But I was full awake as I turned from the window and hurried towards the knocking.

"Moeder?" Bram's voice, hoarse and tired, but tense with concern.

I opened the door to find my son, still dressed in the shirt sleeves he had worn to his father's funeral; behind thick spectacles, his bright blue eyes were swollen and edged with red. His waving gold hair, kissed with copper, was tousled, as though he had been lying down, but the exhaustion in his tone told me that he, like his mother, had not slept.

For a moment, I did not speak but permitted myself to

gaze at him, to remember those dark fearful days when he was still a baby, to admire the brilliant young man that child had become. He is so driven, my Abraham, so upright and curious and intelligent that he had taken a law degree while exceptionally young, then followed in Jan's footsteps and became a physician when the law failed to offer enough opportunities to help the helpless. It became a great source of pride to Jan that his adoptive son should be so much like him; indeed, so like him in interests and appearance that we all came to speak and think of Bram as Jan's own son and saw no reason to disabuse Bram of the notion. Like his adoptive father, he thrives on overwork; yet I could see for the first time the toll it had taken on him, could see the weariness hidden in the shadows beneath his eyes.

He frowned with worry as he scrutinised me and reached for my hand with both of his; after the coldness of Arkady's grip, the warmth of my son's was reassuring. "I heard a scream—"

He spoke in Dutch, as I had intentionally never conversed with my sons in English but let them learn the language at school; and I answered him thus, conscious for the first time in many years that I was speaking a foreign tongue. "It was nothing." I tried to smile, tried to affect a light tone, and failed. "A mouse. I startled the poor thing more than it did me, I think."

"Ah," he said. "I must leave for the hospital early in the morning, but I will remind Stefan to set a trap." He paused, his penetrating gaze never wavering from my face—he is so serious, that one, so unlike his brother—and for a flickering instant my resolve melted. I drew a breath and opened my mouth to speak, to tell him the truth of it all, to warn him, to beg him to flee. Ignorance has brought my children a happy life thus far; will it now bring their destruction?

My words died unborn. Abraham is a dedicated sceptic, the last person living who would accept my wild tale. How shall I tell him? Tell Stefan? I reached out and laid my other hand atop his, tightening my grip, afraid ever to release it.

It served to increase Bram's concern. "Are you quite certain you're all right, Mama?"

I could not release the contents of my heart. No; such a revelation required careful forethought. Instead I nodded, at last managing a weary smile.

"You would not like a draught to help you sleep?"

"No. Go to sleep, Bram."

He patted my hand and withdrew. I shut the door, washed my hands and face in the basin, taking special care to clean my lips—and sat down to pen this entry. From time to time I wipe my mouth with my handkerchief, but the taste of blood lingers.

Dawn is almost here, and still I cannot decide how or what to tell my sons.

What remains of my little family is no longer safe. Evil surrounds us. May God help us all.

⇥4⇤

The Journal of
Stefan Van Helsing

19 NOVEMBER 1871. I am the happiest and most miserable of
men.

I am compelled to write it all down; as penance, perhaps, knowing that someday someone might stumble upon
these words. It would be no less than I deserve.

Here, then, a tale of the Fall: and the truth is that,
recounting it, I feel as much illicit joy as shame.

We buried poor Papa to-day. I was, of course, overwhelmed by grief (shall I use it to pardon the inexcusable?),
of no use to anyone. But Bram was there; always there, and
took good care of Mama. He is much like her: solid, never-
changing, always dependable, so strong that he never once
wept in public. Mama, too, never cried, though her eyes
were rimmed with red.

And I, ever the emotional one, the weak one, stood at
my father's yawning grave braced between those two rocks in
the cloudy morning—I, with my raven hair so different from
their golden waves, my hot tears mingling with the cold mist
that began to fall. I am different from them all—Bram,

Mama, Papa. An outsider, subject to emotions and passions and a restless uncertainty that my calm, steady family cannot comprehend. Indeed, everyone in this city, this tiny kingdom is so industrious, so even-tempered, so conformist and concerned with the practical undertakings of life that I feel out of place.

To please Papa, I followed in his footsteps and became, like Bram, a physician. But my heart is in my poetry.

Gerda understands. She is dark-haired, like me, dark-eyed, and I cannot help thinking we are cast from the same mould. I knew the instant I first saw her, all those years ago: her long hair matted and tousled, her eyes wild as she sat on the floor of her cell, knees hugged to her bosom. Not a pretty woman, but a striking one. Small and fine-boned, thin, with hollows sculpted beneath her eyes, her cheeks, that shadows seek out.

A madwoman, they said, but my brother had seen something more, and I saw from the expression on his face as he peered through the bars at her that she had already captured his heart.

As she did mine that day.

As a boy, Bram constantly brought home stray and injured animals; his generosity is as deep and boundless as the ocean that surrounds us. As a man, he has not changed; but now his strays are of the two-legged variety, and just as needy. She was one of his charity cases, Gerda was, abandoned by her father to the sanitorium, deemed intractably mad.

I remember Bram turned to me that day and, with far more tenderness than his usual clinical air of a physician making his rounds, asked, *There is hope for this one, don't you think?*

Yes, I said. *There is definitely hope.*

I gazed into her eyes: troubled, tormented, and restless, ashine with sensitivity and the skittishness of an untamed deer. I knew at once I had met a kindred soul. No—not met. *Recognised.*

And in one swift instant, my heart was stolen. It has been lost now four years, though I spoke of it to no one; certainly not my kind-hearted brother, who within a matter of eighteen months had healed her, wooed her, wed her. I watched her bloom beneath Bram's protective aegis, beneath my family's. I watched them bear a son.

And I have watched her once more grow unhappy, restless. Bram is a loving husband and father; but beyond his stolid dependability, he possesses his own restless drive, one that he submerges utterly in work and study. He is absorbed in his world of medicine and law; and now that he has salvaged Gerda, he is ever in search of new helpless ones to redeem.

Less dedicated to my medical practise, I have been home when Bram has not. On those occasions when Bram was off studying some new madman, some exotic malady, I became Gerda's squire, a doting uncle to my little nephew, Jan; indeed, I think I know him better than his own father. I contained myself, bore my unrequited love in silence all these years—though I fancied at times she signalled her secret love for me with special smiles and looks, comments that, when weighed carefully, might have carried double meaning.

But I, dutiful brother, did not permit myself to believe; and if I believed, did not permit myself to acknowledge. Bram has always been loyal, kind, tolerant of my temperamental outbursts; when Papa first became ill, Bram filled the role of mentor and fatherly advisor. How could I betray him? Surely my capricious heart would find another object of adoration in due time; I would be patient, and soon my obsession with her would dwindle.

But the more I was in her presence, the more my love grew. Many a time over the past four tormented years have I returned in memory to that moment I first saw her huddled in the sanitorium cell—ah, but it is I who am now the madman, strait-jacketed by my own emotions. And now, what I have long dreamt of, what I have long feared, has happened.

Two nights ago—the evening Papa died—I was sitting downstairs in the drawing-room, in Papa's favourite chair, mourning. It was late, past mid-night, and the others were all asleep or weeping in the privacy of their rooms; Mama was holding vigil over the body. I was too restless for bed, too distraught even to stir the coals or light the lamp. So I sat in near-darkness, staring at the glowing embers in the fireplace, when my eye caught something white and wraith-like crossing through the room.

It moved stealthily towards the mantel, and as it stepped between me and the fire, I recognised Gerda. She wore nothing but her dressing-gown; I can never forget how, that night, the fireglow limned the white silk, revealing the slope of a perfect breast beneath. She took a glass and poured from Papa's carafe of port, then turned, clearly bent on making a quick escape with her prize.

As she did so, she caught sight of me at last, letting go of her glass with a loud gasp.

Fortunately, at that same instant, I rose instinctively, managing with no small amount of fumbling to catch the glass. Wine sloshed onto the fine silk of her robe, onto me, perfuming the air with a sweet oaken fragrance, but the glass was saved. The act left me pressed against her; my first impulse was to immediately retreat and restore propriety, but to my surprise, I moved closer, closer, until I could feel the rapid beating of her heart, until the world receded and I could see nothing but her eyes, as free from sophistication and guile as a feral beast, needing to be soothed and tamed by a tender voice.

She did not pull away. I knew then I had not deluded myself; she loved me as I loved her, and for a long, frozen moment we stood poised on the verge of a kiss.

It was I who finally, reluctantly, backed away. She stared at me a second more, then fled upstairs with her half-empty glass.

I was torn between grief over Papa's death and joy that, at long last, I knew my love requited. That night I shook off guilt and swore that if she appeared to me again under the same circumstances, I would not back away.

This evening—after all the mourners had left, and Mama had closeted herself in her bedroom, and Bram had gone to make his customary late rounds of homebound patients—I sat waiting in Papa's chair again, watching as dusk fell over the grey November landscape, over the flat muddy street, the carriages, the rows of neat brick houses all the same, the windmills beyond, the invisible lurking sea. The chair brings me comfort, for it smells of Papa and his pipe; I found one of his silvered blond hairs on the seat, and his bag of tobacco on the end-table.

I poured myself a glass of his port from the mantel and thought I understood why Gerda had come to drink it: the taste and smell evoked him so—not the sick wasted creature he had become in those final terrible days, but the laughing great blond bear who had loved his children, his wife, his patients with a cheerful, tolerant, expansive love.

I drank until the twilight faded to full darkness, until the street emptied and the house grew altogether still save for the steady ticking of the grandfather clock in the hall. I drank until at last I heard soft footfall on the stairs, then rose and moved to the hearth to stir the fire.

When I turned, she was standing in the doorway, once again dressed in the dressing-gown of white silk; this time, her dark hair fell free onto her shoulders, her bosom, her waist. We studied each other a time like reluctant conspirators, and then she said:

"I heard a noise. I thought perhaps Abraham had returned."

Emboldened by the port, I held her gaze. "We both know he won't be back for some hours."

My directness unnerved her; her eyelids fluttered as she averted her gaze. I thought her on the verge of bolting like a hunted animal, but some strange determination held her back. She squared her frail shoulders and said, "You look so like him, sitting there. Your father was a good man."

I shook my head. "I wish I were good like him. Like Bram."

She stepped towards me, her voice raising with the intensity of her conviction. "But you are! You *are* good. Better than them all!"

"No. I am a dreadful man. Because what would bring me the greatest joy would only bring hurt to those I care for."

Silence. Then softly, so softly I could scarce make out the words, she replied, "Then I am dreadful, too, Stefan."

Her expression became one of such profound unhappiness that I began to weep, my grief over Papa's death mixing with honest sorrow at our predicament.

She moved swiftly to me. We embraced, not so much with lust as pure unhappiness, and she stroked my hair, murmuring, "Hush, hush . . ." in the same gentle tone she uses to comfort her little son.

What happened next I am ashamed to relay. Whether it was the port, the grief, the very nearness of her that loosed the last of my inhibitions, I cannot say. But my lips found the soft white skin of her cheek, her throat, the sweet hollow above her collarbone; my passion was kindled beyond all return, and I reached for her with the trembling desperation of a starving man grasping a crust of bread. Through some miracle, the white silk dressing-gown parted and fell away, revealing the sublime.

With swift desperate hunger, I took her, she standing pressed against the warm stone hearth. Or was it she who took me? She was a lioness, a goddess, full of fire and brazen need, reaching for me unashamed, sinking nails and teeth into my shoulder and gripping me with a fierceness that belied her frail body. Never was my spirit more exalted; never in a church, a chapel have I come closer to the numinous, the divine. It is the world that is mad, not I, to deem such ecstasy sin.

I was transported to the very gates of Heaven. How can this be evil, for two souls who so love each other to unite?

We coupled silently, violently; such was my excitement that I soon was spent. At once, she tore herself from me and hurried off into the darkness, leaving me to sink gasping to my knees upon the hearth.

Distraught at this abrupt abandonment, I struggled to rise, desiring to follow her, to profess my love and gain reassurance from her; desiring only to be near her.

But before I could regain my balance, the front door slammed and I heard familiar footfall: Bram. I smoothed my dishevelled appearance and hid in the shadows, fighting to still my laboured breathing, praying that he would not enter the drawing-room.

My request was heard; he moved back towards the kitchen. I hurried upstairs and closeted myself in my room.

Were it not for the physical evidence that remains on my own body, I would have thought it all a drunken dream, the visitation of an incubus. But her dew, her scent lingers on me still (I cannot bring myself to wash it away), and my shoulder bears the stripes of her passion.

What now? Morning will surely come and bring with it regret and fresh anticipation. Shall I pretend it never happened and live in misery? Or shall I arrange to meet her again? Even now, the memory fills me with such fire that I imagine going to her door and finding Bram heavily asleep, and her restless, waiting for me. . . .

Abraham, my brother! How I have wronged you . . . and how I tremble with guilty delight at the thought of wronging you again!

I have found love at last. But my heart cannot understand the insanity of it all: Why must it be so difficult, so fraught with guilt? Why must my joy bring others such pain?

⊹⊹ ⊹⊹ ⊹⊹

The Diary of
Abraham Van Helsing

19 NOVEMBER 1871. Death and the Devil, Lilli said, and she was right; the Devil has come, and murdered my heart.

Impossible for the day to grow more evil—so I foolishly thought—for it began in the cold grey morning with Papa's burial. It is hard to see a man who brought the world such good turn to dust, as we all shall. I try to take comfort in knowing that the results of his charitable deeds will outlive him by many years.

The funeral was a trial; I survived by comforting the others, which helped distract from my own pain. Mama was, as always, admirably brave, though I know she suffered the greatest loss; but poor Stefan seemed near nervous collapse. I stood beside him as we cast handfuls of damp earth onto the coffin, and supported him; had I not been there, I know he would have fallen. Gerda held my other arm, and she, like Stefan, wept openly, silently, the tears streaming down from her great dark eyes, her pale lips pressed tightly together as though fighting to contain a torrent of emotion.

Gerda, my tortured darling—I know there is no guile, no cruelty in your soul. Have I failed to love you as I ought?

So we laid Papa to rest, and I survived; survived, also, the following houseful of mourners, the platters of food, the flowers. Jan Van Helsing was much-loved, and all of Amsterdam, rich and poor, converged upon us to mourn him. Again I distracted myself by tending to Mama, Stefan, Gerda; and little Jan, christened after his grandfather and too young to understand his abrupt disappearance. Of the terrible memories I shall surely have of this day, one of them will be of my little son, barely old enough to toddle to the front door each time it opened to reveal a new guest, each time peering anxiously beyond them and calling for his grandfather: *Opa?*

And when day had waned and the last caller gone, I (like a fool, I realise now) indulged restlessness and habit and went to call on patients.

I was most concerned about Lilli—that is what she insists we call her, though she cannot remember her last name. We know nothing of her background, for no family has come to claim her despite our efforts to find them; most likely, she is a poor widow. Two months ago, she was found wandering the streets, quite delirious, raving about phantoms that visited her in the night and red eyes glowing in the dark. She was taken to a sanitorium, although she should have gone instead to a proper hospital, for she was half-dead of anaemia. I found her there and made arrangements for her to be moved to a private room in a boarding-house. Now that she has had proper rest and nutrition, the dementia has disappeared—with the exception of one delusion: She fancies herself a seeress of some ability and is quite obsessive about a pack of Tarot cards in her possession.

It seems a harmless enough delusion; she is a pleasant enough eccentric and even jokes with me about it. It is not her mental state that alarms me now but the physical: of late, her anaemia has recurred, despite all treatment. I am making notes on this, for its course is so atypical that I suspect it may be some new disease, for which I am eager to find a successful treatment.

There were many patients I intended to see that evening, but I called first on Lilli; and she received me that night with a great sense of drama. Per custom, I knocked on her door, which was slightly ajar, and entered when she called.

She was sitting propped up in her bed, her thinning white hair tucked beneath a night-cap, her bony shoulders covered by a shawl; in front of her, the pack of cards were spread on the quilt. To either side of her on the night-stands, a dozen tapers burned. They provided the only light in the room, and the effect was quite ghoulish. Lilli's skin was quite pale, her lips grey, and the wavering candleglow emphasised every shadow, every line in her wizened features; indeed, she looked like a child's conception of a witch. As I entered, she looked up from the cards to gaze at me with black liquid eyes, the whites of which were yellowed from age.

"Death," she intoned, with the conviction of a prophetess. "Death and the Devil visit you this night."

Had I not just buried my father that morning, I should have reacted to her melodramatic proclamation with an amused smile; as it was, I took offence. With somber dignity, I replied, "That is beneath you, Lilli. No doubt you have heard of my father's passing."

Her expression softened to one of sympathy—but her response was the opposite of what I expected. "Ah, yes. . . . Yes, I have, dear young doctor! Forgive my stupidity if my foolish words have brought you fresh grief—you, to whom I owe my very life." She paused to lower her face in an attitude of reverence, and when she raised it again, she said, "He was a fine man, your father. There is not one in the city who does not owe him a debt of gratitude. Surely his soul went straight to Heaven."

"Surely," I said, but I could not entirely keep the bitterness I felt from my tone. It would be no small comfort to believe in the Heaven and God Papa did, to believe that he now rests in eternal bliss. The truth, the reality, is dreadful: that he and all his knowledge and kindness and love, all that made him what he was, is now mere fodder for worms. I dare not say so at home—not for fear of disapproval but for fear of breaking Mama's heart. She believes fiercely in the superstitions of the Church; I hope they bring her comfort now.

With a bony arm, Lilli motioned me to take the chair at her bedside. I did, and she reached forth to place a cold hand, with its ridged yellowed nails, upon mine. "Dear young doctor, forgive me; I should first have offered you consolation on your father's death. But the cards . . . they speak so strongly to me to-night! And on *your* behalf."

Her eyelids fluttered; as if dizzied, she closed her eyes and raised a hand to her forehead, then leaned slowly back against the pillows.

"Lilli," I said. "You are not so well to-night." I leaned forward to examine her, holding on to her hand to surreptitiously take her pulse. It was weak, thready, her skin grey and startlingly cold. "The anaemia has worsened a bit, yes? How have you been feeling?"

With her eyes still closed, she gave a self-deprecating little smile, full of good humour. "I have such strange dreams of late. . . . I will die soon, I think." And before I could protest, she opened her eyes and said with sudden passion, "Dear young doctor, you must believe! It breaks my heart to bring you such news—but better you should be forewarned. Please believe me: You have become as dear to me as a son."

I patted her hand. "That I believe, dear Lilli. But why are you so distressed? I know all too well that my father has died."

"Ah . . ." she whispered, her eyes glistening with honest pity for me. "I am so sorry. But your father's is not the death revealed here. Two deaths. Two deaths more are coming, and the horror of the Nine of Swords. And here"—she tapped a dog-eared card—"the Devil himself. Death and the Devil visit your house *this* night. Not yesternight, nor the night before, but—"

"Please," I interrupted sharply; it took her quite aback, for I have never snapped at a patient. She fell into surprised silence as I continued, less harshly, "Let us speak of other things. It has been a long and trying day for me and my family; let us rather speak of you."

So we did, for a time—she is of all my patients the loneliest, and I credit regular conversation and friendship among her most healing medicines. I bade her take her tonic in my presence, a sleeping draught to help her restlessness at night, and a small sip of red wine to help the blood. As we chatted of more amiable things, I found myself growing uncharacteristically morose in her presence, perhaps because I could clearly note her decline. I fear she is right when she says she will soon die.

At any rate, she scooped up the offensive cards and spoke no more of them that evening; not until she fell drowsy, and her eyelids fluttered, then closed at last. Thinking her soundly asleep, I rose and moved towards the door; but before I could close it, she called out to me, in the voice of the prophetess—a voice strange and melodic:

"This is your fate, Abraham: The Devil seeks your house. Take care he does not find it. . . ."

In the doorway, I whirled, angered that her delusion should cause her to toy with my emotions at my hour of darkest grief. But her eyes were closed; she was in a sleep so profound, it could scarce have been feigned. So I left, troubled, hoping to ease my sorrowful anger by directing my attention away from myself and onto those who required it more: my patients.

I intended to visit another three or four, who by chance lived on the opposite side of the city from Lilli. By this time the sun had set and the streets had grown quite dark, but the drizzle had eased; rather than call for a cab, I walked. By the time I arrived once again in my own neighbourhood, the bracingly chill air and the exercise had calmed me. Quite by accident, I found myself once again upon our street, in front of our house—though my plan had been to take a slightly different, more efficient route. Indeed, I felt oddly compelled to return home, and I found my steps slowing as I approached it, suddenly overwhelmed with a growing unease and the desire to dispense with my rounds, to rush inside and make sure my wife and child were safe.

As I stared up at the house—the place I was born, the only home I have ever known—it became to my eyes strangely unfamiliar, even ominous, the way a loved, familiar object becomes, to a child's eyes, a monster in the dark. And as I stared, one shadow in particular captured my attention: a black moving form, the size of an ape, that hovered impossibly near a second-floor window—my mother's bedroom.

The sight of it caused a thrill of fear to course through me. I was convinced that it was malicious, sentient, alive— though *what* precisely it was, I could not have said; I knew only that it meant my family harm. With the panic that accompanies the worst nightmares, I moved silently, intently, towards it.

I never took my gaze from it; but as I watched, it appeared to melt into its surroundings and vanished before my eyes.

At the same time, I saw movement *inside* the window— though this may have been imagination, as my mother's room was very dimly lit. Imagination or not, the sight left me unsettled, and I determined to be sure my family was safe; so it was that I silently made my way up the front steps and opened the door so slowly, it made not a single creak.

Inside, the house was quite dark; everyone had already retired, or so I thought, and Mama had as always left the lamp in the hallway burning for me. I paused in the entryway, drawing in a deep breath so that I might steal quietly up the stairs to my mother's bedroom and listen for signs of trouble. I was torn between the odd, insistent sense of danger (which, I felt, had nothing whatsoever to do with Lilli's unbelievable prediction) and the realisation that my unease might prove to be quite ridiculous.

And as I hesitated at the foot of the staircase, my peripheral vision detected movement to my right, in the drawing-room. I retreated at once into the safety of shadows and peered into the darkness there. Beside the faintly glowing coals in the fireplace, a monstrous black creature writhed.

Or such was my impression; but as I watched, I realised this was not one form, but two, engaged in a cataclysmic struggle.

A low gasp came from one of them: With horror, I recognised my own wife's voice. In response, her opponent raised Gerda's arms—with a flash of the silvery-white sleeve of the dressing-gown I brought her from Paris—above her head and pinned them there, against the rough stone hearth. I almost screamed in fury at the attacker—but his form, too, was oddly familiar, for it was one I had known my entire life.

My own brother.

When Papa died, I thought I had experienced the worst pain I would ever know. But he is buried deep in the earth now, and in time, his mark upon this house and my memory will fade.

Stefan and Gerda I must see every day.

I have tried several times to go the bedroom and lie down beside her, near little Jan's crib. How shall I face her eyes again? It is not in her nature to deceive, to dissemble; her heart is always visible in her face, and I know that when I gaze on it again, I will see her guilt, her unhappiness.

I have not loved her enough. I see it now: I have been all these years a fool, more attentive to my patients than my own wife. For more than a year now, I thought I had detected too much fondness for him in her eyes, but I dismissed it as unreasonable jealousy.

To discover, to-day of all days, that I am right!

I could not confront them: what end would their disgrace have served? Can I blame them, knowing they are both of a piece, and that it was I who so often left them alone?

Instead, I retreated swiftly, then slammed the door with as much force as I could muster in that moment of utter despair.

I hid in the kitchen until I heard first her light steps, then his heavier ones, upon the stairs.

Gerda, Gerda, my fallen love! How shall I reclaim your heart?

And you, Stefan, my only brother . . . how shall I remove the taint and return to the innocent trust that was ours? We grew up so unalike, my brother and I, yet we were of one mind. He was the younger one, the passionate one, the one who constantly required my rescue. Yet his daring inspired me to overcome my natural diffidence at times; and my constancy in turn inspired him.

We are not whole without each other.

Even my medical practise would be incomplete without him, for I am, like Papa, a plodding logician, orderly in my attempts at diagnosis. Most times this is useful, but there are times when it fails; then I rely on Stefan's brilliant bursts of intuition. For me, medicine is science; to him, it is art.

Where should I be without him? For it is he who so sweetly and utterly adored his older brother and taught me to love generously.

Perhaps if I had learnt the lesson well enough, I should not have lost Gerda now.

Oh, the Devil has come indeed; and the first casualty is my own heart.

❧ 5 ☙

The Diary of
Abraham Van Helsing

20 NOVEMBER. Between this night and the last, the whole world has gone mad. The people I trusted most have all taken leave of their senses, and I dare not even trust my own.

I know only that my poor brother is lost to me, whether by his own design or someone else's.

After a dreadful night, I woke wanting nothing more than to convince myself that the scandalous tableau I had witnessed had been only a dream. But what I had seen was all too real; the image of it haunted me so that I rose before dawn and left early for the hospital, unable to face Stefan or my wife.

I immersed myself in work for some hours, which brought some relief—after all, the charity cases are so piti-able that my own problems pale. Who am I to compare my suffering to that of an indigent man blinded by excess sugar in the blood and about to lose his leg to the same cause? Or a twelve-year-old orphan dying of consumption? But too soon, the time came to return home for my afternoon appointments. The temptation was great to stay away and later claim some emergency had prevented me. Stefan, after all, shared my practise and would make sure no patient was turned away.

But I am a miserable failure as a liar; and I knew that sooner or later I should have to face my wife and brother again. Unlike my mood, the day was bright and sunny, the chill tolerable, and so I walked home and arrived there at my customary time, just before one o'clock.

I did not go at once to the kitchen, where I could hear from the clatter of dishes and the click of high-heeled slippers against the wooden floor that Gerda was preparing dinner. For some reason, I could not look upon her first. Instead, I went back to the medical offices and found Stefan, who sat in the examination room, surrounded by anatomical charts, apothecary jars, a human skeleton—the accretion of Papa's forty years of medical practise.

He was sitting at our father's desk, his elbows propped upon the shining polished mahogany, his head lowered, his hands clutching his forehead, his pale long fingers combed into his dark hair. The posture spoke of such abject misery that, strangely, my own eased; I found that I could gaze on him quite steadily—if not with forgiveness, then with pity. All the cold anger that I feared would betray itself in my voice melted away, and I said, quite softly and with honest concern: "Stefan? Are you well?"

He glanced up, startled by my presence. My brother is far better at dissembling than I, but even he could not hide his guilt; he looked away, unable to meet my eyes.

"You look tired," I said. In truth, he looked ten years older than the day before. Older, certainly, than the shadowy image of the lover who had—

I censored the too-painful thought immediately.

But a flicker of emotion must have crossed my face then, for Stefan managed a sidewise glance at me and replied, very quietly, "No more than you."

I caught his eye at last, and we shared a troubled look. In that moment, much passed between us without words; I have no doubt that he understood that I *knew,* but we were each too cowardly to speak directly to the matter. I opened my mouth, determined to end my complicity in this silence.

But before either of us could speak, the office door rang. We both looked up towards the sound; he jumped up as if prodded.

"I'll handle it, Bram. Have your dinner; I've already eaten."

"Are you sure?"

In reply, he went to open the door.

I paused for a moment and watched from the corridor as he escorted the caller inside. A woman—I caught no more than a glimpse of her before I turned to leave, but what a spectacle! She was young and quite beautiful, dressed in furs and brocades and diamonds, with a sable muff and matching cap perched atop a cascade of long red curls. And strikingly tall—the same height as my brother. I took her for a diva or an actress, for her china blue eyes were lined with kohl, and her lips were stained dark red.

Her voice—deep and sultry, heavily accented—marked her as a foreigner, a Frenchwoman. *A chanteuse,* I remember thinking to myself, as it carried down the hall, for it was rich and melodious. A travelling chanteuse who had come to consult a doctor on the care of a much-abused throat, I suspected.

I left her with my brother and made my way to the kitchen, where Gerda and little Jan waited, she setting the plates upon the table, he flailing in his high-chair and crying out happily at the sight of me—holding out his arms, while his mother stood, preoccupied, with her back to me.

Grateful for at least my child's welcome, I went to him at once and scooped him up. He was laughing with exaggerated glee as he pulled at my beard, then released a hearty giggle that came from his belly. His joyful little heart is the one constant in this world, the one truly good thing that has not changed. It was pure balm for my wounded soul, and I indulged in it freely.

"Papa fly!" he crowed. "Papa fly!"

It is our special game. I stretched my arms up, up, so that I held him high above my head, and asked: "Are you an angel, Jan? Papa's little angel?"

"Papa *fly!*" he demanded.

"And so you shall," I said, and tossed him up into the air. He shrieked with delight, waving chubby, dimpled arms and legs as I called, "Fly, little angel! Fly!" and caught him.

Gerda always scolded us fondly, saying, *You'll hurt him, Abraham! Be careful!* But to-day she only watched with a pale smile and, when I turned to look at her, glanced swiftly away and went back to the stove.

"Where is Mama?" I asked, over Jan's repeated demands for more.

She frowned down at the steaming cauldron and, without looking at me, replied shortly, "Resting. She will be down later."

I gave up all attempts at conversation then, knowing they would be in vain. Gerda has always been given to periods of darkness and is sometimes silent and brooding, especially since Papa's recent death; I have learnt not to be overly concerned by it, but that day it gnawed at me, for I felt I finally knew its cause.

She brought me my dinner, but I could not eat it. Instead, I picked at it and watched as she sat beside me and fed the child; he has become our shield from each other. In fact, I was grateful for her concentration upon him, for I was oddly close to tears at the sight of her.

She is so beautiful, so young, with her waving brown hair pulled back with ribbon, like a girl's, and ending just above her tiny waist in one long, loose curl. I know her heart: it is as simple and sweet as little Jan's. There is no guile in her, and no shame, only unremitting sorrow. I knew she sensed my pain and felt it as her own. I wanted to reach out, to rest my fingers upon the hand that fed my son, and ask her for the truth: Did she love my brother more than she loved me? Did she long for freedom?

It cannot happen, of course; Gerda herself would never permit it. She is a devout Catholic, and at best we would only separate, but never divorce.

As we sat in that uneasy silence, laughter came from the medical office: a woman's laughter, in a throaty, flirtatious contralto.

Gerda looked up sharply at the sound and, for the first time that day, spoke to me. "Do you think she is beautiful?"

Her question took me quite by surprise. "The patient with Stefan?"

She nodded. "I saw her from the window."

I hesitated. "She is pretty, yes." I turned towards my wife and fastened my gaze full upon her so that there was no way for her to avoid it, short of closing her eyes. "But it is a —vulgar sort of prettiness. Not true beauty."

And I took her hand. For one brief dazzling moment, she smiled shyly up at me; then the pain crossed her features again, and I thought she would burst into tears.

Just as suddenly, her expression shifted to one of alarm.

She jerked her head in the direction of the office and looked up, frowning. "Did you hear that?"

I considered the question, and decided in retrospect that I had heard a thump of sorts, elsewhere in the house.

Gerda pushed to her feet. "Someone fell."

Her fearful conviction was so utter that I dashed to the edge of the stairs and called up to Mama.

She stepped from her room and came to the landing, looking so troubled, so haggard, so suddenly aged that the very sight of her disturbed me more than the mysterious thump.

"Yes, Bram? What is it?"

"Gerda thinks she heard someone fall." And at her look of confusion, I added, "Perhaps Stefan's patient fainted. I should go see if he needs help."

The sound of sudden heavy footsteps, a panicked shout, the slam of a distant door—

I whirled. As I did, Mama came down the steps so quickly, she nearly lost her balance and fell. I looked back at her to find her expression one of utter panic, her hand upon her heart. I clasped her arm to steady her, and together we ran back through the kitchen, towards the doctors' offices in the back of the house. Gerda scooped up little Jan, who began to wail, and followed.

I ran to the outer waiting room, where the door stood flung wide, letting in the chill winter air and revealing the busy street. On the other side, I espied my brother; he hurried away, his back to me, carrying the unconscious diva, her red curls spilling down over his arm.

A critical emergency, I assumed, as I watched him head for a waiting cab, and was surprised that he had not called for assistance. I dashed to the doorway and shouted out:

"Stefan! Shall I meet you at the hospital?"

He did not turn, did not slow his pace; if anything, my voice seemed to galvanise him to move more swiftly. Quickly, he deposited his swooning patient inside the cab.

"Stefan—" I called again.

At that instant, Mama came to a stop beside me and let go a cry so shrill, so piercing, so anguished that I shall hear it ring in my memory to my dying day.

At the sound, Stefan, who had taken the driver's hand up and swung one foot inside the carriage, paused to glance behind him.

Despite the distance, I knew the face was not my brother's. Certainly the clothes were his, and the hair, but in that strange moment of revelation I saw the build was somewhat smaller, the gait not quite the same. Even the hair was not precisely the same, but slightly longer, a few shades lighter.

"Stefan!" my mother cried, as the impostor slipped inside and the carriage rolled away.

I stood dumbfounded, uncomprehending; and as I stared after the carriage, I caught sight of another man—bald and bespectacled, with a curling white mustache—running down the street in pursuit after them as he signalled for a cab.

None of it made sense to me—but my mother seemed quite sure of what had transpired. She clutched my arm. "They've taken Stefan!"

"But that was not he," I whispered.

She took my other arm and gave me a shake, as though I were a stubborn, inattentive child. "Follow them! They've taken him!"

Bewildered, I dashed outside in my shirt sleeves, waving my arms in hopes of procuring a cab. I ran, staggering through the mud, an entire block without success, until my lungs burned from the cold, sharp air. By that time the diva's carriage and the cab that followed it had both disappeared from view; impossible to guess which direction they both had gone.

I returned, gasping and defeated, and ran back inside, past my mother, wife, and wailing son, into my father's medical office, into the examination room. I had no idea what I was searching for—Stefan, perhaps (as if he could have missed hearing our repeated cries for him!).

There was, of course, no sign of my brother. But in the examination room where he had met the red-haired diva, I detected a faint, irregular odor. And on the carpet near the examination table lay a crumpled lace handkerchief. I squatted down to retrieve it and was nearly overwhelmed by the unmistakable smell of chloroform.

It was at that moment that my confusion transformed into honest fear. I still could make no sense of the events, but I knew something evil had occurred. I raised my face from the handkerchief to look up at my anguished mother and puzzled wife, both of whom stood in the doorway.

"We must call the police," I told them.

"The police cannot help us," Mama said, with such sorrowful conviction that I knew she was withholding some secret, some key that would unlock the mystery.

"Then tell me what else I can do," I countered. When she did not reply, I rose. "Please tell my patients that I will be unavailable until to-morrow."

So I seized my coat and walked down—not to the police house, as was my initial intent, but to the hospital. I hoped, I think, that my eyes had somehow deceived me— that it had truly been my brother who had carried the diva to the hospital, and that I would find him there overseeing her case.

But no one there had seen Stefan that day, and so, discouraged, I made my way to the police.

It was a waste of time. I do not mean to be uncharitable, for I have friends there who have shown me kindness; but my report was challenged, and insinuations made that Stefan and the lady were lovers and had eloped together.

Then I told them of the bald mustached man who had taken alarm and followed. They listened with greater interest there, for they knew of him; he is a retired detective of sorts, and known to the locals. But again, they made more insinuations: that perhaps the lady was married, and her husband had hired the detective.

At any rate, they agreed to hunt down the detective and question him. But until then, there is nothing that can be done to help Stefan.

Dusk had fallen by the time I returned home. All the way, I nursed the foolish hope that Stefan might have returned during my absence. But the house was silent, except for the sound of Gerda in the kitchen. Mama met me at the door. I knew at once from her face that my brother was still lost.

More lost than I knew; for Mama gently took my arm and, in a low voice lest Gerda should hear, said, "I must talk to you alone."

She bade me follow her upstairs to her room. I did, and she sat in the rocking chair before the fireplace—the place where she had so often held my brother and me, comforting us when we were children. I sat across from her, in my father's chair, and for some moments we were silent.

At last she spoke, in a tone that was soft but somehow colder, firmer, more determined than I had ever heard her use.

"My son," she said, "you will think me insane for telling you this, but you must believe. We are involved with powers which cannot exist—but they do. They are not human, but they draw their sustenance from humans and cannot survive without us. And your brother is in grave danger from them.

"It is my fault. All my fault for not going to him last night, when I had the chance. For not telling him . . . and you, when you both had a chance to flee the danger."

She rose, went to her dresser, and took from the top drawer a small tattered book I had never seen. With a sense of reverence, she handed it to me, saying, "These are true events, recorded by my own hand more than twenty-five years before. This is no fiction; you must read, Abraham, and believe."

I read.

I read, sitting in my father's chair while my mother stared, disconsolate, tormented, into the fire. I read, but I cannot believe.

My mother is the calmest, the steadiest, the sanest person I have ever known; in truth, I would trust no one—not even dear Papa, when he was alive—more than I would her.

But the story contained in her journal—it is the raving of a madwoman, a tale of inhuman monsters, of life beyond the grave, of pacts with the Devil himself.

And these forces have stolen my brother in hopes of digesting his immortal soul?

No. I cannot believe. I cannot believe. . . .

The Journal of
Stefan Van Helsing

21 NOVEMBER. I woke this evening to a new existence, a new world where the laws of science and reason no longer apply. Insanity reigns here; nothing is as it seemed, and the small misery that had been my life pales in comparison with the grand, sweeping horror it has become.

I am not even the man I thought I was—Stefan, son of Mary and Jan Van Helsing. No; I am a catalyst for disaster.

Let me return to that hour when I first laid my eyes upon this new world: Full consciousness took its time returning. For some time, I remained in a grey fugue state, neither awake nor asleep. I had a strange dream—which I now realise was no dream at all—of someone undressing me as though I were a sleepy child, removing sumptuous furs and silks, then reclothing me in my own trousers and waistcoat.

Eventually I grew aware of movement, of a rumbling vibration against my back, my legs, my head; later, I recall peering out a window to see an indistinct dusk landscape rolling past. But attempting to focus my blurry gaze prompted a sickly headache and dizziness, and so I closed my eyes and yielded to darkness a time.

When again I came to myself, I found I was sitting in a private compartment of a train with my hands bound behind me; a glance out the window revealed nothing but fast-moving blackness. Across from me sat a young man reading an aged tome bound in worn black leather entitled, in French: *A True and Faithful Relation of What Passed for Many Years Between Doctor Dee and Some Spirits.* He was dark-haired, a stranger: but the face seemed oddly familiar and feminine, with smooth beardless skin and straight perfect features. I detected a smudge of kohl around the blue eyes.

"Who are you?" I whispered. Speech was difficult; my throat was parched and sore. I struggled against my invisible bonds and felt cold metal against my wrists; the nausea provoked by movement soon made me cease.

The man closed his book and set it down on the seat beside him. With a tolerant, faintly condescending smile, he said, "Behave yourself, please. No harm will come to you. In fact, my own safety depends on it."

The voice—it was deeper but still French-accented; I recognised it at once. "The woman. You're the woman who came to the office."

Indeed, my captor seemed effeminate. I could not decide whether he was a woman now dressed as a man, or a man who had masqueraded as a woman, for his (her?) build was androgynous, tall and willowy, with no decidedly masculine or feminine traits.

The instant of recognition brought with it a memory of what had transpired in Papa's office: As I turned away from her following the examination, the red-haired woman had drawn close, had reached out with a gloved hand and clamped something over my nose and mouth. I recalled, with a fresh wave of nausea, the stink of chloroform. I had struggled and been surprised to find my opponent's strength matched my own.

It made no sense, no sense at all. "What could you possibly want with me?" I demanded weakly.

The Frenchman leaned forward to draw a hand across my cheek and whispered, with a lecherous wink, "Ah, you are a lovely young thing. Best not to tempt me with that question!" And when I recoiled, he laughed.

"*I* want nothing with you. You are simply a means to an end for me. As I said, your safety is assured. Those who await you merely wish to . . . embrace you into their bosom."

I pondered this indigestible news a time, then asked, "Where are you taking me?"

"At the moment? Brussels." He held me for a moment with his bright blue gaze, as piercing and curious as a precocious raven's. "Enough of questions for the moment. You are tired. Rest."

The suggestion had an immediate effect on me; I realised at once that I *was* indeed quite drowsy and fell into a doze.

A sharp knock at the door to our compartment woke me sometime later. My companion leapt to his feet, for the first time demonstrating anxiety, and, drawing a small pistol from his coat, pressed against the door. In a voice deep, threatening, and unquestionably male, he challenged, "Yes?"

I know not how to describe the voice that replied, save to call it masculine and unearthly beautiful; the voice of an angel.

"It is I. The prince."

The mistrust etched on my captor's face transformed into surprise and awe. He opened the door at once—only a crack, not far enough to permit even a child entry. Nonetheless, the visitor entered, first growing as two-dimensionally thin as a sheet of paper before my very gaze, then slipping through that crack with impossible ease.

How shall I describe him? His appearance was like his voice: angelic, utterly compelling. His hair was raven, streaked with grey, his eyes the darkest green I have ever seen; and his skin was so translucently pale that the light caught it and glinted pink, pale turquoise, silver, like mother of pearl.

He was, quite simply, magnificent, and neither I nor my companion could take our eyes from him. Yet mixed with that uncorruptible beauty was an aura of sly fierceness, of danger, as though we beheld a bejewelled serpent—graceful, diamond-brilliant, lovely, poisonously evil.

An angel, indeed: Lucifer.

"Prince," my captor whispered, at once lowering the pistol and bowing from his shoulders; then he gestured with his empty hand at me. His demeanour remained one of awe and subservience, but I detected a faint note of fear as well. "As you can see, I have done as you asked. He is unharmed and well. But I did not expect to see you until—"

A gleaming alabaster hand appeared from the depths of the prince's ebony cloak and sliced the air in a gesture for silence. "There is no time for the expected." And he turned and, for a long moment, studied me.

Guessing him to be the instigator of my absurd abduction, I glared back at him with hatred. But he looked on me with such utter unmasked adoration, such sorrowful yearning, that my fury gave way to astonishment. And then he released a long, low sigh, upon which rode a single word— nay, a heartfelt prayer:

"Stefan."

Clearly this dazzling stranger knew me; even more clearly, he loved me. Yet his very presence pricked the skin at the nape of my neck.

Reluctant, he turned from me at last and faced my captor. "So. The time has come for your payment, then." And he reached into his pocket and drew forth a black velvet pouch.

The female man recoiled from it with contempt, and

though his voice trembled faintly, his posture was one of pure determination. "Do not insult me with your offer of lucre, sir; you know my price."

The prince tilted his head and gazed steadily at him with dark glittering emerald eyes; I could think of nothing but that jewelled viper, coiling to strike. I tensed, straining at my bonds, at the sense of imminent violence.

But its eruption was at once halted by the swift movement of my captor. I expected him to fire the pistol; to my amazement, he tore away his starched collar and the top of his shirt to reveal a neck as white and smooth as a woman's, without the slightest sign of an Adam's apple. But its perfection was marred by a small red mark of some kind; from my lower perspective in the dim evening light, I took it to be a razor cut, from shaving—though the skin was free from stubble or any trace of a beard.

"It is this," my captor said. "That you finish what you have started. That you grant me immortality." And he proffered that soft skin to the prince, whose eyes blazed at the sight of it—indeed, literally reddened, as though the blood had rushed there.

With blinding speed, the prince struck—like a serpent, with fangs bared, and fastened his mouth upon the white neck. At that instant, the man cried out softly, indignantly, and despite his earlier willingness, he struggled. But the prince held him fast, and all struggle soon ceased; his breathing slowed, and his eyes glazed, and he soon fell into a trance.

I watched as the prince leaned over his victim, convinced that the chloroform had somehow induced hallucinations—or that I had fallen victim to a brain fever that had fabricated this entire wild episode from my imagination.

Hallucination or no, I stared with horrified fascination

as the prince sucked the wound on my captor's neck for an eternity, until the former's pale face grew ruddy, and the latter's white as chalk. I stared until the victim swooned and fell, and stared still as the predator swept him up into his arms and continued to drink.

At last the prince raised his flushed face from the man draped in his arms and laid the body gently upon the seat across from mine.

He turned towards me. I tensed again, expecting the same fate to befall me and knowing myself still too groggy from the chloroform to put up a successful fight.

Instead, he knelt beside me, his face so close to mine that I could smell his warm, blood-tainted breath, and ordered: "Turn, Stefan. Let me loose your fetters."

What was I to have done? I turned and felt, impossibly, his cold fingers squeeze between my wrists and the tight manacle that bound me.

He grunted; and with two near-simultaneous snaps, I was free. I faced him again and saw on the seat beside me two steel handcuffs, broken in two.

"What do you want with me?" I demanded with a bravado I did not feel, as I rubbed my tingling hands.

"Just this," he whispered, and I am not certain what transpired then: only that his eyes loomed larger until I saw nothing else in my line of vision; then they loomed larger still and became the entire world.

Into that world, a flash of metal entered: a small, sharp knife. I remember an eternal instant when that knife poised above my upturned hand, against the backdrop of those dark, compelling eyes. And then the swift pain of a finger prick, and that finger squeezed, nursed, milked so that it rained bright fat drops of blood upon his waiting open palm.

He licked it—no, that description is altogether inadequate. He *partook* of it, as though it were the sacred Host, the most consecrated wine. And the look on his face just after: that image shall remain with me forever. With an expression of the most infinite bliss and love and sorrow, he closed his eyes, causing a single diamond tear to course down his cheek.

The knife flashed again; but it was his blood now spilled upon my palm.

God help me, I drank. Drank, and gagged on the bitter taste of death and brine. But beneath that bitterness had been something sweet and utterly intoxicating.

I stared back at my benefactor, aghast that anyone should love me so fiercely.

"We are tied now, Stefan," he said tenderly. "If ever you have need, summon me in your mind, and I shall come. Morning or evening, awake or asleep, if danger threatens and you call, I shall come. No ill can befall you without my knowledge.

"But I swear most solemnly: As long as you will it, your mind remains your own. I myself have experienced the horrors that another's mental control can produce; never will I violate your privacy without your call."

And as he spoke, his visage wavered slightly, and his face changed; the features grew less severe, younger, the eyes flecked with brown. Even the silver vanished from his coal-black hair.

"Who *are* you?" I breathed.

A lightning flash of grief contorted his face; for a moment, I thought he would yield to it and weep. But he composed himself and in that handsome voice at last replied:

"I am your father."

⚔ 6 ⚔

The Journal of Stefan Van Helsing, Cont'd.

I had no difficulty accepting that I was not the son of Jan Van Helsing, for I had always known that he had adopted me, an abandoned infant, out of kindness. My childhood had been pure happiness; yet as a boy, I often wondered about my real parents and dreamt of the day I would be approached by a kindly man with dark eyes and hair who said:

Stefan . . . I am your father.

But to hear from this frightening stranger that I was *his* son—this was much to bear.

Yet I believed him; believed because, in tasting his blood, I felt the depth of his love for me. Believed despite the strange murder I had witnessed, despite the fantastic tale he told:

That we were the heirs of a centuries-old monster from an untamed foreign land, and that that monster sought me in hopes of corrupting me, for my damned soul would purchase his continuance. This was the prince of which my captor spoke; and when my father, then a young man like me, attempted to die in innocence in hopes of destroying the monster, he was transformed by the prince's bite into one himself.

Writing it down, it seems all too wild; part of me rejects it utterly. But then a surge of the love I felt during our bloody exchange returns, and I am convinced.

Perhaps I have been bewitched.

Possibly. Even my father warns that the prince, Vlad, will attempt to tie me to him in similar sanguinary fashion, and that this would make me his unwitting pawn. Am I then my father's? (How easily I write the term; too easily, with poor Papa so recently dead!)

He swears that I am not, that my mind is my own and he will never invade its sanctum, that *I* shall have to summon *him,* else he will know none of my thoughts.

The truth? I do not know. I know only that, on that long, strange train ride that literally and figuratively deposited me in a dark foreign land, I trusted him. Trusted even when he pulled open the window and hurled out the contents of my captor's travelling-trunk: fine men's suits; a magnificent array of women's dresses of silks, satins, brocades; and a collection of men's and women's wigs, including the long auburn tresses. And when the trunk was almost empty, he laid the blood-drained body of my former captor into it, covering it with a shroud composed of satin and lace skirts. Then he closed the lid and straightened, saying to me, as though I would understand:

"Vlad has bitten him, and he now will know of my intervention here. His agent has no doubt informed him of your home in Amsterdam. You dare not return there."

My trancelike complacency was shattered; determination pierced the veil of chloroform and languour. "I must! I cannot simply leave without explanation my family, my brother—" I broke off before I could complete the phrase: *my brother's wife.*

The train began to slow; I could see the distant lights of the station.

Fast-moving shadows dappled his gleaming white features as he pondered this a time, his hand upon the now-closed trunk that held my abductor. "Perhaps you are right," he said at last. "Your mother"—and here he lowered his voice, and another wave of unutterable sadness passed over his features before he composed himself—"your entire family is in grave danger. Vlad will stop at nothing to find you, even if it means tormenting and killing them all. He has lost his best agent; to procure fresh assistance, he will require time. Your family will be safe perhaps a week, no more. You must go to them, convince them to take shelter."

How I was to accomplish such a thing, I could not imagine; but as the train pulled into the Brussels station, it seemed quite reasonable.

So, too, did our exchange with the conductor, when he arrived, and my father—whose name, I learned, was Arkady Dracul—arranged for the trunk to be sent upon the next morning's train to his agent in Amsterdam (for what purpose, I shudder to imagine). He paid the conductor in gold and tipped him quite heavily for his trouble, whilst I stood nearby and marvelled at the misleading normalcy of the exchange. For the window was shut, and any trace of the female man's existence—including the snapped handcuffs—was quite gone. Nor did my groggy, dishevelled appearance provoke any curiosity; even Arkady's brilliant handsomeness had faded. He seemed a striking but ordinary man, and together we blended in quite successfully with the crowd that exited the train.

I did not understand why he had not also purchased tickets for our return to Amsterdam the next morning; my question provoked a faint wry smile.

"I am obliged to return to Amsterdam before the dawn, Stefan—and while I could return there much more swiftly alone, I insist on personally seeing you safely back. I shall accompany you for as long as I am able."

Thus it was that, after brief negotiations that involved a startling amount of gold, he procured a small caleche and two swift stallions, and we set off through the cold, dark damp towards Amsterdam.

The emotional exhaustion and chloroform predisposed me toward an uneasy intermittent sleep, which was punctuated by dreams both troublesome and bizarre—but no more so than what I had already experienced in my waking hours. I remember only fragments of that wild nocturnal ride: of my professed father's face and hands, internally aglow like Japanese lanterns against the melting ebony backdrop of his hair, his cloak, the mid-night sky; of his urgent whispers to the galloping horses, who trembled at the sight of him even as they obeyed.

At only one point was I called upon to drive: when, after some hours, we came to the river at Geertruidenberg, the first of the Rhine's three branches that carve their way across the Netherlands to the sea. My companion roused me and with an apologetic smile said, "As it is not the slack of the tide, I must ask you now to drive the horses."

So I did, and we made our way by a long, narrow bridge over the river. Three times we crossed water—the Maas first, then the Waal, and at last the lower Rhine—and three times Arkady handed me the reins and let himself be driven.

By the time we passed from Utrecht province into

North Holland, some fifteen kilometers from home, the darkness was easing to predawn grey. For the fourth and final time, Arkady gave me the reins, saying, "I must go. Tell your mother that my agent will watch your house during the day, to see you are safe; and I shall see you both to-night."

Before my very eyes, he disappeared, and a swirling mist surrounded the carriage, unnerving the horses. Just as suddenly, it moved into the distance and was gone.

I arrived home to a magnificent winter dawn: blood-tinged clouds, edged with sungold, and the air cold, sharp, clean. When I stepped from the caleche and tethered the stallions in front of the house, their warm, quick breath hanging as mist, the door slammed like a gunshot.

I looked up to see my mother, barefoot, running through the freezing mud in her dressing-gown. She said not a word as she sped towards me, then flung her arms about me; but as we embraced, she let go a hitching sigh full of such relief and pain, it tore my heart.

We held each other tightly a full minute, perhaps longer; then she drew back and, still silent, studied me: my eyes and face first, then the whole, then at last my hands. She gazed down at them slowly, reluctantly, turning them in hers so that the palms faced upwards.

And at the sight of the small blood-encrusted cut on the tip of my left forefinger, she let out a piteous sound, half-groan, half-sob, and began to sink to her knees.

I caught her arms before she reached the mud. "It's all right," I told her softly. "It was my father. My father. He rescued me."

"Your father?" She stared at me blankly a moment—in the grey light, her sweet face looked haggard, ashen; I knew she had not slept the entire night—then, with hope asked: "Arkady?"

I nodded.

She released another sigh—this one uncertain—and said: "Come inside. We must talk."

I put my arm around her as we turned to walk inside; but I paused as I looked up to see, in the open doorway, my brother, already dressed, with his wife beside him, her long, dark hair streaming down onto the shoulders of the white silk dressing-gown she had worn the night we coupled.

Guilt stopped me in mid-stride. I saw the anxious joy and tears in Gerda's great dark eyes; she trembled with the effort to restrain herself, to keep from running to my arms. I saw, too, the glance Bram cast at her, and the flicker of anguish that passed over his features.

It was still in his eyes when he looked at me. Our gazes locked, and in that terrible instant, I saw accusation there, beyond any doubt: He knew. My brother knew.

But the instant passed; his expression softened, became that of the loyal loving brother I have always known. He ran down the icy steps, across the frost-encrusted ground and mud, and embraced me.

My poor mother's anguish had left me dry-eyed, but as Bram held me, I wept. Wept and gazed beyond his shoulder at his wife's pale face, radiant with shame and joy, and found I could not meet her eyes.

Like my mother, he drew back and scrutinised me for damage, then glanced over at the caleche with its two handsome stallions and whispered, "But what has happened, Stefan? What has happened?" There was no judgement in his voice, no anger, only concern and typical overwhelming Bram-curiosity.

I left one arm around him, drawing comfort from his unbroken love, and put the other round my mother as we three walked back up the steps. "You will think me mad," I said.

"Then you will not be alone in this house," he replied softly, with a pointed look at my mother.

I think he intended for her to smile; she did not. "I would much prefer the truth be sane, Bram, but to my sorrow, it is not."

Confused, I said no more but gave my sister-in-law the customary chaste peck on the cheek—Gerda, why must it be such hell? Why must it all be reversed?—which only served to underscore the remembered passion of the previous night. I kept my eyes lowered lest they reveal too much.

We all went inside to the kitchen—all but Gerda, who excused herself to tend her crying child; I think she sensed the delicacy of the matters about to be discussed. And in truth, I did not want her to hear them, for her sensitivity is so great, I feared they would trouble her more than she could bear. I have already been the source of enough worry for her.

After much strong coffee, I recounted my night ride to and from Brussels, but I instinctively withheld the supernatural aspects of the affair. I claimed the transvestite was merely overpowered by my mysterious benefactor before being stuffed unconscious into the trunk, and I failed to mention the strange bloody exchange, or the fact that this helpful stranger claimed to be my father. In truth, I was reluctant to admit everything, for my memory of it had taken on a rather nightmarish air of unreality, and I was uncertain whether parts of it had not been inspired by the chloroform.

But when I mentioned his name—Arkady Dracul— Bram started so that he nearly dropped his cup, sloshing hot coffee all over Mama's white tablecloth. An odd look passed between them, then Mama said, "You need not dissemble to protect us or yourself, Stefan. Everything Arkady has told you is true; and I already know the facts about Vlad and the covenant. I have told your brother here the truth, but belief comes difficult for him. Perhaps you should tell us all that really happened."

So I did, reluctantly; and Bram listened all the while intently, his blue eyes peering over his coffee-cup at me with that calm, stoic gaze. His expression betrayed no disbelief, but I knew from the ramrod straightness of his posture, from his perfect stillness, that an internal war raged, for the more troubled he is, the quieter he becomes.

And when I finished, I sighed and leaned back against the chair, exhausted. For a full moment, Bram neither stirred nor moved his gaze; but then at last he turned to my mother and me and asked, "What are you suggesting we do?"

"Leave," my mother said, leaning towards him with such urgency that silver-gold curls spilled down onto her forehead, her cheek; her expression was so animated, so filled with sudden fire that age and exhaustion left her, and I could see the handsome young woman she had been: the woman who had loved the dark, passionate Arkady Dracul. "We must all leave, and go our separate ways; it is the only way to ensure our safety. Otherwise, if we remain together, Vlad will use us each against the other."

Bram rose at once, his eyes and voice filled with a flat impenetrable anger. "This is insanity, of course. I will not leave my practise, my home, my family, all based upon . . . ravings. I do not understand what madness has possessed you both, but I pray you soon come to your senses!"

And he left, his determined rapid footsteps echoing behind him.

I no longer knew what to say, what to do; I leaned forward and laid my weary head in my hands. Mama took my arm then and led me to my room, murmuring soft words of comfort. Like a feverish child, I let myself be undressed and tucked into bed, and sighed at the cool touch of my mother's hand upon my forehead. But before I slept, she sat beside me on the bed and said, very softly:

"I am a horrible woman to have kept these things from you; I should not blame you if you hated me for the way you have been used. Here is the truth of the matter, the whole, entire truth, which I alone can tell."

She told me everything; more than I could have imagined, more than I dare record here, for safety's sake. I was given a choice, which I made, and we wept together at our complicity.

Afterwards, when she left me alone, my heart was too full to sleep. So I have written it all down, and the sun is now high in the morning sky.

I pray Arkady has told the truth, that his agent shall watch over us by day, for exhaustion at last overtakes me. To sleep . . .

⊰7⊱

The Diary of
Abraham Van Helsing

22 NOVEMBER 1871. Can any more tragedy befall us? Within a week, I have seen my father dead and my family torn apart, all of them lost to me in one fashion or another.

After Stefan's fantastical departure and return, and Mama's even more impossible tale of a family's supernatural curse, I found myself trapped in a restless mind that could neither entirely believe nor entirely disbelieve. Logic assured me that madness was not contagious: how, then, could my mother and brother both have fallen prey to the same delusions?

But the thought that I should, based on second-hand reports, let the only family I have known be scattered to the winds—this evoked great anger in me. I was angry, too, that those dearest to me should have taken leave of their senses in a way that brought us all suffering, and so soon after Papa's death. In all fairness, though, mixed with my rage was an undercurrent of bitterness that owed itself to another source of pain.

I saw the look he gave her, and she him, when he returned.

So it was that this morning, after hearing Stefan's wild story and Mama's insistence that we all leave, I lost my temper and left at once for my hospital rounds—a full hour early. Noontime found me in a still disagreeable state; so much so that for the first time in memory, I failed to return home for dinner. I had no office appointments, but any unscheduled patients who might come would be turned away, unless Stefan rose from his bed to tend them. I had no concern, I told myself, for any of them.

Let them worry about my whereabouts, I thought, full of righteous self-pity; and I refused to eat dinner at all, as though this might punish someone other than myself. Indeed, I wallowed in my misery with a great deal of satisfaction, allowing all the jealousy submerged from my boyhood to surface—thinking of how Mama had always favoured Stefan, how she and Papa had spoiled him, never demanded from him what was demanded of me, the elder.

Oh, my brother, if I had only put aside my selfishness and believed you!

I remained at the hospital until the afternoon (and was extremely annoyed when no one from home sent a message inquiring after me), when I made a leisurely round of my homebound patients.

I went to the boarding-house where Lilli was situated last, for she was, she said, always loneliest in the evenings. It was late afternoon; the sun had just set, but even then I had no intention of returning home. Had I not made the terrible discovery—an omen, I think now—perhaps I might not have returned home at all that night; perhaps I might have gone to an inn.

Her landlady told me in hushed tones that Lilli had

worsened in the night and had eaten nothing that day but remained in bed sleeping. After knocking softly on the door, I entered her room quietly—but I need have taken no pains, for the poor dear woman had been dead some hours. I can see how the landlady took her to be asleep, for Lilli lay there quite sweetly, with eyes and mouth closed, and hands resting neatly atop the quilt as though the mortician had already done his work. But her skin—waxen and unnaturally pale, as yellowish-white as her sparse ivory hair—was cool to the touch, and rigor mortis had begun to set in.

An omen, yes. I sat down in my customary place beside her bed and wept a moment; then I dried my eyes and told the landlady to summon the mortician. I might have been generous and offered to fetch him myself, but I was suddenly overwhelmed by an urgent anxious desire to return home.

Indeed, as I made my way out into the bleak winter evening, the grey of dusk rapidly darkening to black, both my pace and pulse quickened as the odd sense of dread increased.

The sight of home did nothing to assuage my unease: rather it only increased it, for as I neared, I saw that not a single light shone in any window. Indeed, the lamp that Mama lit every night in anticipation of my return was dark; the sight chilled me more than the cold night wind.

I bounded up the front steps and threw open the door. The house was utterly dark; to my right, the drawing-room hearth, which should have been blazing by this time, was cold.

But more ominous than these was the soft keening that issued from upstairs—high-pitched, inhuman, full of such abject misery that I responded to it without thought, taking the steps three at once until I arrived at its source.

The door to my own bedroom was flung open. Bitter

cold greeted me as I entered; the sash had been thrown open, and the white curtains billowed in the wind. I rushed to close it and lit the lamp.

Upon the floor at the foot of our bed sat the source of that infernal nocturne: my wife, her collar unbuttoned, gaping open to reveal the frilless camisole beneath, her long hair free and tousled, framing a stark white face broken by three dark depthless pools—mouth and eyes. At the sight, I sank to my knees in pity and horror beside her, for I knew I looked again upon a madwoman, on my poor darling Gerda as I had first seen her, in a sanitorium cell.

Wild and wide and full of unspeakable anguish those eyes were, so far gone into that dark, hellish country that when I laid my hands gently on her shoulders and called her name, she neither saw nor heard me—only continued emitting that high piercing wail, her lovely face contorted in a rictus of despair, her gaze focussed on an invisible terror.

All my questions, all my attempts to comfort, went unanswered, unheard. Helpless, I rose to investigate, knowing that if she could not explain the event that had triggered her relapse, I should have to deduce it.

My first deduction stung like a viper's bite: the bed was not made, as it always was shortly after she rose. The quilt had been thrown carelessly to the floor, the sheets tangled, the pillows scattered and bearing the impressions of heads that I knew did not include my own.

This distressed me mightily, but it was nothing compared to what followed—for I glanced up from that incriminating sight to check my little son's crib, wondering whether he had been witness to the moral outrage that had occurred here.

The blackest terror I have ever known seized me as my gaze fell upon my little son's crib, draped in shadow.

Empty. God in Heaven! Empty . . .

But surely he was in the house, I told myself, though I had never seen him elsewhere but at his mother's side. I knelt down and grabbed my wife's arms, shook her. "Little Jan! Where is he? Where is he? With *Oma?*"

Gerda never saw, never heard. I scrambled to my feet and shouted my son's name into the darkness, searching foolishly for him beneath his crib, his bureau, his toys.

When that proved futile, I rose and hurried downstairs —pausing on my way to knock on Stefan's closed door and call out; receiving no reply, I threw open the door and found only emptiness.

With horror, I dashed to the end of the hallway and Mama's room, calling out for her as I threw open the door.

To my utter relief, I saw my mother lying on the bed, sleeping soundly; but when I lit the lamp and spoke to her again, I found she was in a deep stupour from which she could not be roused. I even took her hand and gently slapped it, only to receive no response.

I rose, glancing round the room for my little son, and found of him no sign. In an utter panic, I ran down the stairs, from room to room, looking even in cabinets, closets, the unlikeliest places.

Gone. Gone, nowhere in the house. But of course, he could not be. What child could have lain quiet, listening to his mother's screams?

In the end, I ran outside into the cold and shouted his name down the street . . .

Only to hear it echo back at me in the evening stillness. And in that dreadful moment when I knew him gone, I longed to join my wife's descent into madness.

I might have stood out there forever, mindless of the winter wind, but Gerda's renewed keening galvanised me. I was numbed by shock, pushed beyond all limits; the strain of the last few days and the pure horror of what had just occurred so taxed my mind and heart that all thought, all emotion abruptly ceased.

In a state of cold, blank calm, I walked inside and with impossibly steady hands poured a glass of Papa's port for my wife.

I ascended the stairs a shattered man.

Thus I returned to Gerda's side. But my wife would not stop her grieving to take the wine; only when I raised it to her lips would she drink.

As she did, I comforted her as I would an infant, smoothing the hair back from her feverish brow with my cool hand, patting her back, whispering reassurances. Though she still did not see me, though her gaze was still fixed on some awful memory, she quieted at last, and I grew bold enough to ask again, "What has happened? Where is the baby? Where is Stefan?"

Her eyelids fluttered, and her parted lips began to move. Certain of an answer, I began to withdraw the wine— but suddenly she raised an arm, with such swift force that the glass was overturned. Port spilled down onto her skin, onto her camisole, staining its snowy whiteness like dark, sweet-smelling blood while she screamed, pointing at the window.

"Gone! She—*she* took them both!"

I turned in the direction of her stricken gaze and saw the impossible: a white face, hovering like a suspended mask outside the glass pane, and clearly masculine (though my wife accused a female, in my confusion, I paid no heed). For a moment, I was honestly frightened, for this seemed a truly supernatural feat, but then common sense seized me. This was certainly a burglar with a ladder, and no doubt the man who had stolen my poor child, perhaps with hopes of ransom. And now he thought to come for my wife. . . .

Full of outrage, I rushed to the window and threw it open, thinking to injure (and thus capture) the criminal by giving the ladder a mighty shove.

There was no ladder, no face, no criminal, only cold wind and black night.

Bewildered, I shut the window once more and turned back towards my wife, only to discover that the man with the gleaming white face and hands stood between us.

The sight of him provoked renewed screaming from my wife. I hurried to her side and held her, covering her with a blanket to ease her trembling, shielding her with my body from this intruder.

He made no advance but said in a low voice so strangely powerful that I heard it easily over Gerda's shrieks: "Abraham. I fear I am too late."

He was a handsome man of indeterminate age, with jet-dark hair and eyebrows, and features that struck me as oddly familiar. I opened my mouth to shout at him, to demand his identity and purpose and the whereabouts of my son and brother, but to my total astonishment, the words that issued from my lips were:

"Do I know you?"

"Perhaps," said he, "but there is no time. They have taken Stefan, and wherever he is, he sleeps now. Tell me what you know."

"He is one of *them,* just like her—and she has taken them! Taken Stefan and Jan!" Gerda shrieked, tearing away from me to lunge at the stranger, and pummelled his chest with her fists. The blanket slipped from her shoulders, exposing the camisole most immodestly, but she was too distraught to notice or to care.

He made no effort to defend himself from her blows, nor did they seem to discomfit him in the least—but her words overwhelmed him with sickly dread. At them, he closed his eyes and whispered, " 'Just like *her.*' Zsuzsanna has been here, then."

I caught hold of her and pulled her from him, covered her again with the bedclothes. "Do you know this woman Zsuzsanna, sir? Were *you* her accomplice? And if so, what have you done with my child and brother?"

He did not reply but peered beyond us at the dark hallway, and suddenly I saw *his* eyes widen with fear. "Your mother," he demanded of me swiftly.

"I cannot wake her," I said, with a small shake of my head.

Before I could interrogate him further, he swept past us —or rather glided by, with preternatural silence and speed. I heard not a single footstep in the hall, but within an instant he had returned, with Mama unconscious in his arms.

The sight of her calmed Gerda, who fell silent and allowed me to continue giving her small sips of the port, and to bathe her warm brow with a washcloth wrung with water from the basin.

We watched as, with infinite tenderness, the stranger lay Mama on the bed; with infinite tenderness knelt by her side and whispered, *Mary.* . . .

That sight, and the look of genuine love and relief on my mother's face when she woke to the sight of him, convinced me more than any other to trust him. I knew that this was the man she had written of in her diary.

"Arkady," she said, and graced him with a smile. "Thank God, you are still with us!" Yet the sad affection on her face soon turned to panic; she sat upright with a cry, and clutched his arms. "Stefan!"

"Gone," Arkady replied. "Alive, but asleep; when he wakes, I will know more. There is no point in following until I know the direction he has been taken. For now, you must tell me what you can."

My mother raised her hands to her eyes and groaned; for a moment, I thought she would weep, but she soon mastered herself and looked up at him steadily. "Zsuzsanna. I was so exhausted this afternoon that I fell into a deep sleep despite all efforts to remain awake; and once there, I dreamt of Zsuzsanna's eyes, beautiful, brown, shot through with shimmering gold. Languour overcame me; I knew this meant that she was trying to enter the house, to steal Stefan from us. . . . I struggled to resist it but was too tired to emerge. I was paralysed, unable to move, to speak, even to open my eyes."

My poor mother let go a hoarse sob. Arkady tried to gather her into his arms, but she pushed him away with a gesture that intimated she was undeserving of comfort. And again she raised her hands to her face and said, "It is all my doing!"

No, I wanted to say, *it is my fault. Had I returned home earlier, none of this could have happened.*

But Arkady spoke first. Gently he caught my mother's wrists and lowered her hands. "I deserve the blame more than any of you. I should have suspected my sister capable of such treachery." And his visage blazed with such abrupt and dangerous white-hot wrath that my mother and I both recoiled from it. "What a fool I was, to think us safe because Vlad was still in Transylvania, because Zsuzsa would never betray me! She must have made arrangements to come days ago, perhaps weeks. Perhaps she even knew of Stefan's whereabouts before *I* discovered them! No," he said, shaking his head at Mama's faint protests, "it is more my fault than anyone else's. Had I been more cautious, Vlad's agent would never have discovered my resting-place; he very nearly succeeded in trapping me there to-night. Thanks to my own mortal assistant, I was merely delayed. But long enough. Long enough!"

He wheeled and gestured at Gerda, who now sat beside me on the floor, resting mutely with her head against my shoulder, her gaze turned inwards. "*She* knows the rest of what has happened here; perhaps she can help us."

"She is catatonic," I said, stroking her hair as though I could smooth away whatever trauma had provoked the rebirth of her madness. To hear myself saying those words again broke my heart. I knew I had lost part of her heart to Stefan—but I had hope, then, that she might be convinced to return to me. Now she was utterly lost to us all. "She has been like this before. She will speak to no one for some time. Days, perhaps longer."

"She will speak to me," Arkady said softly. And he crouched down in front of us and reached a hand towards her—slowly, tentatively, with the palm turned up, as one might approach a wild animal.

She cringed as he neared, and burrowed her face into my shoulder; when he put his hand lightly upon her shoulder, she jerked as though electrified and began to tremble. But then he said, softly—in the loveliest, most melodic and soothing voice I have ever heard anyone, male or female, use: "Gerda. I mean you no harm. But for Stefan's sake, I must know exactly all that has happened."

She glanced sideways at him, her eyes wide with terror, but the instant her gaze met his, her shivering ceased. To my amazement, she turned and faced him, and after a moment of staring deeply into his eyes, hers closed, and she began to speak, in the slow dreamy murmur of one entranced:

"She was here."

"Who?" Arkady demanded sharply. "The woman who looks like me?"

"Yes . . ." my wife answered dully. "In the afternoon. Bram was gone, and Mama and Stefan asleep. I was in the kitchen with little Jan, making the dinner for everyone, when she rang at the door.

"I would not open it, of course. Before he left for hospital, Bram ordered me not to, especially after the man masquerading as a patient stole Stefan away. She asked for Doctor Stefan Van Helsing, saying that someone at the hospital had referred her to him for a complaint. I turned her away, explaining that they were not available and could see no one to-day. But the woman was dressed so prettily, and her face so kindly and so beautiful, that when she paused in mid-turn to glance back at little Jan, balanced upon my hip, she asked, 'Oh. And this is your little boy?'

"Her voice was so wistful that I could not be rude; and she was so very lovely—perhaps the loveliest woman I had ever seen—that I just wanted to continue looking at her. So I answered, 'Yes, this is our little angel. Only he is not so heavenly right now; he is tired and late for his nap.'

"Jan had been crying, so I had picked him up to comfort him; but at the sight of the pretty woman, he silenced at once and stared at her, his eyes growing rounder and rounder.

" 'How handsome he is!' the woman exclaimed with a dimpled smile. 'Such a beautiful child! Is he Doctor Stefan's?'

"No, I explained, it was Stefan's nephew, that I was the other Doctor Van Helsing's—Abraham's—wife.

" 'How wonderful,' she said. 'And how lucky you are to have such a healthy, perfect son.' She began to turn away again, but I saw that her expression had grown unutterably sad, so much so that it touched my heart. I opened the door a crack and asked her what was the matter.

"She faced me then, her gaze intent and steady and so beautiful, I let go a breath. 'I cannot have children of my own,' she said. " 'I have consulted physician after physician and was hoping your brother-in-law could help me.'

"I stood in the doorway, moved by her pathetic story, moved by her grace and charm as a man might be moved. I would have done anything she asked at that moment, no matter how injurious to myself or even my child; and so, when she inquired sweetly, 'Might I come inside?' I opened the door wide.

"She entered smiling, and I—I remember only that I had entered a state of bliss, wanting only to be in her presence, to follow her as a flower follows the sun. When she asked, 'May I?' and held her arms out to my shy son, he stretched out his own eagerly to her, and I let her take him as though it were simply natural to hand him to a total stranger.

"So she took him, and I watched with strange dreamy pleasure as she rocked and tickled and kissed him. When she kissed his lips, his cheeks, his forehead, I felt no alarm; not even when she leaned down to brush his tender little throat teasingly with her lips.

"No, I watched with anticipation; with jealousy, even, for I longed for her lips to touch mine, longed to feel her caress against my skin. I might have pulled her to me and demanded such, but I was in such a languidly euphoric state that I did not want to move or speak. She held my little boy and began to sing to him softly, and I watched as he grew glassy-eyed and silent beneath this creature's gaze.

"Then she laid him upon the kitchen table and turned

to me as I stood, stunned by a strange mixture of fear and longing. She put her arms round my waist, and I felt myself grow sweetly limp, with the same melting sensation triggered by Stefan's kiss. Soon I lay on the floor, and she knelt beside me like a child at bedtime prayer and whispered in my ear, as though we were co-conspirators: 'He is so small, I dare not touch him, while I am so hungry! But I dare not go to Stefan so. . . .'

"While she spoke, she unfastened my collar, my blouse, then ran her palm—so bitter, bitter cold—admiringly over my skin before she bent forward and pressed her lips against the flesh above my collarbone. As I shivered, trapped between fear and anticipation, she parted those lips, and I felt the sweep of her tongue as she tasted the flesh there.

"Then came the pain: cold, electric, piercing, as though small sharp daggers bit into my skin. I cried out weakly and struggled, but as her tongue and mouth pulled hard against the wound, a sudden intoxicating warmth enveloped me, and I fell silent again. Indeed, the quieter I grew, the more pleasurable my trance became, until it eclipsed even the ecstasies of love. I felt myself floating away blissfully from my own body, and wanted it never to end.

"I remember the woman's voice: *Shall I take you across, then? Across the great abyss?*

"I knew she spoke of my death; and I wanted it. Yearned for it, as one yearns for physical release in the midst of passion.

"No. No—yearned for it far more than that. But it was not to be. I remember her high, crystalline laughter as she said, *No. You are more useful to me as a spy.* I fell into velvet darkness a time and was disappointed when I woke and found myself alive.

"My memory fades then. . . . I remember that when I

opened my eyes again, I lay upon the floor in my own bedroom, watching a scene between myself and Stefan as though I were a disembodied observer. Nearby in the crib, sleeping silently—or else trapped in the same stupourous trance—was my little boy.

"Yet I knew it was not me that I saw—but the beautiful woman, who had somehow taken on my appearance. When I concentrated, it seemed I could almost see her face beneath the illusory shell of my own.

"I lay in full view of them both, yet *he did not see me,* as she and Stefan argued tearfully, while I was unable to speak, to warn him, to do anything except watch them both.

"Stefan stood beside my bed, his arms grasping hers, his face gazing down into hers with the love he reserved for me as he told her he was leaving. Leaving forever, so that the rest of us would be exposed to no danger.

"She answered just as I would have: that she did not understand, could not understand, how any peril could be so great that it should tear us apart. She cried, and Stefan—he is so soft-hearted, so kind," Gerda said, smiling sadly in a way that pierced me to the soul. I looked away, unable to meet the others' gazes as she continued, "He could not bear her tears and cried with her. She begged to go with him, but he said no, it would be too dangerous; and besides, she belonged with her husband and child. He had intended to leave without saying anything to anyone—but then he feared they would misunderstand and endanger themselves trying to rescue him.

"So he wrote a letter for us all; but in the end, he could not leave without bidding her—me—good-bye. And I—" She hesitated. "I mean, *she.* I thought perhaps the guilt had caused me to go mad again, to leave my body, so that I now observed myself. It was like watching a play in which I was the actress. *She* said she could not so easily let him go. She showered him with tears and pleas and kisses; he tried to turn away, tried to leave, saying that he had erred once and would not do so again. But in the end, her determined kisses were returned, and she fell into his arms.

"So I watched, unable to speak or move while this strange woman who looked so like me bedded my lover; perhaps it is what I deserve, after treating my good husband so wickedly. That hour was the most bitter of my life, for I was forced to remain silent while another woman kissed my Stefan's face, ashine with tears, and he hers. His final caresses, his final words, were stolen from me, and I could not even weep. Surely she had entranced him so that he did not see her true appearance.

"No, I could only stare as he slowly, gravely undressed this strange and beautiful new Gerda, as though she were a bride on her wedding night. Could only listen to his murmurs that she had never before looked so lovely as she in turn undressed him.

"So they lay down together, and the woman pressed her gleaming white skin against his darker flesh in the twilight. Bodies writhing, they coupled with the same intensity and passion as Stefan and I had that night—"

Here I closed my eyes, stricken at the directness of her confession, shamed for her and myself in the presence of my mother, of this stranger.

"And in the midst of their passion, when Stefan released a hoarse, whispered cry of ecstasy, that cry turned to one of horror. For the woman had resumed her true appearance, and my poor lover saw that he lay with another woman —beautiful, compelling, chillingly malignant.

"He fought to pull away from her, but she clasped her arms and legs about him tightly and, with a strength far greater than his, held him fast. Held him fast also with her gaze; his struggling eased and then ceased as he stared, trans-fixed, into her eyes. Soon he was quiet, wide-eyed, breathing softly, just like little Jan and me.

"And the woman rose from the bed and told him, 'Rise, Stefan, and put on your clothes.'

"Like a sleepwalker, he did so, while she dressed so swiftly, my dazzled eyes saw nothing but a silvery blur. And she went over to the crib, leaned down, and took my sleep-ing child into her arms, then turned to Stefan and said, 'Come.'

"Still I could not move, could not stop them, could only lie cold and shivering upon the floor while my lover obediently followed and passed me without seeing, and soon the three of them were gone.

"Gone. Gone with my baby. . . ." And Gerda covered her eyes and wailed.

And my mother lay sobbing in Arkady's unfamiliar arms. I knew how cruelly the loss of her only grandchild must have weighed on her; yet I was struggling too mightily to free myself from a dark vortex of hysteria to offer comfort.

At the sight of me, Mama straightened and composed herself. Arkady withdrew from her embrace and gazed up at me. "They have taken Stefan and your child; there is noth-ing further I can do for your wife."

"We must go to the police!" I responded. "I will go myself at once—"

"No!" Mama countered. "What shall it take for you to listen to me, Bram? The police can accomplish no more now than they did yesterday! But this man"—she gestured at Arkady beside her—"saved your brother once. I know he will do so again and bring little Jan home to us."

As she spoke, Arkady rose and stepped over to me until

he stood no more than an arm's length away, the black of his cloak contrasting sharply with the unnatural pallour of his skin. "Your mother says she has revealed to you the full truth of the matter; yet you cannot believe. It is imperative that I have your belief, and your trust."

"Sir," said I, nearly mad with despair, "you have neither."

In reply, he slipped off his cloak and waistcoat and set them on the bed; clad only in shirt sleeves, he turned towards me. "Doctor Van Helsing. Will you listen to my heart?"

"I have no time for such idiocy!" I cried, my voice breaking. "We must stop them, find them before they harm my son—"

He looked into my eyes with a gaze so intent, so determined, yet so oddly sympathetic that I fell silent. "I, too, am a father," he said quietly. "And I have lost a father, a brother, and a son. I understand full well your despair. I swear to you: I will find Jan and Stefan. But to do so, I need your help—"

"Not him!" Mama pleaded suddenly, with such vehemence that we two men turned our faces swiftly to stare at her in surprise. "Not him! You cannot take him with you, Arkady. I have one son already in danger; I will not lose Bram, too!"

He listened sombrely, then replied, "Shall we then leave him here with his wife, where she can serve as Vlad's spy against him? No place is safe for any of us now, Mary. I do not relish leaving you behind. But Bram is younger and physically stronger than you and better able to help me with the gruesome task that awaits us."

She fell silent and let the defeat and sorrow on her face serve as her reply.

Arkady sighed in acknowledgement of the unhappy situation. "For his own protection, he must believe." He spread his arms. "You can see what scepticism has purchased me." And he turned back towards me once more. "Doctor Van Helsing: Will you listen to my heart?"

The sincerity and sympathy in his eyes, the soothing undercurrent in his voice, worked together to overcome the near-hysterical frustration of that moment. Oddly quieted, I leaned forward and pressed an ear to the center of his chest.

It was utterly, completely silent; the torso of a dead man.

I drew back slowly in amazement, my gaze fixed upon his face, and gently pressed my index and middle fingertips against his carotid artery.

No pulse whatsoever, and the skin was cool as dear Lilli's corpse.

I lowered my arm, dazed.

"Shall I perform for you?" he asked. "Levitate, as I did when I appeared at your window to-night? Vanish before your eyes? Transform myself into mist?"

"No," I answered dully. "That will not be necessary." A cold layer of confusion had settled atop my panic over little Jan's disappearance. Gerda's story, Stefan's, Mama's, this stranger Arkady's: their impossible tales were all of a piece, too coherent to be the result of individual delusions.

There was nothing left for me to do but trust them. I took my place beside Gerda and listened to Arkady's bizarre instructions of how we might best protect ourselves from this supernatural threat. Listened, too, to his promise that we would find Stefan, as soon as he knew whither my brother was bound. In the meantime, we should rest.

But first, he tried to extract a solemn promise from my mother—that she would remain in Amsterdam with Gerda and would not follow; for to do so would endanger not only her but Stefan and all the rest of us. Vlad would certainly endeavour to use Gerda against those of us who remained here; and someone had to stay and care for her.

"Then let me go with you," my mother cried, "and let Bram care for his wife! He does not understand Vlad as I do."

To which Arkady merely replied, "We shall discuss this when the time comes. For now, you must all rest while you can."

And he would discuss the matter no further. When he left, I took Mama and poor Gerda downstairs, knowing they would not feel safe in their violated bedrooms. I lit a fire in the hearth and dressed my wife, like a child, in her night-gown, then with blankets and pillows upon the sofa and floor, situated them all so that they might sleep. But Gerda was so pitifully wide-eyed and trembling that I administered tincture of opium, which she drank down obediently. Mama refused, saying as always that she preferred wakefulness to the poppy's effects. As for myself, I sat in Papa's chair, won-dering what he would have made of the strange events that had beseiged his family in the week after his death.

When at last the women's eyes closed, I took myself to the kitchen for coffee: I knew I should not sleep to-night, nor for some nights to come, and I had much thinking to do. I sat for an hour, perhaps more, at the table, with my troubled forehead in my hands, surrounded by a storm of thoughts. And after a time, slowly, my overwhelmed senses perceived that I was not alone. I lifted my face to find Arkady sitting silently across from me.

"Forgive me," he said at my startled reaction. "I had to speak to you alone, away from your mother. I have always known where Stefan is ultimately bound. I can go alone and retrieve your brother and son—but their rescue is meaningless. For Vlad will only pursue Stefan again; the danger will persist so long as your brother lives."

"Then what can be done?" I asked.

"Vlad must be destroyed—and that I cannot do." He fixed his gaze steadily upon me. "He—and I—can die only by a human hand. But finding a mortal with the courage and willingness to commit the deed has proven impossible."

I contemplated this silently a time, then said: "You want me to disobey my mother's wishes. To accompany you. To help deal with this Zsuzsanna and . . . Vlad."

"Yes. I know Mary's determination once she has made up her mind; she will never permit you to leave unless she comes with you. The deception is necessary in order for her to remain safe."

In truth, I cared nothing about these so-called monsters, Zsuzsanna and Vlad, about the threat they posed humankind, and I had no intention of setting off on some bizarre supernatural quest to destroy them. But I cared about my little son and my brother and was desperate to do something, anything, on their behalf. And so I said, "Then I will go with you. When shall we leave?"

"Now," he said.

✦   ✦   ✦

I have written all this on the train. I sit alone, gazing out from time to time at the banks of the dark muddy Rhine. Dawn broke some hours ago, and Arkady has closeted himself in his berth with instructions that he not be disturbed until sunset.

The recording of it all makes it no less difficult to believe. To the contrary, the events seem more outlandish pondered in full daylight. But I must find something to constantly occupy my mind; the alternative is to go mad with worry over what has become of my little son.

Would that I *could*—madness would be such sweet relief. But sanity will not release its grip on me.

My life is shattered. Gerda has retreated again into silence, as profound as that in which I first found her; I fear she will never return. To-day I have no father, no brother, no wife, no son.

Here is what, at this sunny hour, I believe: that I have gone clinically insane. That I have fallen prey to a grandiose delusion that pits good against evil and includes Mama, Stefan, Jan, and Gerda in its lunatic embrace.

But this delusion is now my world, and I am required to obey its laws or suffer the consequences; therefore, I shall do whatever is necessary to win back my brother and son.

God, in Whom I do not believe, help me.

⇥ 8 ⇤

The Journal of
Mary Tsepesh Van Helsing

22 NOVEMBER. So now payment comes for all the years of deception, for all the years I have hidden from my sons the truth. You are stolen again, dear Stefan, and there is nothing I can do, nothing I can say; I must simply bear the responsibility for any harm done you to my grave.

Bram, forgive me! I wished only to protect you—but now you, too, have lost everything. . . .

I must bear responsibility as well for what has become of my dear Arkady, for had I not fired the shot that launched him into eternity, he would not be as he is now, would not have spent the past twenty-six years in such hideous purgatory.

I thought not to see him for some time, but he came again last night as I lay upon the drawing-room floor, while Gerda snored softly upon the sofa, lost to the effects of opium.

I had fallen into a light troubled doze beside the hearth. Cold fingers brushed my lips, and I woke instantly, terrified that Vlad had come; but I knew when I gazed up into those loving brown eyes, flecked with green, that it was my Arkady. In such things, I am not easily fooled.

"Hush," he whispered in English, and stroked my forehead soothingly. I calmed and sat up to look about me—and grew anxious again at the realisation that Bram was not there.

"He cannot sleep," Arkady said, smiling faintly in reassurance. "He has gone to the kitchen. I waited for an opportunity to see you alone." I looked toward the hallway and drew some small measure of comfort to see light coming from the direction of the kitchen. Arkady took my hand—I have learnt not to shudder at its coldness—and held it to his breast. "Mary, my darling . . . I have come because we will not meet again."

"But we must," I whispered, my heart at once quickening its pace, for though I dreaded seeing him thus—a monster, his lips stained with the blood of his victims—he was also my beloved, still young, still beautiful, miraculously returned to me from the dead. "We must! When you bring Stefan home—"

He held my gaze steadily, his face bathed in the warm wavering glow from the fire as he said, "Stefan will return alone—after Vlad—and I—are destroyed. I promise you this." A wistful glimmer of pain passed over his features before he added, "Forgive me. This is pure selfishness of my part. I should have let you sleep, should not have troubled you further; you and your family have already suffered enough! But I could not leave without seeing you once more." And he smiled sadly as he reached out to fondly stroke my cheek. "A sight to comfort a man for all eternity."

An eternity in Hell, I knew, and cried out softly. But Gerda did not stir.

My heart has been so badly broken and mended again —stronger than ever now because of its dreadful wounds— that I thought it could never break again. But at the sight of his face, at the knowledge that he was taking his leave forever, beyond death, it shattered.

For the man, not the monster, I reached out and slipped his cloak from his shoulders, unfastened the stays of his collar. With my hands, I freed the soft, shining skin of his neck, his chest, and with my lips, found the sweet hollow at the joining of his shoulder and throat and kissed it. Kissed it to bless it, for I knew it had once been profaned by a wicked, hurtful pair of lips; kissed it to heal it, though I know there is only one fatal way to repair that dark, now-invisible wound.

Then I pressed my cheek there, utterly unafraid, uncringing at the coldness of skin that had once been so warm, and gazed up to see him looking down at me, his eyes filled with tears as bright as diamonds.

We said not a word; our hearts were too full, but we spoke nonetheless, by kiss and caress. Have I sinned? Shall I be damned for loving a monster?

He is my husband; and for that moment, he was not immortal, not undead, but my Arkady, alive and passionate and generous in his love, and I his young wife, emerged from this cocoon of sagging flesh and greying hair. The years and all the evil they have wrought fell away, and we were alone.

I lay with him there on the floor beside the hearth, unmindful of Gerda, of Bram, unmindful of anything save him, save that cold flesh pressed against mine. And my heart breaks now more than ever before, for I know the truth of his existence: that he is still capable of love, both physical and spiritual. His immortality has purchased him no freedom from desire, or loneliness, or grief, and for the decades I thought him sleeping in sweet oblivion, he has suffered all that I have from our separation—and more.

So we made love desperately, silently, clutching each other as though it were truly possible to hold on forever. At the end, I remember the bright flare of pleasure, and the world fading into darkness as I lost myself, drowsy and content, in the ocean of his eyes.

His eyes, his eyes . . .

I woke to an empty house: Empty, I say, though Gerda lay in it; but her eyes are dreadful, vacant. Her heart and soul are not here.

And Arkady and Bram were gone. My love! your passion was sincere, but you used the distraction to mesmerise me. You have deceived me . . . and I you.

And for our deceptions, we and untold others shall pay.

⊰ 9 ⊱

The Journal of
Stefan Van Helsing

22 NOVEMBER. I woke to rhythmic rocking and the haunting strains of a lullaby.

For one dreamy moment, I fancied myself a child again, cradled in my mother's arms—until I opened my eyes to dappled twilight and the loveliest woman I have ever seen, seated across from me. Her skin was the colour of milk, her hair shining indigo, and in her arms she held a child swaddled in a blanket. This madonna was arrayed in fetching finery: a fitted velvet dress of French blue, its daringly low-cut satin bodice trimmed with seed pearls, and a small velvet cap with a net veil that could not hide her beauty. Such large perfect eyes, framed by fine arching brows and long jet lashes! Such perfect full crimson lips. . . .

I longed at once to be the child at her breast, and I listened, captivated, as she sang with a sweet clear voice in a language I had never heard. Italian, I thought at first, but it was peppered with strange, distinctly Slavic sibilants.

I straightened in my seat and found myself once again

upon a train, in private first-class accommodations; beyond the window, an early winter landscape glided past. Not Holland, I realised, for there was no sign of flat lowlands, of polders, dams, windmills, or sea; instead, there were evergreens and the naked limbs of trees against distant snow-capped mountains.

The sight brought with it a rush of fear, and the memory of all that had transpired the night before. I had seen this woman before—when I had lain with Gerda, only to see my lover transform herself into this hypnotically beautiful stranger. . . . Gerda, Gerda, my darling! What has become of you?

The siren across from me ceased her singing and smiled prettily despite my obvious dismay. "Good evening, Stefan," she said in perfect German. "Did you sleep well?"

"Who are you?" I asked, trying to hide my shame at the memory of our nocturnal encounter. My tone was harsh, accusing, but she laughed as though I had said something quite witty.

"I am your aunt, Zsuzsanna," said she, looking me up and down with a frankly lecherous air that was entirely unnerving. "And a pity, too, for it means you shall probably be too scandalised now to repeat last night's behaviour. Nephew or not, you really are quite a beautiful young man."

I felt my cheeks flame as I demanded, "Where are we?"

"Pleased to meet you, too. Really, dear, do you expect me to answer such a question after the shocking discovery I made last night?"

I stared at her, perplexed. "Discovery?"

"Do you always speak in questions? The fact that you're tied to Arkady, dear. My brother. And though I love him mightily, I saw the cut on your finger—on a specific finger in such a specific place that I can't believe it's coincidence.

I really don't care to tell your father where we are at the moment. Of course, he surely already knows where we're going."

"And where is that?"

She smiled, revealing dazzling sharp teeth. "Why, the land beyond the forest."

The child in her arms stirred then and whimpered faintly; she patted its back with a lace-gloved hand. Despite the blanket that hid its features, I recognised the cry at once, with pure horror. "Little Jan! Dear God, you have stolen the baby!"

She blinked at me, her eyes wide. "It's not yours, is it?"

I straightened, indignant, and felt a rush of warmth to my face. "Of course not! It's my brother's."

"Thank goodness." She sighed, then smiled down at the baby and cooed: "Jan. So that's your name, is it, my little fellow? Handsome Jan, my little Dutch boy."

"Why have you taken him? Why have you done such a cruel thing?"

It was her turn to take offense. "I would never be cruel to him, never harm him! I intend to take very good care of him!" As if to make her point, she lifted up her veil and leaned down to kiss the child.

Her face was half-hidden by the blanket; but I could see from the movement of her cheekbones that she had parted her lips. At once I leapt to my feet and grabbed the child, thinking to wrest it from her.

Her grip was twice as strong as mine—nay, stronger, and I came away empty-handed. But the soft blanket that half-covered her prize's face had fallen away, and I saw the boy quite clearly: a nonmedical observer might have thought him sleeping, but I knew him to be in shock. His round little face was ashen, his parted cherub lips blue-grey, his eyes closed; beneath the fringe of golden lashes pressed against his pale cheek were dark half-moon shadows. His breathing was shallow, swift.

He was dying.

At the realisation, all chivalrous instincts towards the gentler sex left me. I tried once more to take the child, this time with every ounce of strength I could muster. It was not enough; and so, fueled by anguish and adrenaline, I struck out with my fist directly at Zsuzsanna's head.

The blow would have knocked a sturdy man from his feet; but in this case it only displaced the small velvet hat, causing a cascade of blue-black curls to spill down onto her swan-white neck and bosom.

She scarcely flinched. The blow clearly provoked no pain—only an anger that was terrifying to behold. She rose to her feet, the child draped over one arm, and growled—a sound that was entirely feral, inhuman. Her face, which only an instant before had been stunningly beautiful, transformed itself into a Medusan rictus, revealing sharp hideous fangs and eyes whose soft clear brown had grown opaque gleaming gold.

With a movement so swift I was taken off-guard, she struck back—with one arm sending me reeling backwards, off-balance, so that I slammed against the seat and slid to the floor.

The impact knocked the air from my lungs. I half-sat, one elbow propped upon the seat-cushion, and fought to recover my breath while her quicksilver visage transformed again from beast to beauty.

She smiled tenderly down at the pale cherub in her arms and smoothed the hair from his forehead. "I would never hurt you, would I, darling? No . . . I only give you kisses—the very sweetest—so that you can stay and be my little man forever." And she lifted him higher in her arms and brought her face low to his small white neck.

I forced down a gulp of air and lunged at her.

Again she struck out with a slender blue satin arm, this time not even bothering to remove her attention from the tiny victim in her grasp. But her second blow hurled me against the window-seat with such force that I heard, upon impact, a loud crack and knew not whether it was my own skull or the wooden seat-frame.

I collapsed, dazed; I may have spent a few seconds unconscious. And when I came to myself I saw my little nephew lying horridly limp and motionless in Zsuzsanna's arms, while she sat with her red lips fastened upon his neck, her own pale throat working mightily as a single crimson drop spilled upon her white bosom and threaded its way down between her breasts.

And as I watched, poor Jan emitted a death-rattle; his murderess raised her face and graced him with a bloody smile. "There, now," she said in the most maternal, soothing tone. "Sleep, my sweet. Sleep, and when you wake, your new mama shall see that you have everything you desire!" And she wrapped the small corpse more tightly in the blanket, patted its backside, and hummed the strange lullaby as though it were a living drowsy child.

I could bear no more. I had seen the mother stricken with guilt on my account and could only imagine her agony at finding her child gone. Now to see little Jan killed, my dear nephew, while I watched, unable to prevent it . . .

I covered my face and burst into hoarse, loud sobs.

Almost immediately I felt a cold, feather-light touch upon my arms, my shoulders. In the midst of my racking grief, I expected her to strike out again, to beat me into silence; yet I was too overwhelmed to raise my hands in defense, to do anything other than weep. I should not have cared had she killed me then.

But no blows came. Her touch remained light, and I came to realise, after the first horrible wave of sorrow passed, that she was gently stroking my hair and murmuring reassurance. *Comforting* me, and when I looked up at last, my vision blurred by tears, I saw she had left Jan's swaddled body upon the seat and knelt beside me; and in her eyes shone genuine compassion.

"Ah, my poor Stefan," she said, tenderly wiping my cheeks with her cool gloved hands and leaning her face next to mine so that I smelled her breath, bittersweet and metallic. "I know how difficult all this is for you. But do not cry for your nephew! He died gently, in a state of pure bliss— this I swear to you, for I have done it myself. He felt no pain, no fear; and when he wakes, he shall never, never feel pain or fear again. He will live forever! And I shall see to it personally that he will always be loved and cared for. I spent my life a lonely woman, without the love of a man or child. Please—do not deny me this."

I could answer her only with more tears. She put her cold arms round me as I wept, rocking and shushing me as though I were little Jan. I yielded utterly to grief and guilt, and how long we remained thus I cannot say.

But after a time I had no more tears and came to myself enough to realise that I was still in her arms, my cheek nestled against her neck, her shoulder, her perfumed hair. I lifted my face and found it pressed against her bosom; I drew back slowly, reluctantly, aware of the sudden rapid beating of my heart, of her desirable beauty. Remembering the passion of the night before, I drank deep of her seductive, laughing gaze and wanted nothing more than to embrace her cold perfection. . . .

To my utter disappointment, she pulled away from me with a bemused grin; I think she quite relished my reaction to her loveliness and enjoyed the flirtation. "Ah, yes, you are a lovely young man, Stefan. But if I yield to one appetite, it is not so easy to control the other—and I have not fed sufficiently for that now. Were I in passion's throes to give you one of my special kisses, *he* should never forgive me." And she smoothed a hand over my cheek, my neck, down to the centre of my chest, where she lingered coquettishly. "Perhaps later, my dear. But if there is anything else you should require during your journey—anything within reason—just ask, and I shall see it provided."

I looked away, disgusted that such thoughts should enter my head at such a heartbreaking moment, when the child of my lover and my brother lay dead before me.

I spent some hours staring out the window at the changing countryside, contemplating when and how to make my escape. Thus far, I have had no opportunity; Zsuzsanna does not sleep and is quite watchful—despite the fact that she still holds my little nephew's corpse in her arms and coos at it from time to time. I attempted once to bolt from the compartment, thinking to jump from the train—to death or freedom—but she restrained me all too easily.

Like my dear dead nephew, I am her prisoner, her pet.

So I demanded paper and pen, which amused her—*you come from a family of inveterate journalists,* she said—and I spend my time writing it all down. Now I await another chance; but from her hints, it is clear that someone else—a human woman, I think—is somewhere nearby, armed with a pistol, and that she will serve as my guard when day comes again.

Arkady! Where are you? *Summon me in your thoughts,* you said, *and I will come. . . .*

I have summoned, but I know not where I am, only that dark place whither I am bound. The dying of the light brings with it fear; at the same time, it brings hope that rescue will come.

But I look over at the cooling flesh of Bram's boy, as he lies stiffening in the arms of his diabolical nursemaid, and know I do not deserve to be saved. I am glad, now, that I cannot give Arkady direction. Let the darkness take me. I have destroyed my brother's life, his wife's, and now his little son's; let the sacrifice of my own bring them some measure of peace.

❧ 10 ❧

The Diary of Arkady Dracul

23 NOVEMBER. I shall not be able to control the hunger much longer.

Travelling is problematic. Without my Amsterdam henchman, I have no means for feeding without creating others like me—and this I have sworn not to do. The world suffers enough from *my* existence; let me spawn no fresh monsters.

Perhaps if I can control myself, drink but a little and permit my victims to live, then pray that I and Vlad will soon meet with destruction . . . but I fear I have gone too long without nourishment for such self-control.

In my desperation, I thought to-night to broach the subject with Abraham. I have sensed Stefan's thoughts and know the fate that has befallen his little nephew, Jan; I cannot bring myself to tell the father this heartbreaking news. But Bram will learn of the grisly art of setting a vampire to rest one way or another. Why shall he not learn of it now?

But it is too soon, too soon.

I trust Abraham; trust him as I have always trusted my beloved Mary. He is so like her—even, coincidentally, in appearance, for being Dutch, his eyes are blue and his colouring fair, though the gold in his hair is kissed with red. But it is in temperament that they are so utterly alike that one might think she bore him. She has raised him to share her calm, her strength, her loyalty—and even her stubbornness.

I will need to rely on that strength and determination when we arrive in Transylvania. Before then, there are many things he must be taught, for Stefan and Jan's sakes as well as his own. But I can see my trust in him is not returned.

After rising this evening, I found him in our compartment, lost in thought as he stared out at the grey wintry landscape, a writing tablet on his knee, one hand absently fingering his golden beard. He did not hear my approach; and I saw in his pale furrowed brow, in his blue eyes, slightly magnified by thick spectacle lenses, such worry and love that it touched my cold, unbeating heart. I have spent a quarter-century immersed in a decadent, predatory world, with only the hope of revenge and the fading memories of my dear ones to keep my humanity alive; my life as a murderer has calloused me.

But experiencing once more Mary's love, and her goodness, is sloughing the layers of coldness away. (I worried that my very touch might taint her—but no. I am convinced that, for all my wickedness, our act did not, could not sully her goodness; if anything, it redeemed and elevated me. For the first time in twenty-six years, at her caress, I felt a surge of honest warmth course through my being; I am ready now to face whatever fate awaits me. Mary, dear, can you forgive me for putting you gently to sleep afterwards? I cannot save your one son without the help of the other—and I remember all too well your resolve; I knew you would not let us leave without you.)

Bram's goodness, too, reminds me of the horror I have become. I saw the anguish he suffered the night of his wife's terrible confession of betrayal in the presence of us all; but his concern for her suffering, and Stefan's, eclipsed his own pain. He showed her naught but forgiveness and gentleness afterwards; nor has he once mentioned her transgression, or his brother's.

Without opening the door, I slipped inside the compartment and said, "Doctor Van Helsing."

I expected to startle him; but he was a man too burdened, too drained, to waste energy on such a frivolous emotion. Slowly, he withdrew his focus from the dark, changing scenery on which it had rested—though I knew his mind was not there but far, far distant in space and time: in Amsterdam, in his wife's bedroom, at that terrible moment when she recounted her tale of violation and betrayal. His gaze went inwards a moment, then at last emerged and discovered me. There it rested, and he beheld me in silence, waiting.

Damn the hunger! It assailed me as I caught his scent, and for a fleeting second, reason left me: I could think only that here was a healthy victim, full of fresh strong blood, yet too worn, too distraught to put up much struggle. And we two were alone, unwatched. . . .

Only an instant of weakness, no more: I forced it to pass. He glimpsed it, I am sure, but the weary blue eyes behind his spectacles showed not the slightest hint of fear.

He drew a long breath—one in which I heard that infinite exhaustion caused by emotional pain—and said at last, "Certainly, sir, these circumstances are too desperate and familiar for formality. My name is Abraham; my family calls me Bram."

"Abraham," I said. "As a father, I can understand your suffering. Please know that you have my full sympathy."

He turned his face back towards the window and kept it there as I continued. "Before we arrive at our destination, there are things of which we must speak. First and most important, you must be trained to protect yourself from creatures such as I. As a man of science, you will no doubt find some of the methods bizarre, even fantastic; but I assure you, before my transformation, I was myself the greatest of sceptics."

"Tell me what I must do," he said softly to the window.

I spoke to him then of what I had learned—both as a terrified mortal and an undead patron of the Scholomance. I began with the basics: the protection afforded by sacred relics, and the simple skills of inducing self-trance, of concentration and meditation, of the need to build the aura through imagery so that another might not easily penetrate; of the need to recognise and resist another's attempt to invoke trance.

With the theories of Franz Mesmer, he said he was as a physician familiar, but that he lent them little credence; they were useful for stage performers and the circus, nothing more. For he, he stated emphatically (and with more than a little of the arrogance I have seen in current-day practitioners of medicine), could not be mesmerised. I wasted no time arguing.

Abraham, I said without moving my lips, and his eyes, startled and ingenuous, focussed instantly on mine.

I had him at once. With the thrill of the hunter knowing the prey is his, I leaned towards him until our faces were almost touching; his went utterly slack, and the pupils of his eyes dilated until only a tiny rim of blue, blue iris could be seen. His breathing grew slow, shallow. He sagged back against the seat, his hands limp at his sides, awaiting my command.

Your life and death are in my hands, I told him—and meant it, for I realised that my little demonstration was a grievous mistake. I was almost as helpless as he—helpless in the face of my own appetite. I was near enough to smell his warm, warm skin, feel the heat of his body, hear the gentle, barely perceptible throb of his heart and the murmur of rushing blood.

Unfasten your collar, Abraham.

I had not meant to issue the command, but it came forth unbidden, and I watched, hypnotised myself by desire as he unloosed his cravat and removed the stays.

And then the appearance of skin, flushed with blood, pulsing, ruddy against the stark white of the open collar . . . I found myself drawing closer, closer, until my lips tingled from the heat; until they hovered a mere inch from his bared throat.

The shrill cry of the train distracted me an instant; it was enough to rescue us both. I pulled back in dismay and thrust him from me—too roughly, I fear. He struck the wall beside the window and tumbled to the floor, then gazed up at me, his spectacles askew, in complete astonishment.

"We will discuss this at a later time," I said abruptly, and left the compartment while I still could.

To-night! It shall have to be to-night; if only I can control myself. . . .

The Diary of
Abraham Van Helsing

23 NOVEMBER. Darker and darker it grows. Darker and darker . . .

I was sleeping in the wagon-lit, secure in my privacy, knowing that Arkady would be gone until daybreak. In truth, that sleep was restless and long coming, for the earlier incident in the compartment with him troubled me. I had indeed lost control of my will, and the immediacy of the experience—and its frightening culmination—brought home the notion that perhaps what was happening *was real.*

He came close to killing me to-day; I know it. And if Arkady is capable of such sudden arbitrary violence, then what of Vlad?

And Stefan, and Jan . . .

Stop. That way leads to pointless torment.

To continue: After some hours, I had fallen into an uneasy sleep only to be abruptly awakened by a hoarse groan.

"Abraham . . ."

I opened my eyes to see Arkady sitting on the berth across from mine, face buried in his hands in a gesture of utter despair. I sat up, instantly alert, heart pounding, convinced that he had somehow come across terrible news: that Jan or Stefan was dead. "What is it? What has happened?"

He looked up, revealing an expression not so much of grief as of shame. I sensed at once that something was different; his pallour had vanished. Indeed, his face was quite flushed, as some men's become when they overindulge in drink, and his lips cherry-red. "I need your help," he said in a voice drowsy and faintly slurred, which increased my suspicion that he was drunk. "In the compartment."

He faltered, until I demanded: "Out with it! If you must interrupt my sleep, do so efficiently!"

He was silent a moment, then said, more calmly, "Very well. In our compartment, you will find a man. A dead man. I had not intended this to happen, but I should not have waited so long—"

My voice dropped to the faintest whisper. "Are you saying that you killed him?"

This time he met my gaze steadily; his own was heavy-lidded, as though he fought imminent sleep. "Yes. Inadvertently. And I require special assistance."

I did not wait to listen to the rest but climbed from my berth and hurried, barefoot and clad in only a nightshirt, to the compartment. Time was of the essence; many times the untrained eye and ear may fail to detect a pulse and proclaim death prematurely. If Arkady was wrong, I wanted to provide whatever medical assistance I could.

And if he was right, I had to see the evidence with my own eyes.

The lamp had been extinguished. The compartment was unlit save for full moonlight, which streamed through the unshuttered window and was broken by the occasional denuded branches of tall trees, which dappled the scene with fast-moving bands of dark and light.

I stepped into that ever-changing chiaroscuro and nearly stumbled over a body upon the floor, quite hidden by the darkness.

I did not light the lamp but instead knelt down at once to conduct an examination, making use of the fleeting moonlight and the degree to which my eyes had adjusted to the dimness.

It was a man, lying on his side in a sprawling pose that suggested he had lain upon the seat, then rolled off due to the train's motion. He was well dressed, white-haired, with a long, drooping mustache, and so portly he took up most of the floor between the passengers' seats; I could scarce find the room to kneel beside him.

With difficulty, I rolled him over that so that he lay supine, and pressed an ear to his chest. The heart within was silent; nor could I find the pulse in the wrist or neck—but at the throat was a small dark stain. I touched it with a finger, and raised it to my face, and smelled cooling blood.

Arkady had been right; he was dead, but the skin was still quite warm. The murder had taken place recently.

"I was careful," Arkady said softly, his tone one of regret and dismay. I glanced up to see him sitting, knees clasped to his chest, upon the seat beside us. "Quite careful not to drink too much—but of a sudden, he simply . . . collapsed."

"Light the lamp," I said.

He tilted his face, curiously phosphorescent in the moonlight, in a gesture of disbelief. "Impossible. Someone might pass by. For me, incrimination presents no difficulty; I can easily find a means of escape. But for you to be seen with the corpse—"

"Light the lamp."

After a moment's pause, he did so, and the results of his appetite stared sightlessly back at us in uncomfortably distinct detail: a grandfatherly man, a Papa Noel, with snowy waving hair, jowly neck, small pale green eyes behind gold-rimmed spectacles, and apple-round cheeks. I continued my examination, grateful that my habitual professional demeanour allowed me some control over the emotions that assailed me—especially at that moment when I wiped away the congealing blood upon the man's throat with my kerchief and saw the indisputable evidence of two small puncture wounds.

The same wound that I had seen on Gerda's neck.

I can no longer deny the reality of all these insane events. But that does not mean I must participate in them.

Arkady sat in clearly miserable silence until at last I looked up and said, "You are right; I do not think he died from loss of blood. Look at his colour: his lips and gums are still pink, and there is a faint flush still on the cheeks."

His expression grew hopeful. "Then I did not kill him?"

I made a half-hearted attempt to keep judgement from my tone and failed. "I did not say that. See the eyes? How one pupil is much larger than the other? It is indicative of bleeding in the brain: apoplexy. His fear may have triggered an attack."

"I tried to ease his fear. I did not think that—" Arkady began quietly, then looked up in mild alarm as I rose. "Do not go just yet, Abraham. I did not bring you here to confirm what I already knew."

"Then what assistance *did* you need?" My emotions were already taxed to their limits; I felt disgust, anger, that he should have committed such an act, then asked me to be party to it. I felt anger, too, and sorrow, for the sake of poor dead Papa Noel. "I am a physician, sir; this man is beyond my help."

"In fact, he is not, Doctor Van Helsing. In two nights, perhaps three, if not prevented, he will rise to be one such as I."

I had seen and heard enough in the past week to check my scepticism and replied only, "Then what must be done?"

Arkady's voice dropped so low, I could just make out

his reply. "The head must be severed, and a stake plunged through the heart."

I recoiled as I realised, from his expression and demeanour, that he intended *me* to carry out such desecration. I turned and moved at once for the door, pausing there only long enough to say, "This is your crime; yours alone, and yours alone the consequences."

Resolute, I stepped out into the unlit corridor. He followed, silent, gliding, melting into the darkness, and whispered into my ear—as though he were beside me, which was impossible in that narrow space: "You do not understand: I cannot do it myself, else I would not come to you. Realise what you are doing—creating another monster, one who will bring more grief to families such as yours."

Unmoved, unhearing, I hurried back to my berth and crawled inside. My tormentor, now invisible, followed.

"Van Helsing, help me! I am damned and cannot destroy another vampire—"

"Then be damned and go to Hell, sir," I whispered to the night, my voice trembling. "And cease tormenting us poor mortals."

After only a second's pause, he answered, with an audible flicker of pain, "I shall, Abraham. I shall, as soon as it is possible. But that I cannot do either without your help."

I pulled the blankets over my face, and there remained —awake, perspiring—until dawn.

This morning when I went to the compartment, the corpse was gone, disappeared as though it had been nothing more than a bad dream.

I will go to Transylvania and find my son and brother, and return. But I will not be drawn into Arkady's evil world, will not be party to murder, will not execute grisly rituals or fill my head with his bizarre mental training. I *will not.* . . .

❧ 11 ❧

The Journal of
Stefan Van Helsing

25 NOVEMBER. We are getting closer to home now.

To Transylvania, I mean; I have heard the word *home* so often used in reference to that country that I have come to call it that myself, though I have never been.

The days and nights begin to blur together. The servant woman, Dunya, watches over me by day, Zsuzsanna by night, but from time to time they overlap.

I was terrified of my situation at first, and fearful for my life; but Zsuzsanna has shown me only kindness. I want for nothing—our accommodations are sumptuous, and we have our own car—and dine on the finest food and wine. Vlad must be enormously wealthy to have made these arrangements; for I have yet to see a conductor or waiter. Food appears, and it magically disappears, and our quarters remain tidy. Either Zsuzsanna or her serving-woman are doing this unaided, or the details all are tended to while I sleep.

Until to-day, I thought we might have our own private train. Now I see that that would have inconvenienced Zsuzsanna too greatly, for reasons I shall soon explain.

My diurnal guardian, Dunya, is a small thin woman, with colouring similar to Zsuzsanna's, except for the reddish cast to her dark hair. Clearly they are from the same racial stock, but Dunya is of a different class, sheltered, uneducated, a lowly servant of a sort not seen in Holland. Perhaps this accounts for her shyness; she speaks to me only in monosyllables, and at times her frightened dark eyes grow vacant (when Zsuzsanna or Vlad controls her, I have decided).

They are most often vacant when she brandishes the pistol in order to prevent my escape. This morning, in fact, at dawn, the mental dullness and confusion that plague me when I am in Zsuzsanna's presence departed, and I had a moment of clarity when I sensed Arkady was following, and that he urged me to try to break free. (It seems to me these periods of lucidity come at sunrise, noon, and dusk; I shall have to keep a record to see if my perceptions are accurate.) I made up my mind to leap from the train—for I know Dunya will not kill me—Zsuzsanna swears that they intend me no harm, and I believe her.

The guards had changed; Dunya had taken her place, with weapon at the ready, in the compartment. And I rose, under pretense of stretching my legs and visiting the water closet.

Instead, I hurried to the rear of the car and tried to open the exit; but it was locked or jammed, and before I could do more than jiggle it, Dunya appeared, with the pistol levelled at my legs, ready to shoot.

What could I do except meekly follow her back to the private compartment? Perhaps she does not mean to kill me, but I cannot be certain of her aim . . .

And then there is the matter of Zsuzsanna.

When I am with her, most times I forget myself. Her

eyes have an uncanny power to sway me, to make me do her bidding. I colour with pure shame to record that she has again appeared to me as Gerda, and again I took her in my arms in the travelling compartment and ravished her. . . .

Or was it she who ravished me? I am even more ashamed to report that when she let Gerda's image drop and appeared as her beautiful self to me, I did not stop myself, did not turn away in revulsion at what I had done. Worse: last night, she did not bother to change her appearance at all, and still I embraced her, knowing full well she was my father's sister, a cold-blooded creature who had killed my brother's son.

We are lovers each night; and each morning I wake filled with remorse, determined to abstain the following eve. But her eyes, her eyes! I fight, but cannot resist them.

I have questioned her carefully about the blood ritual; she says little, but from what she does reveal, I think that the ritual that tied me to Arkady has kept me from being a complete automaton now. But the further I move away from his influence and the nearer to Transylvania, the more confused my thoughts become.

For at times, I know how Zsuzsanna is attempting to manipulate me; but in the evening, I come close to believing her when she says it is Arkady who seeks to betray me, and Vlad who is good.

But to-night was distressing—as troubling as the first day, when I learned that Amsterdam was no longer to be my home.

Dunya held watch by day. After my early attempt at escape, I drowsed through most of it in a warm patch of sun beside the window. When night fell, I rose to stretch my legs and in the corridor encountered Zsuzsanna.

She was as provocatively lovely as ever, but to-night she

was beaming with special brilliance. For holding both her hands and tottering in front of her was my little nephew, Jan.

Oh, he was radiant! a shining cherub with golden curls and sapphire eyes, dimpling and cheerful as I have ever seen him—when only a few nights ago, he had lain pale, grey-lipped, unmoving, in Zsuzsanna's arms.

Weeping with joy, I dropped to one knee and spread my arms wide for him.

He cried out in delight as he let go her guiding hands and, with sudden remarkable agility and grace beyond his eighteen months, ran to me.

"No!" Zsuzsanna called after him, but we were far too caught up in our happy reunion to pay her any heed. "Be careful, Stefan, it is too soon—"

I grabbed him and rose, whirling him about; he has always loved to be lifted, and swung, and tossed into the air. But this time, he did not giggle with childish glee, or beg to "fly," as he calls it. Instead, he wrapped his chubby arms about my neck and looked solemnly at me with great blue eyes—eyes that were peculiarly magnetic and beautiful to gaze upon, but cold and soulless as an inanimate object: like the ocean, or a glittering jewel. And then he bent to kiss me.

"*Jan,*" Zsuzsanna chided, and swiftly plucked him from my grasp. "Not Uncle, darling; not Uncle." She swept him away down the corridor while he wailed, his round little face peering over her shoulder at me, his little hands reaching out to me.

How could I not follow? They disappeared swiftly into the next car. I followed, of course, but found the exit again jammed or locked. Before I could scarcely react to this realisation, they returned.

Not alone; they were followed by a kind-faced matron

who reached out, smiling and playful, to little Jan as he leaned over Zsuzsanna's shoulder and in turn peered shyly at his newfound friend. Each was clearly transfixed by the other.

They went into the private sitting compartment. I joined the trio at once, falling into that pleasant, dull passivity Zsuzsanna's presence so often evoked, and completely forgot all desire to escape, forgot anything but my desire to remain in her company.

A pleasant round of introductions were made in German. This was Frau Buchner, travelling to her cousin's funeral in Bratislava and quite lonesome for her grandchildren. She was a sweet simple woman, soft and round, with sloping shoulders and the beginnings of a dowager's hump, and braided grey hair coiled round her head beneath a lace scarf. Something about her reminded me of Mama: her gentleness, perhaps, or her clear blue eyes, or perhaps the sweet smell of ladies' talcum. But she was older, paler—though her pallour may have been due to the severe effect of her mourning clothes, for she was dressed from head to toe in black. The only spot of colour rested upon her broad bosom: a large gold crucifix.

And this, she avowed with a nod at my nephew, in a voice that had just begun to quaver with age, was simply the prettiest child she had ever seen—

"Who is lonesome for his grandmama," Zsuzsanna offered graciously, aglow with maternal pride. With Jan in her arms, she settled down beside the older woman whilst I sat across from them. Beside us, the unshuttered window opened onto deepening twilight and the distant black waters of the Danube, a diamond strand of lights draped along its curving banks.

"And what is our baby's name?" our visitor asked.

"Jan," Zsuzsanna answered proudly, as though she had christened him herself.

"Jan. A good name," she told the little boy. "Where I come from, we would call you Johann."

"Oma," Jan chirped, reaching a pudgy hand towards Frau Buchner; but when she smiled and reached back towards him, he withdrew at once to the safety of Zsuzsanna's embrace. The nearer she came, the more he recoiled, determined not to let her touch even the wipsy golden curls upon his head. Yet the whole while he stared over at her with those wide, crystalline-cold eyes—the eyes of a charmed cobra.

"Oma," he said again sweetly, and when I smiled despite myself, Frau Buchner turned to me for explanation.

"It is the Dutch word for 'grandmother,' " said I. "You remind him of her."

Her whole face brightened with pleasure at the compliment. "Ach, a pretty little Dutch boy. Yes, darling, I am an *oma,* with grandchildren of my own." And she reached for him again, unsuccessfully.

I took advantage of her distraction to whisper softly to Zsuzsanna, "But how is it possible? Only two days ago, I was sure he was dead." Writing these words, I realise that I knew, deep in my heart, what had happened. But in Zsuzsanna's presence, all that I had learnt from Arkady and Mama was forgotten; I lived in a pleasant, confused fantasy world where no evil was allowed to intrude, where little Jan and I were her happy, willing travelling companions.

"What is this?" Frau Buchner tilted her head, half-listening.

Zsuzsanna looked down at her charge and ran slender, long fingers fondly through his curls. "Our little darling was very sick. But to-day he is all better."

Frau Buchner nodded her head, the picture of sagacious

experience. "I tell you, that is the way it is with these little ones. One day, they have a fever so high you think they will never live. And the next day"—she snapped her fingers, which drew renewed interest from Jan—"Poof! They are ready to play again." She leaned forward towards the child again; the crucifix on her bosom dangled between them. "Isn't that right, my darling?"

She reached for his hair again, but Jan recoiled this time with a loud whimper, though his gaze remained fixed on her.

"So, are we the shy one now?" She smiled, but it was clear that she was desperate to win his affections, and that his rejection vexed her.

"I think your necklace frightens him," Zsuzsanna said, an abrupt coolness in her tone.

The woman looked down at it with puzzlement. "My necklace?" She fingered it, then gazed back up at the child. "Oh, my dear, what is there to be frightened of? That it is shiny?"

Zsuzsanna watched her with the same intent, predatory stare that recalled a tigress with her cub. "Perhaps that's it."

"See, darling?" Frau Buchner lifted the chain with two fingers so that the pendant dangled in front of Jan's owlish eyes. He squealed and burrowed his face into Zsuzsanna's shoulder, while she struggled not to show her own discomfort. "It's just a golden pretty," the older woman cooed. "See it shine? Just our Lord Jesus on the cross."

"Take it off," Zsuzsanna demanded, her voice harsh.

Frau Buchner blinked up at her in gentle surprise. "What?"

"Take it off."

The look Zsuzsanna gave the other woman was so intent, so piercing that I felt the hair on the back of my neck lift; Frau Buchner's expression went slack almost immediately. Slowly, she lifted the heavy gold chain and slipped it over her face, over the fat coil of grey braids on her crown, and held it out, at arm's length.

Zsuzsanna drew back from it in obvious disgust, shielding the child in her arms with her body, and turned to me, her eyes narrowed, her face a hard pale mask. For the first time, I saw beneath her beauty; saw a flash of something indescribably hideous. . . .

I hesitated, unwilling, instinctively knowing what would happen next without knowing *how* I knew. For a moment, the golden chain with its heavy gleaming burden dangled in the air between us.

"Take it," Zsuzsanna growled, her lower lip curling to display a row of teeth, each one white and hard and culminating in a fine sharp point, a deadly row of razor-keen stakes. It was the mouth I had seen the terrible night she had killed little Jan: a monster's rictus.

I looked swiftly away, closed my eyes.

A faint metallic cascade. I looked back to see Frau Buchner, her eyes distant, unfocussed, her fist open. The chain had slipped from her grasp to the floor in front of my feet.

"Oma!" Jan crowed happily, and she came to herself again for an instant, laughing as the boy bounded suddenly from Zsuzsanna's arms to hers. *"Oma!"*

"Oof! Careful now, little one," she said, smiling indulgently as the child carelessly flung his arms around her neck and buried his face there. She laughed again as she patted his back and turned to say something to Zsuzsanna—then grimaced with pain and let go a startled little scream.

"Aah!" She caught his hands and moved to pull him away—but abruptly her arms dropped. Her eyes grew vacant once more, and she grew quite still, mouth open, lips pursed in a surprised "O."

Zsuzsanna nestled back against the cushion and watched, her eyelids half-lowered in sensual approval—while I sat, frozen with horror and confusion. The compartment grew silent save for the rumble of the train and the child's loud, unselfconscious sucking, while his little fists waved about like a nursing infant's and clenched and unclenched the black silk of Frau Buchner's dress.

After a time, the matron's eyes closed, and her veiled head leaned back against the seat. Not long after, Jan lifted his face—cheeks and lips and chin smeared with bright blood—and sought Zsuzsanna's arms.

"That's my good boy," she said, producing a handkerchief and proceeding to wipe him clean; when that was done to her satisfaction, she cradled him in one arm. "Sleep now, little one."

And with the other, she reached for Frau Buchner.

It was not easily accomplished, but in the end, the older woman slid sideways in the seat so that one cheek rested upon the dozing child's belly and the other turned up towards Zsuzsanna, who leaned down to drink.

Only a moment; and when she was done. Zsuzsanna gently pushed her upright, then leaned over to pat the poor woman's hand: "Frau Buchner."

The woman woke with a start and lifted a dazed hand to her forehead. "What is it? Did I fall asleep?"

"Yes, dear. Are you tired? Perhaps you should go to your berth."

Buchner's eyes were vacant, troubled, the eyes of a soul who wants badly to remember and cannot. "Yes. Yes. Perhaps I should. Excuse me, dear."

Her face was ashen, her balance uncertain. I rose at once to take her arm and helped her to the other car.

When I returned, Zsuzsanna was rocking Jan in her arms and singing the strange lullaby I heard the first night on the train; she interrupted her song to gaze up at me and order, "Pick it up and dispose of it, please."

I knew she spoke of the crucifix, which still lay atop the coiled chain on the floor. Even now, I cannot explain why her request seemed logical, why I did not question it. I picked Frau Buchner's necklace from the floor, pulled down the window-sash, and tossed it out towards the darkly glittering banks of the Danube.

It is shortly after dawn. My mind is returned to me once more, and I have just made another unsuccessful attempt to escape, by wriggling through an open window. Now Dunya sits, tight-lipped, watching over me hawkishly with the gun. I can do nothing but reflect on last night's events again with horror.

If I am so swayed now by the vampire's glamour . . . what shall become of me when I arrive in Transylvania and fall prey to Vlad?

❧ 12 ❧

The Diary of
Abraham Van Helsing

26 NOVEMBER. And ever darker still . . .

I am in a different world. Holland seems in retrospect
so modern, airy, light: all white-washed brick, clean streets,
and wide flat expanses of land and sea and sky. When we
came to Buda-Pesth, I knew the civilised West was far behind us. The city's air was distinctly ancient and corrupt: a
dark place, with narrow cobbled streets and crumbling Ro-
man ruins.

Yet I was restless, sick of travel, eager to stand on terra
firma again. It was evening, and I convinced my bloodthirsty
companion to step from the train for a few hours' respite—
and for myself, a decent meal.

Arkady led me to a restaurant in the old town of Buda
—one where he had, he said, dined many, many years ago—
and neither drank nor ate but entertained me with conversation as I did both. I drank *barak,* the fiery apricot brandy,
ate a rich fiery dish of chicken sauced with cream and pa-
prika, and stared out at the dark hills that overlooked the

wide black Danube and the great unfinished bridge spanning it. Looked out, too, at the spires of a great cathedral—Saint Stephen's, Arkady said, with grim irony.

I know he senses my abject disgust at his capacity for murder; he is trying now to win back my trust. Certainly he never seemed to me more human than when he told me, with a sly smile, of the reputation of Hungarians and Roumanians both for wiliness and for moral disregard, and he made a small joke:

What is the difference between a Roumanian and a Hungarian?

Either will gladly sell you his aged mother; but only the Roumanian will deliver.

I did not laugh; could barely manage a small smile. The strain of travel and worry have begun to wear on me. I can think of nothing else except what has become of my child and my brother; at the same time, my weary body wanted nothing more than to stop and spend a night in a comfortable—and stationary—inn. But the urgency of our quest forbade it.

So we reboarded the train and continued our journey until the wee hours of the morning, when we arrived in Klausenburgh, which Arkady calls Cluj, our first stop inside the Transylvanian border. There we were forced to find accommodations—where we remained until late afternoon, which caused the innkeeper no small amount of consternation and cost us no small amount of coin; we were forced to pay for a full night's stay.

Arkady is free with his money and insists on separate lodging, which satisfies me. I have no desire to know the details of his existence; after the incident with the poor apoplectic in the compartment, I already know far more than I ever wished. But I sense that the hours are irregular for him as well, for they appear to have taken a toll on him; his striking youth and handsomeness are no longer so pronounced, and once, when we were conversing over my Buda-Pesth dinner, he turned his face to gaze mournfully out the window—and it was as though a mask suddenly slipped, revealing the profile of a haggard, aging man.

From Klausenburgh we took the train to Bistritz (spelled Bistrita, which Arkady pronounces *Bistritsa).* I thought the Austrian trains were slow, but the Roumanian rail system is slower still, and maddeningly unpunctual. Our train departed more than an hour late, and took nearly six hours to make a trip that in Holland would have taken less than three.

I am waiting, now, in a hotel in Bistritz that is renowned for neither its comfort nor its food—but it is the only one in town that, according to Arkady, is safe. There is a coach that leaves every afternoon for Bukovina, which it seems bore Stefan and Zsuzsanna and my son—my son!— away to-day. (I could not keep a groan of relief from escaping my lips to hear that the small golden-haired child who accompanied the woman was the picture of radiant health. Thank God, they have not harmed him.) We are only two hours behind; and so we dare not wait until to-morrow for the next coach. Arkady has gone to try to procure horses and a carriage, and we will make the trip as soon as he returns.

I have asked him why they have taken my child; he only answers darkly that he does not know. But I sense there is more he does not tell me.

＊ ＊ ＊

LATER ENTRY. I have written this in the carriage, so I do not know whether it will be legible to anyone other than myself; but I felt compelled to put it all down, though I can scarcely see in the gathering gloom. If we succeed and recover Stefan and Jan, then we shall all someday treasure this record of the darkest event in our family's history.

And if we fail . . .

Arkady drove the horses, for he is familiar with this region, and his vision is keener than mine: although he clearly craved more rest, I did not argue, for the land is wild and rugged, with mountains whose like I had seen only in the Swiss Alps. I had no desire to be the one responsible for keeping the carriage from going off the narrow winding pass over the cliff's edge—and I was grateful that the sunset had dimmed the view of our perilous ascent into the Carpathians.

The external conditions seemed to reflect the state of my mind, for the weather quickly turned raw, and as we set out, a light snow began to fall. Our carriage was an open caleche, with only enough roof to cover our heads, so that the blankets covering our legs quickly grew damp; I grew both chilled and grateful that I had brought the bottle of *barak* my Buda-Pesth host had generously pressed upon me.

Shortly into our journey, after we had left the town behind and ventured up into the mountainous forest, Arkady reined the horses abruptly off the path. The suddenness of this action caused my pen to leave a broad mark across the page (for I had just begun to record this entry); I looked up to see an astonishing sight. The mountains—which had stretched before us into infinity—had vanished, and we appeared to be in a different area altogether: a glen, sheltered beneath thick branches of towering pine. So sheltered, in fact, that the snow stopped, and the air grew warm and faintly hazy with mist. But most remarkably, soft *sunlight* filtered down through the branches—the sort of pure streaming light used to depict the favour of God pouring down from the heavens—giving the place an otherworldly aura.

This realisation left me quite speechless; I thought I had either dozed and dreamt that I had left with Arkady just before sunset, or that I dreamt now. But my perceptions were all too real, too keen.

The horses slowed their pace and calmed as they trod softly over a thick carpet of pine needles; and then Arkady reined them to a stop and turned to me.

"Abraham," he said in his melodious voice; the air had grown so pleasantly warm and damp that even the vampire's breath hung as mist between us. Beautiful though that voice still was, I saw that his handsomeness had waned even more; indeed, it had faded the instant our surroundings grew charmed, and it seemed to grow more mortal, more human, each moment we remained there.

"What is this place?" I asked in reply, my voice hushed with awe.

He did not answer but continued: "There are many things you must understand before we arrive at the castle. There is a chance we will not arrive in time—before Vlad has a chance to perform the blood ritual. If he drinks Stefan's blood—by chalice, lest he make him undead—and Stefan his, then your brother will be under the vampire's sway. For the rest of Stefan's life, Vlad will know where he is and what he thinks. And he will to some extent be able to manipulate him. This I know because it was done to me when I was mortal.

"I performed the ritual upon Stefan myself—not out of any desire to invade your brother's thoughts, but out of hope it would minimise Vlad's control. So you see"—and here he smiled unhappily—"I understand how you must feel, finding yourself unwillingly in the employ of a monster."

"For the rest of Stefan's life?" I asked, aghast. "Then if this happens—he will never be safe."

"True. If we take Stefan from him, he cannot follow; but there are always men who favour money more than goodness, who will fetch him for a price." And he turned his face towards mine, his dark eyes suddenly afire with a radiance I knew sprang not from immortal glamour but from the desperation of a human heart.

"But there is a way to end the danger to him forever. Abraham—you *must* help me to destroy Vlad. To destroy myself, and what I have become. You must believe that I take no pleasure in this existence—but if I die now, I only help perpetuate the greatest of all vampires.

"Will you help me destroy him?"

I could not quite meet his intense gaze. "I will do what is necessary to save my son and brother."

He sighed in disappointment and was silent a time; then said: "I cannot let you go into Vlad's lair unprotected." He looked up, and I followed his gaze, astonished to see through the rising mist, that a stone building—what appeared to be a small monastery, windowless except for a small spired chapel—stood directly in front of us.

"Arminius!" he called in the utter silence, a silence such as I have never heard before or since; the air itself seemed to absorb his words so that they did not echo. Another moment later, the black wooden door opened to show a figure in the shadows. Arkady turned back to me and said wryly, "I thought to advise you never to speak of this place to anyone; but it does not matter. They would think you mad anyway." His expression grew suddenly wistful. "I had never thought to bring anyone here, except perhaps my own son. But I know you can be trusted." He gestured with his chin at the waiting figure. "Go. He will give you what you need."

I hesitated in disbelief and confusion.

"Go," he repeated, more firmly. "I cannot."

I crawled down from the caleche onto heavy dew-soaked ground; the air was redolent of evergreen and damp cool earth. Aware of every clumsy sound I made in that silent glen, I crossed to the doorway and found within a pair of ancient eyes.

As ancient as Vlad's; perhaps older. Yet these eyes were not shrewd and cunning but wise—and calm, as silent as the glistening oasis surrounding us, as dark as the night beyond. They beheld and saw everything without passing judgement, without making demand; I could have turned from them at any time and gone but found I did not want to.

Their owner, the presumed Arminius, was an unprepossessing man dressed in a monk's black robe—wiry and small, with long white hair and beard that spoke of age, and a straight, strong spine that spoke of youth. The silence between us did not discomfit him; he merely waited, watching, until I stammered in German:

"I am . . . Abraham. I require . . ." I hesitated, trying to remember what I had read in Mama's diary: "A crucifix." It seemed forward to ask for an outright gift; I fumbled in my pockets and realised the only currency there was Dutch. I pulled it out and proffered it to him. To my surprise, he laughed aloud, grinning in a way that seemed entirely ingenuous and certainly unmonklike.

He ignored the guilders in my palm, instead nodding with his chin at Arkady and the waiting carriage. "You wish for something to repel the vampire, yes?"

"Yes," I said, and felt myself blush at the outrageously superstitious admission; at the same time, I wondered how well he knew my travelling companion and whether he thought I might be using these items against Arkady. It was at the very least a preposterous situation, that a vampire should deliver me here to collect the items to ward him away. Yet Arminius seemed to find nothing unusual about the situation or my request, though I was not at all certain he even understood it. Still wearing his idiot's grin, he gave a small bow from the shoulders, then retreated, closing the door behind him.

After some moments, he returned with a small pouch of black silk, which he unceremoniously handed to me. I nodded thanks and turned to leave with it.

"Abraham," he said in strangely accented German; upon reflection, I have decided his native language was Hebrew.

I turned and allowed myself to be irritated by the unselfconscious amusement in his eyes.

"You have in your hands two gold crosses and the sacred Host. Do you understand what these things are?"

I was raised as a child in the Catholic Church, though as an adult, I had left such beliefs far behind. Exhaustion and strained nerves had worn away the last of my civility; who was this man to address me as if I were a simple-minded child? *I* was the one who possessed superior scientific knowledge; he knew only superstition and folk legend. Did he think himself my better?

"Yes," I snapped. "Two pieces of metal and a cracker."

He slapped his thigh and with a burst of hilarity doubled over, then straightened and threw his head back. "Ho ho!" he crowed. "You give me hope, Abraham! You are the first ever to give a sensible answer."

I almost replied snidely that I had not known this was a test—but was distracted to notice for the first time that his black robe was neither a priest's robe nor a monk's, and that he himself wore no crucifix, no symbol of faith. I stared back at him, frankly curious.

Wiping happy tears from his eyes, he gestured at the pouch. "You are quite right, of course, that these are no more than what they appear to be. But to use these properly, you must understand. Any symbol, any scrap of metal or crust of bread, is holy only to the mind of him who makes it so. And it is useless unless properly prepared: Relics are only as powerful as the will of the one who charges them, whether consciously or unconsciously. The cross can be worn to ward off the vampire, and the Host used to seal places of entry and exit. Keep them in the pouch, and they will not disturb your . . . friend. But know that, if exposed, these will be very strong—if you trust."

"I will try," I said, with a cynicism I know showed in my face and voice.

All mirth fled his manner, transforming him into an entirely different man, one of awe-inspiring authority and conviction, with eyes full of passion and power. "Try—and you and your brother are lost. There is no room for trying, Abraham. You *must* have confidence. I'll not waste my efforts on those doomed to failure."

That he should know of Stefan startled me into silence; I tried to remember when Arkady might have had the time to tell him, to precede our arrival by telegramme. Perhaps that night my brother was taken, in the hour or two before he came to me in the kitchen . . .

At the same time, I was annoyed that he should speak of wasting *his* efforts, when it was my life and my brother's at stake. What had he done except provide me with a few relics?

"I will not fail," I said, with a heat I felt on my face. "I will do whatever is necessary to save my brother."

"Good," he replied. "Then perhaps I will see you again."

I turned, only for an instant, back towards the carriage; but by the time I looked again at the old man, he had vanished, and the great black door was once again closed. I hurried back to Arkady and the waiting caleche with my prize, and when I climbed in and gazed back at where I had stood, only mist and prismatic sunlight remained.

A dream, no more.

So it seems now as I sit beside Arkady, hurtling through the snowy darkness towards the Borgo Pass. But my right hand clutches black silk, and cutting into my fingers and palm are the sharp and all-too-tangible edges of a golden cross. . . .

❧ 13 ❧

The Journal of
Stefan Van Helsing

26 NOVEMBER. I doubt there will be time to write it all down.

I am prisoner in a strange castle in a strange land. I write now in a room with walls and floor of cold stone, and no warmth except the hearth, which I have lit. Beyond the single high, narrow window lies the night and no doubt a spectacular view of the spiralling Carpathians and the thick evergreen forest. From the carriage I saw the mountain range in all its splendour, at sunset when the highest snowy peaks were tinged with an unearthly rosy glow; at the very same moment, a chorus of wolves echoed mournfully in the distance. Despite my fear, I could not help but be impressed by the land's wild, dangerous beauty.

Zsuzsanna ceased to mesmerise me—and this I mean both in literal and figurative senses—sometime after the carriage left Bistritz, which is when dread overcame me. I suppose she realised I was in her grasp, so further efforts were not necessary; appearing in daytime seems to wear on her. And she was preoccupied with little Jan, who slept covered by a blanket until the sun set, and our sweet companion, Frau Buchner, who now seems just as comfortable as I had been earlier with our strange travelling arrangements. Zsuzsanna spirited the dear woman off the train with us at Bistritz, and from there into the Bukovina diligence, which we took to the Borgo Pass.

The frau seems cheerfully oblivious to her previous destination and her cousin's funeral, and quite unaware of her role as bloody nursemaid to little Jan, who rose once darkness fell to suckle contentedly at the woman's neck, whilst she stared vacantly out at the passing black scenery. She is now quite happy and anxious to be going to meet the prince. (Or is it the count? I have forgotten how Zsuzsanna referred to him.)

Little does she realise where she is truly headed. And to what fate, poor creature? To what fate?

Still, Zsuzsanna's control was sufficient to keep me silent when we boarded and disembarked the Bukovina coach, and also when the prince's carriage arrived, driven by a grim-looking older man whose face was partly hidden beneath a thick scarf to ward off the chill.

It was after nightfall when we arrived at our final destination: the castle, a craggy black monolith, with crumbling spires rising into the sky. Our driver disappeared at once, and Zsuzsanna smiled drowsily at us mortals, the slumbering child in her arms, as I helped Frau Buchner from the coach.

"Come with me, my dear," she said to the older woman. "I know the prince will be anxious to meet you at once. And as for you"—she turned to me—"I will show you where you are to rest until we come for you. But the prince must prepare first so that the ritual may be accomplished."

I gazed stricken at the matron, who stood smiling with sweet innocent excitement as she smoothed her hair and wrinkled skirt, eager to make a good impression on her royal host. I opened my mouth to warn her, reached forth my hand to grasp her arm, to rescue her—

Zsuzsanna struck it down with bruising force, so swiftly that I do not think my eyes would have perceived the blur of movement had I not also felt the pain. Certainly the other woman never saw, never suspected, but maintained her nervous, anticipatory smile, her pale eyes wide and vacant, while I struggled to speak and found no words came.

So like a puppet I followed and let myself and Frau Buchner be led dumbly to the slaughter. I was brought to this room, with its moodily eastern European flavour: dark stone walls, upon which hang dust-covered mediaeval tapestries; a generous, centuries-old carved bed, with a headboard of gargoyles and a cover of fine brocade, its gold threads gleaming in the firelight. Everything here speaks of age, of glittering corruption, of night.

Buchner is gone, and now I sit awaiting *my* fate.

Bram, my brother! I do this for you. If this record survives me, my prayer is that you will know my love for you, and my grief for having wronged you. . . .

⪦14⪧

The Diary of
Abraham Van Helsing

27 NOVEMBER. Shortly after midnight we arrived at a place as dark, malignant, and forbidding as I could imagine: Vlad's castle, a great turretted fortress of grey stone, clearly many centuries old and constructed to discourage invaders.

Surely I was among the most discouraged of them; at the sight of our destination, my heart quailed to think of my little boy and my brother inside such an evil place. So vast was it that not one of the many windows shone with light, but at my murmur of dismay at this we approached, Arkady whispered, "They are here, and there is light. Somewhere deep inside."

My fear did not ease—not to think that we would have to foray deep into the belly of the monster, on such a night when stars and moon were blanketed with thick clouds. The clearer weather of that afternoon had vanished, and snow rained down upon the dark silent landscape. But as Arkady leapt soundlessly down from and tethered the worn, still-anxious horses a short distance from the front entry, I reached once again into my pocket and drew an odd comfort from the crosses and Host wrapped in black silk.

"Put it on," Arkady said, meaning one of the crucifixes, as I rose to climb down. "But realise that it prevents me as well as Vlad from touching you. And . . . you will need something from your medical bag. Chloroform, if you have it; something soporific. But do not keep it inside the bag—it must be ready at an instant's notice."

At this, I looked at him askance; he directed his gaze away from mine, towards the castle.

"We may already be too late. And if we are, Stefan will not come with us willingly."

I was too far gone already into this mad adventure to question such a point; I possessed a small amount of ether for the direst emergencies. I poured a bit of the volatile liquid onto my kerchief, careful to hold my breath all the while, then wrapped it again, then a second time, in small towels from my bag before stuffing it into my waistcoat. And then I took one of the crucifix necklaces from the pouch and slipped it round my neck.

Immediately, I noticed Arkady move a slight distance away; and never during the whole fateful night did he violate a certain area around me. It was as though I were cushioned by a pocket of air that he could not pierce. For the first time, I felt safe within his presence; I had never entirely trusted him, especially since the terrible incident with the apoplectic.

"I will bring the bag, too," I announced, as I stepped with it down from the carriage.

"It will be no use to you," Arkady said.

"How can we know? If they have harmed Jan or Stefan—"

His expression hardened. "Little Jan they cannot harm in a way that can be mended using the contents of that bag;

and Stefan they would protect at any cost. Their existence is tied to his life."

I would not abandon the bag but took a step towards the castle, my jaw set. He gave a faint sigh and reluctantly moved alongside me. "This way," he said, gesturing with a nod away from the great front door, adorned with inhospitably sharp metal spikes. "It is the fastest."

He led me round to a side entry, inside the stone walls up a sloping sweep of dead grass—past large gardens that had clearly been untilled the previous summer and were left to go to seed until all died with the first winter frost; past untrimmed grape arbors that threaded their way off trellises to wind around nearby bare-limbed fruit trees. There were wooden fences rotting in disrepair, and chunks of stone that had fallen from the castle face and lay ignored; clearly, this had once been a vast, thriving estate that had housed and fed many people. But any mortal who had dwelt here had long ago fled in haste.

And one of them—dead now—served as my guide, moving quickly, silently, his feet gliding over the snow-dusted frozen grass without the soft, squeaking crunch my own boots made. Despite the absence of moonlight, his pale skin glowed with that curious incandescence, which strangely reassured me, for I could easily follow in the fluctuating dark. He moved with the assurance of one who knows the route and whither he is bound; but beneath his sharp, slender nose, his lips grew thin and taut and lined on either side, and his large dark eyes narrowed. He was struggling to contain emotion, and I realised, as I emerged from my self-made cocoon of grief and fear, that monster or no, he suffered as I did. For it was his son, too, who lay within these walls, and he knew better than I what was to be feared; he had paid a price greater than death. I saw as well the pain and hatred provoked by the sight of this so-familiar place.

When we arrived at the door—clearly the servants' entrance—he stopped and turned towards me, careful to maintain a comfortable distance from the golden charm that hung over my heart.

"Once we enter," he said, "I may communicate with you—though not aloud. But you must not speak unless I question you, or unless it is the deadliest emergency. Even so, Zsuzsana and Vlad will hear your footsteps after a time, if they are not utterly distracted; as we near them, they will hear even your breath."

"And you?" I asked.

"They will not hear me until I make myself known. This is the training of which I spoke, that of containing the aura." And at the look of guilt that crossed my face, he added, "Even had you begun on the train, there would not have been time, I think, to perfect it. You are not a sensitive by any stretch of the imagination."

"Thank you," I said, managing a tone of irony despite the fact that my hands had begun to tremble slightly in my pockets; it was, I told myself, the cold.

Wryness flickered in his eyes a moment, but he dismissed it at once and said, "Do precisely as I tell you. I realise you desire nothing better than to rush inside and demand your son—but that would merely cost you your life or worse. Vlad is more than a vampire—he is a sadist, and at the first opportunity he will use those you love to torment you, and use you to torment those you love. Disobey me, and your failure is guaranteed. Understood?"

"Understood," I said, but in truth his first point was quite right: I understood only that my child was somewhere nearby, and my brother. I would have said anything to bring myself closer to them.

We stepped inside the castle. I took a deep breath and released it with a gasp, almost gagging, which drew a backward warning glance from Arkady. The air, though cold, was stale, utterly devoid of oxygen, as though no window or door had been opened in many a year. And foetid, so much so that I became convinced this was the kitchen, whose servants had fled in the midst of preparing a large meal, leaving the food to rot. At the same time, I was grateful that the room was shrouded in total windowless blackness, lest my surmise prove incorrect. The only light was that provided by my radiant host, whom I followed through the dark, trying to muffle the ringing of my boot-heels against the smooth stone floor.

We passed through several large rooms whose contents I could not divine, then up a narrow winding staircase, with shallow steps built for a shorter people than mine. At one point upon them, Arkady paused and, without turning, without *speaking,* said:

"It was here, long ago, I first met your father."

And I, forbidden to question, to raise my voice, could only recall my mother's chronicle of the past and imagine what had occurrred there and then.

During our journey, he paused only once more, this time in front of a large portrait rendered in faintly Byzantine fashion. This was quite visible, for it was flanked by sconces, whose lit tapers cast a wavering glow upon the subject: a lean, hawk-nosed man with a drooping black mustache and curls that flowed onto his shoulders. Arkady, I thought at first sight, but this man's eyes were a striking shade of dark green, such as I had never seen before, and his feathered cap and dress—and the painting itself—were clearly from a century long past. In one bottom corner was a shield bearing a winged dragon; in the other was what I took to be a familial crest—an ominous one, with the head of a great grey wolf resting atop the coiled body of a serpent. I knew from what I had read in my mother's diary that this must be the likeness of the mortal man, Prince Vlad, known to some as Dracula, the son of the Dragon; to others as Tsepesh, the Impaler.

Arkady saw where my gaze rested finally, upon the dragon impaled by a double cross, and again he spoke; I glanced over at him, startled, and saw with my own eyes that his lips never moved.

The Order of the Dragon. During my life, I foolishly believed it had been a secret political organisation, nothing more.

We moved on and at last arrived deep in the castle's windowless interior, in a corridor lit by more flickering sconces. Soon we passed one open door that revealed a richly appointed bedroom with a roaring fireplace—yet here, too, the furniture and coverings spoke of decadence and faded glory. My guide slowed his pace, growing even more intent and stealthy, until at last we stood in front of another door left ajar.

Arkady paused, the private distress he felt at entering this particular place telegraphed by his pale clenched fists, by the arms held tightly at his sides, as though he fought the urge to physically recoil. At last he stepped inside and I followed, to find that this much-dreaded chamber was but an ordinary drawing-room, brightly lit by a modern lamp and warmed by a fire, with three high-backed chairs—two gentleman's and one lady's—angled to view each other and the hearth. Between the two larger chairs stood a table, upon which rested a cut-crystal carafe and three matching goblets, each containing pale spirits poured from the carafe and glittering with the orange light cast by the fire. Two of the goblets were full, untouched, but the third had clearly been drunk from; it was only a quarter full, and lip prints showed clearly on the crystal rim.

The whole scene seemed innocuous enough, but Arkady hesitated at the sight of the third glass. His expression darkened so that I knew at once, without hearing, what he thought: that we were indeed too late.

Still, he turned away from the sight, away from the fire, towards a closed door gilded with a ribbon of light. And as he did, I heard his voice once more inside my head:

They surely know you are here; we cannot prevent that. But stand aside, and do not enter until I call you. And above all else—do not look into their eyes. You are not yet strong enough.

Obediently, I stood behind him to one side, my right hand grasping my doctor's bag, my left the pouch containing the other crucifix—which, I swore to myself silently, my brother would soon wear (for my little son would be in my arms, protected by the cross on my own breast)—and the blessed communion wafer, which I had decided to use to seal the door behind us mortals once we made our escape. And in my right pocket lay the ether-soaked cloth—protection against more human foes.

Arkady straightened and grew utterly still; he was preparing himself for the strike, I knew, and though I could not see his face, I got the impression he had closed his eyes and slipped deep into a trance.

Suddenly he spoke silently once more inside my mind.

The room beyond . . . it has been sealed off on three sides by the placement of holy relics. A trap for me—but let us use it against Vlad instead.

And when I addressed to him the thought that I understood, I sensed, rather than saw, that he faintly smiled in acknowledgement. But his tone immediately grew grim again.

It means that he has utilised a mortal agent recently—one who is, even now, nearby. I hear breathing, the rustle of clothing. . . . Be prepared for attack, mortal or immortal, from any quarter.

Another instant of stillness; and then I felt a cold force like a bitter winter wind sweep through the room. It howled down the chimney through the hearth, extinguishing the fire, pinning me shivering to the wall as it whipped my clothing and hair against my skin, then blew beyond me, past Arkady—who, though his hair and cloak were ruffled, stood immovable, straight and still and regal as an ancient bas relief of an Egyptian god.

With a powerful gust, the door in front of him slammed open, cracking the wood with an ear-splitting bang.

I was once a rational man, a man of science, proud that, since childhood, I had never entertained a single superstitious thought. But in that moment reason deserted me, for that door opened not onto another room; nay, it opened onto another world, which I knew—not saw, nor smelled, touched, or heard, but *knew*—contained such brazen decadence, such pure *evil*, that the skin on the back of my neck turned to gooseflesh, and a chill coursed down to the base of my spine. I suddenly understood how desperation had provoked ancient man to rely on charms and superstitions and prayers as protection from danger. At that moment, all scepticism deserted me, and I was profoundly grateful for the black pouch Arminius had pressed into my hand. Its presence alone brought comfort.

Even so, with the door open, I could see nothing beyond Arkady, save an empty narrow foyer lit by the glow from an interior room. Fearful of being seen, I advanced slowly, timidly as he entered, his movements swift and strong and unafraid. While I hid, peering around a corner of wall, he passed through the foyer into a grand high-ceilinged chamber, a place that might have served as a mediaeval banquet hall—or a cathedral, in this case one dedicated to the worship of wickedness.

On his left as he entered was a black curtain that hung from ceiling to floor, concealing an area large enough to be a small theatre; directly before him, a grey stone wall with a closed door leading to another chamber.

And on his right stood an ancient throne, set upon a dais of dark gleaming wood; and each of three steps leading up to the royal seat was inlaid with gold to spell the phrase: *JUSTUS ET PIUS.*

The throne was flanked by candelabra as tall as I, each bearing more than a dozen flickering tapers, and upon it sat the man I had just seen in the portrait, dressed now in flowing robes of scarlet and an ancient handwrought crown of gold and rubies. But he had changed, aged: his mustache and the hair that flowed onto his shoulders were now snow-white, and his face was so pale and gaunt, with the skin stretched tight over bone, that it appeared skeletal. There was not a speck of colour to him except for his lips (which were as deeply red as the jewels that glittered in his diadem) and his eyes.

His eyes . . . My instinct, when first I saw him, was to turn in disgust from his bloodless, ghoulish appearance. For he lacked Arkady's compelling handsomeness—I knew at once I looked upon a monster, an unnatural fiend. Whatever magical glamour he might once have possessed had long faded; or so I thought, until I gazed upon those eyes.

Even at the distance I stood from him, they commanded notice. Their colour was utterly remarkable: evergreen, dark and eternal, yet as brilliant and flashing as the jewels in his crown. To look upon them was to be lost in that forest, entirely unmindful of the fearsome countenance in which those gems were set. I found them almost too beautiful to bear—and as seductive as the sirens' song, impossible to turn away from. But Arkady's advice returned to me, and reluctantly, I forced my gaze away . . .

To the golden chalice, studded with a single large ruby, which rested in his bone-white hands.

To my brother—dear God, to Stefan!—unharmed and whole, still dressed as he had been when I last saw him. He sat upon the stone floor a short distance from the throne, at the base of the three stairs. The room's chill seemed not to bother him, for his waistcoat was unbuttoned, his arms behind him, propping him up, his legs sprawled out in front. The effort to sit up seemed almost too much for him; his head lolled drowsily, his dark hair tousled, uncombed, as though he was fully exhausted—or inebriated.

Yet his gaze was fixed on the occupant of the throne—until Arkady approached, causing Stefan to turn his face towards the intruder.

Ah, the love in that gaze! The utter grateful devotion! I thought it was directed at Arkady, his rescuer, and felt a surge of emotion that brought me close to joyful tears.

Then Stefan turned again to face his enthroned captor, and I saw—with a thrill of the bleakest horror—for whom that rapt adoration was meant.

"Arkady," the Impaler said in a voice as musical, as hauntingly lovely as his eyes, and just as incongruous coming from such a ghastly, lifeless face. "We have been expecting you. For it is the duty of every father to deliver me his son, just as your father so long ago brought you here to this room and with his own hand pierced your flesh, that you might be tied to your destiny—to the covenant."

When he uttered those last, I realised that upon his lap lay a dagger—silver, gleaming, bloodied. And round my brother's wrist was wrapped a white kerchief, stained with a single crimson blot.

The Impaler, Vlad, continued: "But you are late, Arkady; you should have come here the very day Stefan was born. Even so, we have waited, so that we might share with you our moment of familial celebration." And he raised the chalice in his hands like a priest offering consecrated wine to Heaven. "Stefan, thus I tie you to me, and this I swear: You and yours I shall never harm, so long as you support and obey me. Your blood for mine."

While he spoke, Arkady moved with immortal speed towards Stefan—who still stared with oblivious, drunken devotion at Vlad—then past him, towards the throne, clearly intent on retrieving the golden goblet. Before he could succeed, a small dark-haired woman in Roumanian peasant garb stepped between them, a crucifix held high in one hand.

Arkady recoiled at once and cried aloud: "Abraham!"

I was already in motion, propelled by love and fear, dashing into the midst of that conflict as fast as will and body would permit. My goal: to fling myself upon the woman and remove her from Arkady's path. For I remembered my mother's diary and Arkady's warning—that once Vlad drank of Stefan's blood, he would possess his will and know his every thought. How, then, would we ever protect him?

But I was late, too late; ere I reached her, there was a flash of gold as Vlad upended the chalice and drank—and a sudden harsh cry from Stefan who clutched his skull in pain, as the talons of Vlad's control seized his mind.

At the same instant, the peasant woman lifted her other hand to raise one more protective relic—this one made of wood and bright, gleaming steel. And before I could halt my progress towards her, she leveled the pistol at me and fired.

I had advanced to where my brother sat—some few feet in front of my opponent—before the bullet struck at close range. It grazed the side of my left shoulder, gouging its way through flesh and deltoid muscle before passing through.

Fortunately, my forward momentum continued to carry me to her, and the gun's report threw her off-balance. I knocked her from her feet, staining the front of her white apron with my blood. Both weapons clattered to the floor.

I stumbled down onto one knee and grabbed the kerchief soaked in ether. Before she could rise or retrieve the pistol, I clamped it down over her nose and mouth. With my other hand, I pinned her waist to the floor.

She flailed, pummelling my brow, my cheek, my chest. I managed to hold fast until her writhing grew feeble, then ceased altogether, and when her eyes closed and her head rolled limp to one side, I lifted the cloth, lest she inhale a fatal dose.

The act left me dizzied and groaning in pain. I sank onto the floor before the throne, struggling to retrieve my wits, to flee from the intoxicating fumes of the ether, un-awares at that instant that the woman's fallen crucifix—and I, with my cross—lay between Arkady and Vlad.

Vlad's drink, Stefan's cries, the pistol shot, my struggle with the woman: all had taken two seconds, three, no more. I lay with my head on the cold stone, blearily aware of Arkady on my left side, calling for me to rise, to move aside, and Vlad on my right. Through pure force of will I pushed myself to a sitting position and saw:

Vlad flinging the chalice against the wall, with such

force that the gold rim was dented with a loud clang. Rising, gripping the gleaming dagger with such force that the ivory bones appeared to emerge from the skin, emerald eyes transforming, literally, impossibly, to the dazzling brilliant red of flame.

"Liar!" he screamed, in a voice no longer music, but the deafening rush of thunder, of all-consuming hellfire borne on wind. His face was contorted beyond recognition, his ruby mouth a rictus, spewing spittle, revealing the sharp deadly teeth of a predator. Of a serpent; of the dragon. *"Betrayer! Deceiver!"*

In my daze, I knew not whether he spoke to Arkady, to Stefan, or to me . . . but now I believe he addressed us all.

I crawled at last to one side. Immediately, Vlad flew from his throne towards my brother—moving so swiftly that I believe he *actually* flew, for a blur of scarlet glided down the JUSTUS ET PIUS steps without ever seeming to touch them and collided almost at once with the hurtling blur of black and white that was Arkady.

The two struggled—again, travelling at a pace almost too fast for the human eye to record, the sound of their movements like the rushing of wind, the sound of their blows like the ring of stone against stone, not flesh against flesh. Around the chamber they spun, until at one point Arkady hurled his older, frailer nemesis against the black curtain, the gold and ruby crown falling with a loud clatter and rolling across the stone. The weight of Vlad's body upon the curtain caused it to tear with a loud rip; half remained hanging, but half dropped silently in a heap, to reveal a macabre vision in the shadows:

A mediaeval torture chamber, equipped with rack, strappado, oiled glistening stakes of various sizes; and upon the wall, a set of black iron manacles, from which hung—

God give me strength to write it, to set it down. It was a sight so obscene, so pitiful, I turned my eyes away at once as though stung by vitriol.

A woman; a poor elderly woman hung from the manacles. Naked and quite dead; bare, blue-veined feet swinging ever so gently in the air. Her arms were spread to form a wide V, at the base of which her head hung forward, blessedly hiding her face. But I saw her hair—still neatly braided and coiled and pinned, the grey-white hair of a grandmother, the same colour as her bloodless flesh, as the large drooping breasts whose nipples pointed downward to a soft, ample belly. That flesh bore red stripes—jagged lacerations inflicted by a particularly cruel nail-studded whip, a cat-o'-nine-tails.

Though I looked away, her image will be forever imprinted on my memory.

Arkady paused, stricken by the sight; a second, no more, but it was time enough for Vlad to recover and whirl towards us all.

And from the depths of his scarlet robes, he raised an arm, white and sinewy, and hurled the dagger.

So quickly had he moved when he descended the throne, I had not realised he had taken it. Amazed, I watched the silver flash as it flew past Arkady as he turned in dismay to follow its path—and saw a blur of black and white as he vainly tried to snatch it from the air.

I watched until it found its mark: not Arkady, no; he was not Vlad's target.

Not Arkady, but my brother's heart.

My brother's heart.

Stefan, my brother, you have done no wrong that can equal my failure to save you; that can ever outweigh your sacrifice.

The act seemed to me pure madness, for everything I had understood about the covenant suggested that Vlad would do anything to protect Arkady's son; that Stefan's mortal wound had just signed the Impaler's death warrant. Such pure madness it was that Arkady and I froze, unable to do anything but watch in horrified disbelief.

Stefan gave a single sharp cry and fell back. That sound, that single dreadful moment of realisation, galvanised me like an electric shock; relieved my pain and lifted me to my feet, propelled my legs so that I staggered to my brother's side, dragging with me my doctor's bag.

Ah, but it could have done no good.

Arkady was already kneeling at Stefan's side; I knelt at the other and cried aloud myself to see the dagger's handle protruding from the centre of his chest. His shirt and coat were already covered with blood, which spilled onto the floor, onto my knees; the blade had pierced his heart, but it might just as well have pierced mine.

I did not remove it; it would only have caused him further agony. He was already grey-skinned, panting, with lips parted and eyes dimming yet still filled with bewildered love as he looked up at me.

He could not speak. I know not for whom that loving gaze was intended—whether he was still under Vlad's sway or whether he recognised my face. But I know now he meant his final loving act for me; so I claim that look as my own and prefer to remember that moment between us as unsullied, untainted by the evil surrounding us.

Arkady and I held his hands as he died, still wearing an expression of sweet devotion. In my sorrow I did not look up as a loud thump came from behind the closed door to the inner chamber, did not react as that door opened. Had any more of Vlad's human agents appeared, I should have sat, a willing target, while they emptied the pistol. Even the strange, evil new world I had entered had flagrantly disobeyed its own rules and gone insane; all meaning, all sense had vanished.

I glanced up at last at the sound of a feminine scream, to see in that doorway an astonishingly beautiful woman with long, dark hair and features that betrayed her relation to Arkady and Vlad. She gaped stricken at Stefan's death tableau, then up at Vlad, who now stood in front of his throne, blazing with wrath.

"Fool!" he shouted at her, with a vehemence that made her recoil. "Vain, witless harlot! You have brought me *the wrong man!*"

His words provoked from her, from Arkady—from me, despite my grief—a gasp. Again, my overwhelmed mind could not grasp his words, could not understand them; could not understand why he had not killed me instead of my brother, even when he stretched out his hand to me and, with once-more dazzling emerald eyes and the most dulcet of tones, said:

"Stefan, my child, in this very house you were born; and fate has decreed that to this house you would return. Come to me now. . . ."

⊰15⊱

The Diary of
Abraham Van Helsing, Cont'd.

I looked up from my brother's cooling body, from his vacant, slack-jawed face, his clouding eyes, emptied now of any trace of the love that had dwelt there, and was overcome by fury towards his murderer.

Towards myself. In the passion of the moment, I still did not understand why Vlad had addressed me as my brother; I only knew that he was not worthy to speak Stefan's name, nor I to claim it.

"My name is Abraham," I told him bitterly.

Beside me—reaching out as if to shake me back to sensibility and stopped by the invisible shield created by the crucifix round my neck—Arkady urged: "Do not speak to him! Do not look at him!"

But I, in my foolishness, thought my hatred sufficient to protect me from that magnetic evergreen gaze. Too overcome to speak, to think of a curse vile enough, I glared at Stefan's murderer as though my eyes could pierce him like the dagger that pierced my brother.

Yet he responded to my hatred with the same beautiful voice and eyes, holding out his hand, beckoning. "No; that is the name your mother gave you—after she brought another child into your house, a child she has used cruelly, selfishly, to keep you from your birthright; to deceive us all. To deceive, I see now, even your own father."

I drew a breath, ignoring Arkady's pleas, which suddenly seemed muted, very far away. "How—how do you know such a thing?"

"The truth is carried on the blood, my son. And I have tasted it. This false Stefan—this impostor—had been recently instructed by your conniving mother to deceive us both. *Justus et pius,* my son; I am harsh, but just to those who betray the covenant. And the penalty for betrayal is death."

Reading what I have written now, I recognise that his words reveal his megalomania, his utter self-absorption—and a total callous disregard for the man he had just murdered. But hearing them then, I heard only the beauty in them, the logic, the love. His gaze had captured mine, and I felt myself falling, down, down into that same dark and sensual vortex into which Arkady had pulled me upon the train, when he had nearly taken my life. I felt a distant thrill of fear, of desire to struggle, to emerge from that void—but it was superseded by a dreamy euphoria, a sense of forbidden ecstasy. The effect was much like that of opium, yet far more intoxicating. My grief blessedly vanished, replaced by the deepest pleasure I had ever known. Why should I not remain there? Evil had triumphed; but was this really defeat? Vlad's actions were merited, given his situation—and he would never, never harm me.

I would be cared for here. I would be treasured . . . and if I wished, I would never need experience sadness again.

Indeed, all my sorrows were the result of struggling against my proper fate; and if I yielded, if I embraced my ancestor, no more harm would come to anyone. And I could spend the rest of my life in this dreamy bliss. . . .

I rose, scarcely mindful that the knees of my trousers, my legs, were soaked with Stefan's blood; and that the shoulder and arm of my jacket and coat were soaked with my own. Scarcely mindful of Arkady's shouts, both within my mind and without, I took a step towards the throne, then paused and, with my right hand, pulled the gold chain of the crucifix over my head. I held it out at arm's length, and for a tantalising moment—feeling like a ready virgin who holds the last obstacle to her seduction—watched it dangle in the foreground of my vision, against the backdrop of Vlad—waiting, himself fascinated, mesmerised by the turn of events.

Nothing could have penetrated my trance, or prevented me from dropping the cross and taking my place beside Vlad: not Arkady's cries, nor his desperate presence as he stepped between me and my distant ancestor, nor the sight of poor Stefan's corpse. . . .

Nothing, save the faint sound of my son, in the other room wailing . . . and his subsequent appearance in the lovely vampire woman's arms.

I turned towards the inner chamber to see her in the doorway, holding Jan. He was beaming, my little son was, beaming at the sight of me—and perfect, unharmed, his pale skin glowing with health, his round cheeks faintly flushed. Such a welcome sight! It drew me from my stupour, so that my grief over Stefan's death, the ache in my shoulder, came flooding over me once more; but alloyed with that pain was tearful joy.

I withdrew the arm that held the cross and kept it in

my one hand as I held both arms out to my boy and cried his name.

And he chuckled, a sound that was pure balm to my stricken heart, and reaching for me in response, he called out: "Papa! Papa! Jan fly! Jan fly!"

To my dismay, Arkady again stepped between me and the object of my desire. With a wrath as blazing and awesome as Vlad's, he shouted at the woman: "Zsuzsanna! How could you betray me thus? You, my own sister!"

I cried out in disappointment, tried to move around him to my child as I called Jan's name. With blinding speed, Arkady moved again, again, again between us, blocking me from the reunion I most craved, calling out to the woman: "Why have you betrayed me? What heartless creature have you become, Zsuzsa, that you are capable of this? You are indeed nothing more than his whore, for him to command!"

Little Jan wriggled from her arms, falling to the ground but regaining his balance at once with unchildlike grace. Meantime, the woman's exquisite face had grown livid with wrath in response to her brother's accusation. Yet despite her fury, her great dark eyes filled with tears, which soon spilled down her cheeks.

I expected, from her magnificent rage, that she would strike out at him. Instead, she drew herself up with dignity.

"And what of you, Kasha?" she hissed, which such vehement force that her words seemed to lash out at him like a whip. "Have you remained so noble and untouched all these years? How many have *you* killed in the name of your martyr's vengeance? Do you drink their blood only out of the desire to save your son—or do you continue to walk this earth because you, too, find this unlife seductive? Because you, too, cannot let go? Or are you truly so eager to experience the eternal delights of Hell?"

Her words struck him with far greater force than any physical blow; he fell silent and hesitated an instant, no more.

It was enough. Enough for me to surge past him, to open my arms once more to my child, who cried out again, with heartfelt glee: "Papa, *fly!*"

"My little angel," I murmured happily as he bounded to me—for a toss over my head, I expected, for his favourite game. But instead, my child leapt up and—impossibly—hurtled towards me with preternatural speed *through the air.*

"Papa! *Jan* fly—"

He came to a sudden stop, his tousled curls mere inches from my outstretched hands, and there he hovered, his sweet brilliant smile turned into a grimace of aghast fury.

I stared back at him, heartbroken, spellbound, not by the mesmerising embrace of his bright blue eyes—his *oma's* eyes—but by the very horror of what he had become. Still holding the cross aloft, I closed my own eyes before that gaze engulfed me, and sensing Arkady beside me, I heard at last his words:

He is lost, Abraham. For all our sakes, we can do naught but leave.

"But I cannot abandon my child," I whispered. "How can I leave him here—in such a place?"

They can hurt him no further. Nor, at this time, can we help.

Still I wavered, torn, and opened my eyes to see Jan hovering in the air before my hand—the hand that held the cross—like a malignant cherub. Testing, I lunged forward with it, shoving it into his face; he recoiled, hissing like a threatened cat, baring his teeth to reveal tiny fangs just as sharp, but far more deadly.

"Leave him!" Arkady ordered, giving me an abrupt

shove—though he never touched my flesh; but the ripple created by his hand sweeping through the air almost made me lose my footing. "Leave, Bram! There is nothing we can do: Your child is dead."

He flanked me to my left; as I struggled for balance, I became aware of a crimson presence to my right: Vlad, who sidled alongside, speaking directly to my confused mind.

Join us, Stefan. See how your poor child longs for you? I ask only one small thing: the blood ritual. Permit this, and I swear to you that your little son can return home with you. No harm will come to any of you, if you allow this one thing. . . .

His plea was joined by that of little Jan:

Papa, come. Oh, Papa, come!

Arkady spoke as well: *Bram, my son. My son! I know you are strong-willed, like your mother. Remember her now—and listen to me—*

But his voice was drowned out by the others. I hesitated, torn, the cross held loosely in my palm. I had only to overturn my hand—such a small movement, so easily accomplished—and let it drop to the stone.

In the midst of this mental chorus, a distant part of my mind was peripherally aware that the woman had, amazingly, fought off the effects of the ether and gotten to her knees; Vlad's mental urging was apparently stronger than the drug. She crawled past us towards the grisly torture chamber, ignoring the elderly woman's hanging corpse, and disappeared behind the remaining velvet curtain.

Again I say, I noted this with a distracted portion of my mind—a portion that, at that moment, was scarcely cognizant, for the voices in my head had nearly overwhelmed me.

But I am a father; and the one I heard most clearly was my son's.

Papa, Papa, come. . . .

His little voice was full of tears, near breaking with childish desire as Zsuzsanna picked him up to soothe him, patting his back in a purely human maternal gesture, whispering sweet reassurances; she looked at that moment so like Gerda comforting our boy that I scarce could bear it.

I spread my fingers and let the cross slip between them, then took a step towards my child.

Arkady and Vlad both descended on me at once; but Vlad was the swifter. He wrapped a strong arm round my shoulders, in a gesture that was both welcoming and restraining. His touch was icy—so cold that it penetrated layers of fabric, raising gooseflesh on my skin. But I was mentally in his grasp as well and felt no fear, just a swift sinking sensation of the descent into the vortex.

In the next blurred second, Arkady took hold of me by the shoulders, pulled me from Vlad's grip, and hurled me down.

In the fleeting instant of contact when Arkady's hands were upon me, my mind cleared and I came to myself, enough to hear his urgent message: *My son, flee!*

Swift instinct made me break the fall with my open hands; they struck the stone with such bruising force that I cried out in pain. But the distraction of it passed as I discovered, beneath one swelling and cut palm, the crucifix.

I snatched it up immediately and glanced up to witness a second horror:

In order to free me, Arkady had stepped into Vlad's grasp, taking my place. The two struggled mightily, each leaning into the other, straining with effort to move the other into position and thrust him backwards. It was a trap; for the peasant woman had reappeared from behind the black veil and staggered drowsily towards us. Again she bore a weapon—but not the pistol. In its stead, clenched in both fists just below her heart, was a sharpened wooden stake the length of half an arm.

I scrambled to my feet, crying out a single word in warning, one that rose unbidden from the deepest recesses of my soul: "Father!"

He heard. I know he heard, for in the midst of his battle with Vlad, his gaze met mine, and I saw there love and gratitude, mixed with deep concern.

We shared a look that said we had, after so many years, recognised each other at last; shared it a fraction of a second, no more, but it was enough to seal his fate.

"*Go!*" he gasped aloud, and the moment of inattention was enough. Vlad spun him round and, with a mighty thrust, sent him hurtling backwards.

Against the peasant woman. Both went flying against the remaining black drape, tearing that, too, down to reveal a butcher's table stained with blood and flanked by a grisly assortment of knives and stakes.

They slammed against the far wall: and for a terrible instant they stood flattened against it—Arkady atop the woman, his eyes wide, stunned by pain, the sharpened point of the stake protruding from the center of his chest.

I ran to him, unmindful of Vlad and the others, and crouched down at his side as he slid slowly down until he sat, knees bent, upon the cold stone. There was no blood; no fluid at all, only a gust of air like lungs deflating, like a sigh, and on it was carried a barely perceptible whisper:

Mary . . .

Pressed to the wall behind him, the woman half sat, her head lolling to one side at an impossible angle, peering out just beneath his shoulder with wide sightless eyes. I did not need to touch her to know that her neck was broken and that there would be no pulse.

"Father," I said again, but he could not hear me; he was already gone, transforming before my stunned gaze from immortal to a man. The vampire's luminescent glow died like a suddenly extinguished flame, and streaks of silver spread through his black hair as though molten metal had been spilled upon his crown, then trickled downward. His face, too, rapidly aged until I found myself staring at an utterly mortal man, my mother's age—a man whose face was lined by grief and despair, whose shadowed eyes were full of pain and desperation.

For the first time, I gazed upon my human father's face; the face of sacrifice, worn by the heavy burden of generations past and future.

He was dead, I knew, but I still heard his voice in my head, as though he spoke to me:

My son, go. Go. . . .

Whilst the heart-rending metamorphosis occurred, Vlad laughed, saying, "You have failed, my boy, after all these years, just as I foretold. You are a fool to think you possessed my cunning, my strength. None can destroy me! None has the power!"

At the same time, Zsuzsanna had collapsed, sitting on her heels with her gown fluted out around her, my child still clutched in her arms as she sobbed: "Kasha! Kasha! You are right—what have I become? Forgive me!"

Vlad turned upon her, sneering. "I thought you would be strong enough by now, Zsuzsanna. Spare me your shows of grief! By to-morrow you will have forgotten your brother and will be laughing again, in love with your own beauty. It was necessary that he be destroyed; there was no time left us for mercy. Or would you prefer that we both perished in his stead?"

All this they said while I knelt at Arkady's side, the crucifix still clutched in my hand.

Then Vlad approached me again, stretching forth a ghostly white hand, the scarlet robes spreading beneath his arm like a bloody veil between us. "Know that this pains me, my child, as it does you; but I cannot permit betrayal. He sought to steal from you your birthright. You have seen my harshness; let me show to you now my generosity, to which Zsuzsanna and Jan can attest."

And he fixed his green eyes upon me once more. I would not meet them. Instead, I looked down at Arkady's mortal, aged corpse; and away, at my beloved brother's body. These two were the only convincing things in this chamber of horrors, the only things that had any reality, and I focussed on them to the exclusion of all else, until Vlad's words faded and became no more meaningful to me than the buzzing of a fly.

There is a measure of anguish that the human mind can accept; beyond that, each new blow brings only numbness, the heart's anaesthesia, for it can tolerate only a finite amount of anguish. Even writing this, I find I cannot weep for them all at once; the loss of Stefan brings a different pain, a different sorrow, from the loss of my little boy, or of Arkady.

Intense grief brought with it a liberation from reason: any remaining scepticism I might have possessed died that moment with Stefan, Arkady, my son. Perhaps I might have surrendered then, in despair—but I could not so disrespect my father and brother by falling prey to the evil they gave their lives to overcome.

Instead, I clutched the cross in my hand and felt its warm tingling emanation. I lifted it high—higher, fending off the undead murderer that approached me—and felt its power course through my arm and beyond. My surge of confident belief seemed to extend the range of its power: Vlad lowered his hand, and snarled, retreating one step, then another.

I used the opportunity to dash to the exit, where I broke the sacred Host and placed half at the doorway behind me, preventing Vlad and his consort—and what remained of my Jan—from pursuit . . . at least until a human hand removed the holy relic.

Down gloomy corridors I ran, down winding stairs, out into the night, where the carriage and horses waited. I staggered out of blackness into a world of white and grey; the storm had turned to blizzard. At that moment, I felt I had lost so much—father, brother, wife, child—that I hoped only to lose myself in the all-consuming whiteness.

I climbed into the carriage and drove the horses onwards, onwards, away from the castle and into the very heart of the storm.

⇥16⇤

The Journal of
Mary Tsepesh Van Helsing

27 NOVEMBER. The past week has been a difficult one. Were it not for my daughter-in-law, I should have broken my promise to Arkady and followed them to Transylvania.

But Gerda is as helpless as a child. This must certainly be the way that Bram discovered her, mute and vacant-eyed, in the sanitorium. For love of him, I cannot desert her, nor hand her back to her former captors; they would lead her at once to an empty cell and bind her in a strait-jacket behind a locked door, treat her as an object rather than the tormented soul she is. Bram would never forgive me.

But I shall never forgive myself, if harm comes to him. I shall never forgive myself regardless.

To-day was the hardest day of all. I spent it as I had the others, in a house that a mere fortnight ago was filled with contented voices and laughter: my husband's, my sons', my grandchild's. Now it stands empty and silent. Gerda neither speaks nor moves but submits passively as I spoon-feed her, bathe her, dress her, sit her before sunny windows in hopes that the scenery outside will spark a response, will somehow pierce the veil that separates her from the outside world. Once placed, she will remain motionless if left to herself, and she responds to nothing I say.

I talk to her nevertheless, forcing my tone to remain falsely bright as I speak of Bram and Stefan and little Jan as though they will return to us soon; chattering away as though our lives had not been destroyed by darkness.

And I watch carefully for changes in her. The small bite marks that Zsuzsanna left on her neck have not healed—which I think may actually be a good sign. For I remember when, long ago, Zsuzsanna was herself bitten, and how the wounds Vlad inflicted disappeared the day she died. Gerda appears to be in no danger of imminent death. But she eats so little; I worry for her health. And I dare not leave her alone, not even to go to market, for fear she might harm herself. If she was to die . . . what would she become?

I must not think such things. I am not sure I am physically or emotionally strong to do what would have to be done.

To-day, for the first time, she spoke.

She was sitting at the kitchen table while I stood over the stove, stirring pea soup. It was the hour before dusk, when the sun was low in the clouded sky, filling it with a reddish glow. My back was to her, but I was as usual talking away, about the women in the church and how kind they were to have brought us food. She was freshly washed, and I had sprinkled her with talcum and dressed her in a pretty frock in hopes of raising her spirits and mine, then brushed out her long, lovely hair. It lay in dark waves upon her thin shoulders, catching the red glow of the dying sun, while she stared dully ahead.

I was in mid-sentence when she interrupted with a loud

shriek. It startled me so that I dropped the spoon; it clattered loudly against the floor as I whirled round to see her on her feet, eyes wide and wild, mouth a perfect O, the chair over-turned behind her.

She stood for only a breath; then sank at once to her knees, still screaming. I rushed to her side, clutched her elbows, tried to lift her up.

"Gerda! Gerda, darling, what is it? What's wrong?"

The sound chilled me to the core, for it was the same terrible cry that had been wrung from her the night Jan and Stefan were taken from us. But she would not answer me, would not hear, but closed her eyes and abandoned herself to sorrow and such wild, tortured sobbing that I could not re-strain my own tears as I knelt down and held her.

"Gerda, please. What's wrong?"

To my astonishment, she drew in a hitching breath and wailed: "Stefan! Stefan! They have killed him. Killed him!"

My heart froze in my breast. For one tortured moment I grasped vainly at hope—to tell myself that this was simply another symptom of her madness, all illusion, untrue. My son could not be dead.

But I knew her mind was tied, however faintly, to Zsu-zsanna's; and I knew, also, with a mother's instinct, that what she said was true.

I collapsed myself with grief, and for several moments, we two wept, kneeling together, I embracing her. In the midst of it, I could not resist clutching her arms and beg-ging: "How did it happen? Did he suffer? And what of Jan, and Arkady?"

But she only shook her head and would say no more; would not eat, or drink, or sleep when led to bed.

I left her there, her gaze once again dull and empty, though her eyes are now red and swollen from so many tears.

And I came here to mourn alone and write down my confession.

My son, my son! I tell myself it is not true, that it is Gerda's wild imaginings, but my heart knows otherwise. . . .

I am twice a murderess; for it was I who killed Stefan, as surely as I fired the bullet that pierced my first husband's heart. I know not how he died, but I know why.

Because of the fear that haunted me my first year in Amsterdam. I saw that my little son resembled me rather than his father, Arkady. But I was still terribly frightened: What if I were mistaken, and Arkady had not died? What if Vlad had somehow survived? What if he someday hunted us down and took my child from me?

The fear gave me no rest. And so I thought: If I changed Stefan's first name and married Jan, took his surname, then we would be safer. In all honesty, Jan had wanted for some time to marry me; but I did not love him. I still loved—and love to this day—Arkady.

But Jan was a gentle man, and kind. He convinced me we would be safer wed, and my little boy better off with a father. For my baby's sake, it was done.

Then one day soon after, an infant boy was discovered abandoned in the city and was brought by a kindly soul to Jan's office. The little orphan was deathly sick, and we kept him many days in the house, caring for him, certain he would not survive.

I took care of him myself and was struck by his dark colouring and eyes, so similar to my dear Arkady's. And I began to think wicked thoughts: What if we adopted this child, took him into our family? Gave him the name Stefan —and if Vlad ever threatened, he would surely mistake this child for Arkady's.

I told myself that if God permitted this dying child to survive, I would take it as a sign He had sent the boy to protect my son. Miraculously, the child lived—and we took him as our own.

And I named him Stefan.

It was a cruel, selfish thing to do, a heartless one, but I could only think then of my own baby, whom I had re-named Abraham. Jan indulged me in this, for he understood my terror, but he felt that both children were perfectly safe, that no harm could come from this change of name.

So when I gave that innocent child Stefan's name, and in turn named my son for Jan's father Abraham, hoping his fair hair and eyes would fool the world into thinking he was a Van Helsing rather than a Tsepesh, I felt great relief.

But it was no solution at all; for I quickly came to love this second Stefan as my own son and grew just as fearful that harm would come to him. But over the years, my terror began to ease. And Jan reassured me that my nightmares would never come to pass. So I saw no reason to frighten my children with stories from a bloody, horrific past; nor did I see any cause to change their names again, for it began to seem fitting that my natural son was called Abraham, and my adopted boy Stefan.

And Stefan was by nature more emotional than Bram, more temperamental, more artistic—all traits he shared with Arkady, so that it became easy even for me to think of him as Arkady's son. And while Bram for the most part inherited my calm nature, at times he displayed Arkady's scepticism and determination. But to this I turned a blind eye, afraid even to admit the past to myself, lest it return to torment us.

Now it has. When Stefan was rescued from Brussels and returned to us, I told him the entire truth and begged him to forgive me. I wanted to tell Bram, too, and warn him and

Arkady. But Stefan would not let me, insisting, "This is my name now, and my fate: I must do what you chose me to do so long ago—protect my brother. The fewer who know his secret, the safer he shall be."

After hearing Gerda's tortured confession, I might have thought he had insisted out of guilt, because he wished to make amends for his adultery. But I know him as well as my own blood son; his heart was good and brave. He loved Bram. Guilt or no, he would have done anything to save his brother.

Stefan, Stefan! My brave child! Forgive me! I would rather have died myself rather than let evil befall you. I can only pray you sleep sweetly in God's arms, untainted by the wicked forces to which you so willingly sacrificed yourself.

⊰17⊱

The Diary of
Abraham Van Helsing, Cont'd.

Even now I am uncertain of my intent in urging the horses to the southwest, towards the Borgo Pass and the way I had come. Certainly at least a part of me desired death; another, help. But I felt no fear. My overwhelming desire was not to flee from Vlad but simply to escape pain, regardless of the method; to drown in the white oblivion surrounding me; to forever blot out the images of my brother's and father's dying eyes, of my little boy's undead ones. Without Arkady's help, I had no hope.

That the horses did not lose their footing and slip off the narrow winding pass down the mountainside, dragging me and the carriage with them, I consider a bona fide miracle. For the night had turned blinding white, snow blowing sideways, covering the poor animals, covering the blanket so that it lay sodden in my lap. My damp feet and legs began to ache from the cold, then went blessedly numb as the chill ascended to my hips and then my chest, where it inflicted burning pain.

It distracted and troubled me not at all, for mere physical inconvenience could not compare with the heartache I endured. As a physician, I realised with clinical detachment the imminence of frostbite; yet this, too, seemed quite unimportant, as meaningless as the fact that the horses had slowed and laboured with great difficulty in the mounting drifts, or that the rational remnant of my mind knew we were lost in both a literal and a metaphoric sense.

Yet the horses struggled onwards, and I wiped my spectacles with my gloved hand and shielded my eyes from the stinging onslaught of snow as I turned to peer at the forest, to see whether I was nearing the place where Arkady had taken me: Yakov's hidden glade.

Abruptly, the horses' forward momentum ceased, though I urged them on; the carriage rolled back half a foot, then stopped. With great care, I coaxed the animals to reverse their steps, hoping to free the wheels, two-thirds of which had disappeared in snow. It was no use; we were hopelessly stuck.

I felt sorry to know that I should be responsible for the deaths of the innocent beasts, but for myself I could not mourn. I could only pray that death was what I had always believed it to be—mindlessness, nonexistence, oblivion. But I could no longer be certain of anything; not now, when reality had become so utterly different from the logical scientific world in which I had put my faith—so much more dangerous and evil. If a creature such as Vlad existed, how then could I be sure there was no Heaven or Hell?

I huddled beneath the wet blanket and closed my eyes, ready to welcome my fate. For some moments I sat, thinking of my wife, so far removed from me by emotional and geographical distance, and of my little boy, whose future had been stolen from him, and of Arkady—and of Stefan, the most fortunate Van Helsing, for he at least had been released from suffering.

Then I remembered my mother, whose heart would surely break were she to lose both sons. In the midst of my surrender to the elements and despair, her image bade me take action. I opened my eyes, the lashes heavy with melting flakes, and climbed down from the carriage—staggering, snowblind, into hip-deep drifts.

I could scarce move, but some force beyond me propelled me sidelong into the silent forest, beneath heavy-laden pine branches that released small avalanches when I clambered beneath them. With all my strength, I shouted Arminius' name; the swirling snow swallowed the sound, permitting not even the faintest echo.

Still I screamed—a cry that was neither a summons nor a demand, but the most heartfelt prayer, though I could have explained neither its contents nor the hoped-for reply. I screamed—*Arminius, Arminius!*—until my numbed feet and legs would carry me no further, until I pitched forward and, gasping, rested my bearded cheek against the snow.

Never in my life had I been so defeated, never in my life so willing to embrace death. Exhausted, I let go a sigh and with it let go all hope, all fear, all desire, even the tormented remembrance of my loved ones. The snow rained down softly, steadily, until it buried me; beneath it, I shuddered a final time, then yielded to stillness and darkness.

⁘ ⁘ ⁘

And from the midst of the darkness, Arkady came to me—alive, a mortal man, with silver gilding his jet mustache, his hair, and sorrow in his gentle eyes.

Bram, said he, *it is not meet for you to be a stranger to your heritage. Come. . . .*

And he led me out of the blackness into a soft spring dawn, onto a knoll abloom with wildflowers, whereupon sat a vast home—or more properly, an estate, of a far more modern Roman-influenced design than the castle and significantly less sinister in appearance and aura. No doubt this had once been a pleasant family home—but it possessed a deep undercurrent of sadness, an air of tragedy, perhaps because of the tangled vines that had overgrown many of the windows, almost obscuring them. Or perhaps I was influenced by the look of sorrowful nostalgia upon my companion's face.

I followed him across the knoll to the house; and as we entered, I could see in the pre-dawn grey the distress caused him by the dust and dirt and disrepair.

This had once been a fine house; finer, certainly, than any I had seen in Holland, for we Dutch, even those of us with some wealth, disdain ostentation. But here there had been no such restraint; there were hallways and great drawing-rooms (more drawing-rooms, I think, than any family, no matter how large, should have use for), all appointed with the finest furniture. There were huge gold and silver candelabra by the score, some of them bearing more than twenty candles at once; and the finest lace tablecloths; and walls hung with tapestries such as I have seen only in museums; and chairs covered in brocade threaded with real gold; and everywhere, large Turkish rugs of the finest wool. Arkady led me into a study filled with books.

For several moments I stood staring at the portraits on every wall, most of them of slight, dark-haired, dark-eyed Roumanians whom I would never know—but one of them was of a seated young Arkady Tsepesh, his short dark hair combed in the style of thirty years before, his mustache neatly trimmed, a faint shy smile beneath his moody poet's hazel eyes.

And standing behind him, her hand resting gently on his shoulder, stood my mother. Young—so young, younger than I had ever seen her, and beautiful, her blue eyes radiating the sweet calm nature I have so grown to love. There was a softness to her young face that she has lost now; an innocence, a trust that has been replaced by a faint hardness, a faint pain about her eyes and lips.

"Stefan George Tsepesh," Arkady murmured, and I started to find him standing beside me. His gaze followed mine, to the image of the lovely young blond woman with the soft curls, and for an instant his eyes were those of the sensitive, hopeful young man in the portrait. "Your mother named you George—for the saint who slew the dragon; and I . . ." Here he faltered and bowed his head, for a moment unable to speak. When he gathered himself, he continued, "I named you Stefan—after my dear brother, whom Vlad slew."

He faced me then, smiling unhappily. "Bram . . . I understand now that it is no accident you favour my wife, in eyes and temperament. I can see now my dear mother's face, and her Russian blood in the red cast to your hair." He paused a moment, then pointed to the hallway, and the stairs. "Go, and see your past."

Compelled by curiosity, I wandered up, trying to recapture the feel of the home's inhabitants, trying to retrace my mother's, my father's footsteps. Upstairs I found a bedroom that must have been theirs; in it was a small jewelry-box full of women's earrings and a golden locket. And at a small desk was a quill and a square bottle of black ink, long ago dried. I stared at it for some time, wondering what sad words had issued forth from it. Had Mama sat here all those years ago and penned the startling journal she had only recently given me?

Next to the bedroom, I found a small nursery with an old wooden cradle—and upon the wall, an icon of Saint George slaying the dragon above a burned-down votive. On the floor near the cradle were adult blankets and pillows, and at the window hung a wreath of braided garlic, dried to paper and dust. Clearly, this had once been a hiding-place from the forces of evil.

At the sound of Arkady's voice, I turned in surprise to see him standing beside me.

This is where your mother sought protection in the nights before your birth. Come. . . .

Again I followed as we moved outside the house, back to the flower-covered knoll, where I saw for the first time that across from the main house sat a small chapel of Eastern Orthodox design, with a dome and spiral. This he entered, leading me just inside the door. The feel was distinctly Turkish, with a high cupola and walls entirely hidden by glittering Byzantine mosaics of saints: Mary at the Annunciation; Peter, denying Christ as the cock crowed; Stephen the martyr, pierced by arrows. At the other end of the room was a small altar curiously devoid of religious symbols.

We paused near the entrance, at a great wall covered with gold plaques, all marking crypts labeled with the surname TEPES.

Tsepesh, he pronounced, *which means Impaler. This was Vlad's mortal name, and thus it was the name taken by his human offspring. But when he became undead, the peasants, out of fear, gave him the name Dracula: son of the dragon, of the Devil. When I became immortal, I adopted the name Dracul, which admits my evil genesis, for I did not wish to dishonour the name Tsepesh.*

I peered thoughtfully at the names and dates upon the golden plaques. Ancient crypts these were, some almost four hundred years old. And as I gazed upon them, I became aware that we did not stand alone: in front of us materialised the ghostly images of men, each dressed in the costume of a different era—one wearing the short waistcoat popular during the time of Napoleon, another in mediaeval tunic and woolen leggings. Some were still in the prime of youth, but most were older, with greying hair and bowed, beaten faces; and all of them with eyes so full of anguish, I could not bear to directly meet their gazes.

I knew then I looked at an historical spectrum spanning the last four centuries.

These are your ancestors, Arkady said. *Seventeen generations. These are the men who suffer in Hell so that their families would be protected and spared from knowing the truth: that Vlad corrupted them by pressing them into his service—a service that required them to provide him with the blood of innocent, unwitting victims. These are the men whose souls have purchased continued life for the Impaler.*

I am the eighteenth generation; my soul has now purchased him a fresh span of life. And you, Bram, are the nineteenth.

Suddenly I no longer stood inside the chapel but in that terrible chamber where my father and brother had died. There sat the Impaler upon his throne, magnificent in scarlet robes and golden diadem; as brilliant as the sun, as fiercely proud and beautiful as a lion. I watched as the first generation of those bound to his service cringed before him: the father weeping as he pierced his squawling infant son's finger with the dagger, then milked that young blood into the chalice.

And Vlad upending that chalice, as he had poor Stefan's, and drinking . . .

Generation after generation after generation I watched the sad pageant repeated; seventeen stricken fathers, seventeen wailing sons.

Let it end with me, Arkady's voice said, though I looked about me and saw I stood alone. *Dear Bram, let the curse end with me.*

And I watched, from the lofty perspective of a god staring down from heaven, as generation after generation Vlad savoured the slow descent of each individual soul into terror and corruption when the chosen son came to realise who his "great-uncle" Vlad truly was and what was expected of him.

I saw, too, the covenant at work: the castle as a thriving estate filled with servants, with peasants toiling in the fertile fields. Like a great feudal lord, Vlad provided sustenance and protection for an entire village. And they in turn colluded with the eldest son to provide sustenance for him—agreeing never to warn the unwary travellers seeking lodging, or those lured to the castle by the son's invitation.

So this unholy alliance continued, until the day Vlad's arrogance overcame him, and he dared to prey upon one of his own: Zsuzsanna. Terrified that the vampire might now attack any of them, the villagers fled, and the castle fell into disrepair, abandoned by all except Vlad and his two consorts, the immortal Zsuzsanna and the mortal Dunya.

And I saw again the family estate, and myself as an infant, being carried away in the hands of the gentle blond giant I had come to know as Papa. And my parents fleeing in the opposite direction in a carriage, desperate to cross the river before sunset—my mother pale and exhausted after a difficult labour, covered with blankets to ward off the spring chill, my father's face grim, taut with desperation as he drove the horses hard towards sanctuary.

I saw them fail. Saw the sun slip lower in the sky until

the last fading rays had vanished, saw the carriage suddenly beset by a pack of snarling grey wolves. One leapt into the carriage, at my mother's throat; and my father turned and killed it with a single shot from the shining steel revolver in his hand.

From out of the darkness Vlad appeared and moved close to threaten Mama—leaping like the wolf onto the carriage, between my parents, spreading his cloak, like a great evil bird descending on his prey. My poor brave mother— her face wan, her hair tousled, her eyes narrowed with terror and determination—grasped the gun from my father's hand and with a look of infinite love and grief, fired it.

Not at Vlad, but Arkady—who with his dying gaze, beheld her with such gratitude, such devotion, as I have never seen.

The horses shrieked, bolted, carrying my mother with them; my father, dying, tumbled from the carriage onto cold ground, while Vlad knelt beside him, lifted him, embraced him evilly.

This was their suffering and their sacrifice, freely given for me. Had my father been permitted to die innocently at that moment, the pact would have been ended; Vlad would have been destroyed. I would be in Amsterdam today alive, happy, my little boy still at my side—and both of us blissfully ignorant of the great price that had bought our freedom. But the Impaler befouled that noble act by sinking his teeth into my father's neck.

Arkady's death should have purchased Vlad's destruction; but his second death had now purchased Vlad's survival.

Was I to let such a bitter loving sacrifice be negated?
Let it end with me, Bram! Let the curse end with me.
I looked to see Arkady once more at my side. But as I

watched, he was transformed before my curious gaze—grew shorter, thinner, white-haired—until at last I realised I stared not at my father but at the mysterious idiot, Arminius.

And Arminius smiled his wise-simpleton's grin and said, *The covenant is a two-edged sword, Abraham. A two-edged sword. . . .*

I said, "I do not understand."

It cuts both ways. Vlad has corrupted many of his family's souls. But should you destroy him, Abraham, you will set them free: your father's soul, and those of your ancestors. Accept the burden, and you can redeem them.

＋ ＋ ＋

When I woke I was warm, lying beneath blankets not of snow but of coarse handloomed wool, upon a hard narrow mattress stuffed with straw. I did not recognise my surroundings, which looked as though they belonged to a much earlier century: the walls were rounded, earthen, bearing the prints of the builder's hands; the floors nothing more than packed sod strewn with straw. An oil lamp at my bedside table illumined the room, as did the fire burning in a nearby stone hearth, which emitted a cheering warmth. But beyond the window and the crude handmade wooden shutters covering it, the wind howled fiercely as the storm continued.

I pushed myself to a sitting position to discover my shirt and waistcoat and cloak had been removed, replaced with a coarse woolen undershirt that itched against my skin. My bandage had been replaced as well, with a fresh one of loose-woven, handloomed fabric.

I remembered the snowstorm and marvelled that my feet and legs seemed quite free of any sign of frostbite, and that I felt generally well and rested. Even my wounded arm had ceased aching. I almost swung my legs over the side of the bed, intending to rise and examine the room, when I chanced to glance to my right and saw lying on the floor beside me a wolf.

A large silver-white wolf in its thick winter coat, quite soundly asleep (or so I thought), curled in a comfortable half-moon. As I sat gaping, it lifted its head and stared at me with quizzical colourless eyes.

Had the cloak with the gun and ammunition been nearby, I would have seized a weapon at once. But the beast merely yawned, to display pink tongue and gums and a fearsomely sharp set of fangs, then set its great head down upon its front paws and gazed up at me with an air of canine boredom.

Cautiously, I pulled my legs back under the blankets and sat straight and still, paralysed by uncertainty.

As if in reply to the animal's yawn, a man entered the room: Arminius, still in his plain black robe, bearing in his hand my—or rather, Arkady's old—shirt. The shirt appeared somewhat new; that is, I suspect Arkady had purchased it without ever having the opportunity to wear it, and it had lain unused, untouched, for over two decades in his closet. At the same time, its style and faint yellowing marked it as old-fashioned. Arminius impressed me the same way: a very young very old man, with white hair and beard but the smooth rosy skin of a newborn, and eyes as bright and ageless as the white wolf's. His skin was the pink of the animal's tongue, his hair the same colour as its fur, and they, combined with the sparkle in his eyes, seemed utterly incongruous with his sombre black vestments.

He smiled at me first, then at the animal—who grinned, tongue lolling, as it thumped its tail like a dog in greeting—and asked the creature kindly, "Is he awake, Archangel?"

And he bent down to scratch the wolf behind the ear. Archangel closed his eyes appreciatively and began clawing the air wildly with a rear paw.

I dared then to rise—still keeping one eye on the grinning four-legged predator—and took the proferred shirt. So awed was I by the entire tableau, and by the very fact that I had survived, that my voice was reduced to a whisper: "How did you find me?"

His smile never faded, though he shrugged as if the answer were not important. "I have a way of finding those who need my help. Come; you are hungry."

He was quite right. I let him lead me to a kitchen with a much larger hearth, where a black iron kettle hung from a spit. He indicated with a nod where I was to sit—at a rough-hewn table and bench made from a few split logs. So there I sat while he ladled some of the contents from the kettle into a handmade bowl and brought it to me, then handed me a piece of brown bread. I waited for a spoon, but it was not forthcoming; instead, I lifted the bowl to my lips.

It was peasant fare: beet and cabbage and barley stew, but delicious and hot. I ate two bowls while my host crouched on his haunches on the dirt floor in front of the fire. The wolf joined him, curling upon the heated stones of the hearth while its master stared into the flames and stroked its head distractedly. I watched them both curiously as I ate; animal and human resembled each other in colouring and had the same gentle, placid demeanour.

I ate until I could eat no more; and at the very instant I set my clay bowl against the unfinished wood, my host turned his face towards me to reveal his soft smile.

"Now it's time for you to talk."

How could I not? The man's air was such that I had trusted him with my very life the instant I first saw him; and the devotion the huge wolf showed him impressed me no less.

So I told the story: of my life in Amsterdam, of how it was shattered by recent events, by Arkady's appearance and my brother's kidnapping and death, by my son's transformation into a vampire, by Arkady's destruction. I spoke, too, of my shocking discovery that I was Arkady's son and Vlad's heir—and that I was weak, powerless to do anything to help those I loved.

Desperate, I begged Arminius to come with me to the castle—to set my little boy free, to destroy Vlad. For I sensed that he was most learned in these occult matters, and very powerful—powerful enough, perhaps, to overcome the Impaler.

To my embarrassment, my voice broke many times during the telling of the story; more than once, I paused to remove my spectacles and wipe away tears. Yet I should have wept oceans of them if I thought it might convince Arminius to aid me. I was determined that he knew precisely what help to give.

He listened to my emotional plea in complete silence and detachment, his gentle dark eyes focussed on mine the entire time. And then he turned his face again to stare into the fire. The wolf woke and nudged his hand, and he stroked its head once, twice; the creature settled down again and soon fell into a dream, its front paws twitching faintly.

"I cannot go with you, Abraham," he said at last. "I am, like Vlad, tied to my dwelling, to some extent. Even if I were not, I could not raise a hand against him. *You* are the one who must accomplish this task, my friend. You have been awaited many generations."

My frustration, my anger, were too great to hide. "But I am not strong enough!"

He nodded at the fire, as though he were addressing it. "Not now. But if you choose the correct path, you will be." And then he gave a single, abrupt sigh. "Of course—once you know what is required, you will resist."

"No," I said, vehement, intent on vengeance. "I will do whatever necessary to destroy Vlad. Only tell me what I must do."

He turned his whole body then from the fire and faced me directly, sitting back and folding his arms round his shins. "Were you evil, I would send you to the Scholomance —the school where the Devil trains his own in the mantic arts."

"If there's a school for evil," said I, desperate, leaning across the table towards him, "then surely there must be a school for good."

He smiled at that, his thin lips curving easily into a half circle. "Such a place dare not exist openly—nor even have a name, as it would be under constant attack from its enemies. Here is the problem, Abraham: In order to fight evil, we must know evil. In order to prevail against Vlad, you must possess equal power in order to defend yourself and those you love. But such power brings with it terrible temptation."

"If I am to defeat Vlad, then I have no choice."

"No." His expression saddened. "No choice, to fight one such as Vlad. Others have tried; none has succeeded."

"Have you tried?"

His eyes widened slightly with surprise before he quickly averted his gaze; he rose to his feet and half-turned towards the fire, which cast a tiger-lily-orange glow upon his face, his sparkling white hair.

"No. I have not tried, though I have advised others. But they did not possess the . . . unique opportunity you do."

I lifted a curious eyebrow. "Which is?"

Again, he studied the fire rather than meet my gaze and, after a long pause, replied, "You have your mother's strong will. Believe me, you will need it. Even during his life, Vlad was cunning and bloodthirsty, known throughout his small kingdom of Valahia—better known to you as Wallachia—for his acts of sadism and torture. Oh, his people loved him for the victories he won over the Turks—but his ferocity in battle had nothing to do with courage or honour or love for his land. Only two passions drove him: the thirst for blood and power. The passing centuries have only made him crave them more."

His eyes looked upwards and sideways, beholding the past; curious at the conviction in his voice, I said, "You speak as though you knew him."

He glanced back at me, his lips curving upwards ruefully, shyly, as though the truth embarrassed him. "I did. Born under the sign of Sagittarius, the year the English burned Jeanne d'Arc as a heretic—perhaps an omen of other evil to come.

"I knew his father, Vlad Dracul, sent to the city of Buda as a hostage of Sigismund I. And his grandfather, Mircea the Old, who ruled many years, and his great-grandfather Basarab the Great, who defeated the Tatars." The wolf beside him growled in his sleep; Arminius laid a hand upon him. "Yes, I know, Archangel. The Draculas, as they have since come to be known, were a family of great intelligence, great shrewdness, great political ambition—but, I am afraid, not great wisdom, despite the fact that many of them joined the *Sholomonari*."

I frowned at the term—though I was far more puzzled by his assertion: Did he truly mean that he *knew* Vlad's forebears? That he was *older,* by at least a century, than the Impaler?

"From King *Solomon*," he explained. "The *Sholomonari* were comprised of the most brilliant minds in Eastern Europe. They devoted themselves to alchemy—the search for immortality; or, if you will, the philosopher's stone. But after a time, many of the *Sholomonari* devoted themselves to evil rather than good. Those inclined to wickedness studied at Sibiu, over Lake Hermanstadt, at the Devil's Scholomance; and each learned the art of pact-making, some for temporal gain, others for more lasting treasure. Vlad's father and grandfather were *Sholomonari,* as was Vlad himself. He and his forefathers used their powers to further their political careers.

"But Vlad possessed a streak of cruelty and craving for power beyond theirs—perhaps because his own father cold-bloodedly surrendered him as a child to the Turkish sultan, as a hostage—and he soon discovered a way to have eternal life, eternal blood. Thus was the pact you know as the covenant born. Like his own father and grandfather, Vlad thought nothing of surrendering his own kin, if it brought him gain."

A terrible realisation came to me. "So if there have been and are many *Sholomonari* . . . then are there also many vampires?"

"After a fashion," he said. "The sort you know have all been created by Vlad's bite. There are others, though, of another nature—as many kinds, perhaps, as there are bargains with the Devil. Different men seek different things. Vlad sought immortality laced with blood and terror, for such brought him pleasure."

"And how is it you know all these things?" I asked; my curiosity had bested me, although the question seemed impudent, almost rude. "About the Scholomance, the *Sholomonari,* and Vlad?"

I expected he would not answer; my head was swirling with romantic superstitions about a secret organisation of *Sholomonari* dedicated to uphold good, and his being sworn never to reveal the source of his vast occult knowledge. But answer he did—after a moment's pause to stoop down and thoughtfully stroke the sleeping wolf's flank—with words I could never in all my life have imagined:

"Because, my dear Abraham—I, too, am a vampire."

⇥18⇤

The Diary of
Abraham Van Helsing, Cont'd.

I could do nothing but stare at him, thunderstruck by his admission; a sudden chill of fear overtook me. Had I been so wrong to trust this quiet stranger? So wrong about the atmosphere of goodness I sensed here? Had I fled Vlad's castle only to walk into the beast's very maw?

He saw my discomfort and a sad, self-deprecating smile fleetingly curved his thin lips beneath his drooping mustache; then his expression once again grew sombre. "I do not mean to frighten. But it is the truth."

"Who *are* you?" I demanded softly, without knowing I intended to pose the question.

"Just what I appear to be: a humble Jew born many years ago in Buda, before it was joined to its sister city across the Danube."

"How many years ago?"

He shrugged, as if it were too insignificant to mention. "Some few centuries before Vlad. Suffice it to say that I left my native Hungary to escape the Black Death and certain reprisals against those of my heritage, and found a safe haven in the wilds of the Wallachian Forest. There I acquired an interest myself in alchemy and those things labelled occult."

"You were one of the *Sholomonari*, then?" I no longer worried that my questions were uncourteously direct; his startling admission negated any right to privacy on the matter.

"Yes. As it was the fashion then to take on a Latin name, I became known as Arminius, the mage. So I am known even now." He sighed unhappily at the memory. "I was as greedy, in my own way, as Vlad. But I did not crave blood or political gain; no, I desired simple immortality, and personal powers. So I did what others have done before and after me and shall continue to do in the future: I used my magical knowledge to forge a pact. But such bargains are never without price. I sacrificed the souls of innocents—"

He broke off suddenly and turned away from me, hiding his expression; I suspected he did so to hide his grief. Archangel woke at once at the movement and pressed a muzzle against his hand, as though to offer comfort.

After several seconds' pause, Arminius continued. "Yes, I sacrificed innocents, just as Vlad now does, in order to purchase my immortality. Unlike him, I had no desire to play generations-long cat and mouse games. No, I wanted simple power, not blood; and I obtained it by draining my victims psychically."

"Psychically?" I could not keep the scepticism from my tone.

"Arkady spoke of it to you, did he not? Of the physical aura, of the life-force?"

"He has mentioned it," I said with unease. It is not so easy to change from cynic to convert overnight. Yes, I had seen with my own eyes that the vampire existed; but talk of auras and animal magnetism and psychic forces still struck me as purely ridiculous.

"I can hear you still do not believe. A pity, because you must learn to contain yours, to protect it, if you are to prevail against Vlad," he said sternly. "My victims never had such knowledge and died as a result. For I knew how to attach my own aura to theirs, to pierce it, to obtain from them all their energy and life. Thus was I strengthened, whilst they weakened slowly to the point of death. And with each new life I absorbed, I gained increased knowledge, increased ability such as you have observed in Vlad and your father: super-normal hearing, vision, smell—even the ability to know others' thoughts.

"As for my victims: I knew their thoughts all too well. Not in the crude manner that Vlad gleans them, a snippet here and there, from the blood—but intensely. Deeply, for my contact with them opened the innermost recesses of their minds and joined them with mine. It was at first a pleasurable process for me, for I saw the faceted jewel-like intricacies of each shining soul, the incredible, infinite wealth of knowledge stored within each memory. But over time, the very beauty of what I stole began to haunt me; and the treasure I accumulated preyed upon my conscience until I could bear the guilt no more."

"And what did you do?" I asked, spellbound, scarcely daring to breathe.

"I repented," he said, turning to face me once more. "I made amends."

My heartbeat quickened; I could think only of Arkady. If my father had only been able to repent, to somehow redeem himself— "Arminius," I said, "my father's soul is lost. Is there anything I can do—"

"Just one thing. And I suspect you already know what it is."

"Kill Vlad," I replied grimly.

He answered with a solemn nod and, in a tone that reminded me eerily of my dream, said, "The covenant works both ways, Abraham. Destroy him, and you release your father's soul from Hell—and those of your ancestors. You alone can redeem them.

"But you should also know: His final loving sacrifice for you in fact saved you. Because every time one of the Draculs overcomes evil and chooses good, it weakens Vlad. It is probably the only reason you were able to escape the castle without being trapped by his hypnotic powers."

I considered this in silence a moment before I asked, "And now—are you mortal again?"

At this, he laughed suddenly; the sound brought Archangel to his feet. "Who knows? I suppose it depends on whether I have truly found the philosopher's stone. You are a scientist, too; no doubt you can understand, I have no empirical evidence except"—and he swept his arms out, looking down at the scrawny body beneath his robe with amusement—"I do not seem to have died *yet*."

As he laughed, he brought out a crudely formed cup from a nearby cabinet and set it on the table in front of me, then fetched a smaller kettle from the hearth and poured a dark-looking brew into it. "Drink," he said, in a suddenly stern tone that allowed no contradiction. "It will do you good."

Tentatively, I raised the cup to my face, pausing to smell the muddy brown liquid. "What is this?"

"A medicinal draught of herbs. To cure what ails you."

I frowned. "Nothing ails me. At least, not that a tisane of herbs can right."

A glimmer of hilarity passed over his features, then was firmly repressed. "You are indeed a physician, aren't you, Doctor Van Helsing? Do you not trust me? Do you think that I have rescued you, bandaged you, fed you, provided a warm bed for you, only to poison you now?"

I hesitated perhaps a second longer than was polite (which seemed only to cheer him all the more, a fact I found rather irritating). "No. Of course not. But I would like to know what purpose this serves. Out of . . . professional curiosity."

"To stengthen you, my friend. For your return to the castle. Have I offered you anything here that has not brought you good?"

He had a point. I had, after all, gulped down the soup without a second's thought; and Arminius had obviously managed to successfully treat my wounded shoulder and the impossibly nonexistent frostbite.

But I had always scoffed at folk medicine, which I felt was as liable to kill as to cure. I scowled uncertainly down at the liquid in the cup. It looked somewhat like plain black tea, but the smell was altogether different and peculiar, with strong overtones of earth. I took a small sip and could not repress a grimace; indeed, it was all I could manage not to spit the "tea" back into the cup.

My less than gracious response again faintly amused him, but his demeanour remained one of firmness. "Yes, it is bitter. Many things are, but they are necessary. Drink. *Drink.*"

His insistence took me aback. I did not quite understand it, except that he obviously felt the concoction had some value. I opened my mouth to inquire as to its specific purpose, but he spoke first.

"Since you share an interest in the medical arts . . . I

have seen many changes over the years in medicine—some good, others not so very. You doctors have lost too much of the old herbal knowledge; it would do you good to add such things to your practice."

"Herbal knowledge?" I asked.

He looked pointedly at the cup in my hand; I gave a sickly smile and took another tiny sip. Bitter, indeed—to the point of inducing nausea. Had I not trusted him, I might have thought it was poison. But he smiled again at my pained reaction as I swallowed, and replied:

"Such as the proper use of wolfsbane. And garlic. And the petals of the wild rose. We will speak of this again, Abraham, when you return."

I glanced at him askance—and took another sip of the terrible tea at his insistent look. Apparently, he expected me to depart, then come again. But his expression remained enigmatic, and he supplied no answer, even when I asked in jest, "Am I leaving again so soon?"

Instead, he changed the subject and began speaking at length about the subject of homeopathy, while I slowly drank the vile brew; about how ingesting a small amount of what ailed a body in fact often brought a cure.

I could not resist arguing against it, in defense of my profession and beliefs. I cited many an example, all of which he attempted to refute; in desperation, I at last gave what I believed to be a compelling comparison. "It is as foolish," I said, "as attempting to avoid the vampire by allowing him one small bite."

At that, he grew quite silent and gazed at me searchingly. "You are more correct than you know, Abraham. To 'cure' the vampire, you must become the vampire."

His words chilled me to the core. Quite literally, for I suddenly realised that my arms were freezing cold. I rubbed them in an effort to warm them, then glanced back up at Arminius to see he smiled encouragingly, despite the alarming statement he had just made.

As I stared at him, I realised that, behind him, the fire had grown exceptionally colourful, the flames changing from red and orange to green and blue and violet before my eyes. The room, too, was changing in perspective, seeming suddenly enormously large. Arminius himself was transforming, from a white-haired man into a handsome white wolf like Archangel, who still lay sleeping in front of the fire.

I realised of a sudden that I, too, had changed; that I could see a strange glow around Arminius and Archangel, which seemed to undulate with their breath and movement and change colour. And I could hear everything: our breathing, the beating of our hearts, the sound of our digestion. I could even hear that the snow outside had stopped falling.

Suddenly compelled by a sense of wild freedom, I ran towards the door and discovered I was no longer in the body known to Abraham Van Helsing but in a young, strong animal body—that of a wolf, like Archangel and Arminius. The knowledge filled me with exhilaration and euphoria, like a prisoner suddenly released who has heretofore never known he was in jail.

As I approached the door, it opened before my very will.

Outside, the night was bright and clear, filled with a moon shot through with prismatic glints of violet, red, blue. So brightly did it and the stars shine down on the sparkling fresh snow that it seemed day, not night. I bounded off into it in my wolf-body, but within an instant I realised I was not running at all—nor entrapped within any body, but gliding easily upon the cold breeze.

I rode the wind over high, glistening white mountains,

over valleys, passing by isolated cottages until I found a suitable large town. There, looking down from my avian perspective, I saw a radiant warm glow—like that cast by a fire—emanating from the peasant cottages upon the hillside and the finer homes in the valley. Like a feather I floated down, past homes and shuttered windows, marvelling at the sound of breathing that came from within, of the beating hearts, at the smell of warm flesh as unmistakable as if my face were pressed against it. . . .

I chose a large house—an inn, according to the sign above the door chime—where the sounds and smells were particularly inviting. There I felt myself coalesce in front of a shuttered door.

I looked down to see my hands—but not *my* hands; they were someone else's, and I realised that this was not my body. I held those stranger's hands up to the moonlight and realised, with a thrill of horror and intrigue, that the flesh was pale and radiant; I spread one out in the cold air and turned it this way and that, like a woman admiring a diamond ring upon her finger, and watched with childlike amazement as different colours, beautiful quicksilver mother-of-pearl hues, pale blue and rose and green, glittered in my skin as though it were polished opal.

I lowered it again at the sound of footsteps—upstairs, I realised with oddly mounting euphoria—and listened impatiently as, step by lumbering step, my victim neared. Surely time had slowed for me, for it seemed hours before at last the door creaked open.

Behind it stood a woman in a large shapeless nightgown—a middle-aged woman, stout and sagging from childbearing, two waist-length brown braids emerging from beneath her white cap, a large mole sprouting two dark hairs just above her upper lip. She squinted out at me, tucking her chin atop a fold of pasty flesh, and snapped, "It is late to knock!"

She spoke in Roumanian. Impossibly, I understood every word, as though she had addressed me in perfect Dutch.

A faint red glow surrounded her like a gauze veil; I knew at once that this was the phenomenon Arkady and Arminius had referred to as the aura. Hers spoke of animal strength and determination, of unalloyed life force, and it flickered with dark brown sparks of annoyance.

Make no mistake: She was a plain woman, even homely, a woman who would have incited in the mortal Doctor Abraham Van Helsing not even a flicker of lust. But the scent of her drove me to madness. Such a marvellous smell! Earthy, warm, bittersweet; the smell of healthy blood, accompanied by the beautiful music of a strong heart thrumming in her ample bosom. A robust woman, with blood dark and rich and red—I almost could not answer her. My desire made me near swooning, evoked the same weak-kneed sensation I had felt the first time I carried Gerda to the marriage bed and kissed her.

All this I noticed in my curiously expanded time, before she had even uttered the first word; I could scarce control my impatience whilst she spoke. Yet as desperate as I was to embrace her, some intangible force held me back.

I knew I must await her invitation.

"I seek a room," I said, and marvelled at the sound of my own voice. For it was *not* my own but a stranger's, richly melodious and deep. I looked over at the heavy peasant woman with true longing—an emotional and physical ache, like lust—though it was somehow not as coarse but more refined. I yearned not for her body and a moment's pleasure but for her essence, her very life.

Yearning so permeated my entire being that I could direct it through my eyes, like a beam of light; and when I gazed into her eyes, I sensed the red glow surrounding her—protecting her—weaken round her heart. As I continued to stare at her, it glimmered, then went out altogether, like an extinguished candle flame.

I surged forth, feeling my very desire precede me, filling the air around her with darkly sparkling indigo mist. Her eyes at once went dull, confused—the same terrible dazed look I had seen in the eyes of the peasant woman in Vlad's castle. I knew then I had established a connection, similar to the one Arkady had attempted with me on the train: I knew, beyond all doubt, that I was free to place thoughts directly into her mind.

"Of course," she murmured, her wide-eyed gaze focussed entirely on me; it was, in fact, the answer I had ordered. When she opened the door and gestured me inside to a dimly lit corridor, I felt a wicked thrill. Yet I began to struggle against it, suddenly realising what it was: a thirst, a hunger, all-consuming, all-compelling, so desperately painful that I could scarce bear it, could scarce stand.

For a few passing seconds, somehow I fought: somehow held back, not understanding how I could have so suddenly found myself inside a vampire's skin. Not willing, most certainly, to kill. But my restraint lasted only briefly; and then the ache grew to such intensity—far, far beyond any emotion, any sensation I have known as a mortal man—I could endure it no longer.

It is a dream, I told myself with relief. *The dream of a dying man trapped in the snow.* None of it—Arminius and his white wolf, the glade, perhaps not even Vlad and Arkady and Stefan's death—was true. Perhaps I was even home at bed in Holland, so delirious with fever that the entire last few weeks had been nothing but hallucination. Perhaps even poor Papa was still alive.

Thus I rationalised my next action: to yield to the blood-hunger and seize the woman in the corridor, pressing against her sturdy body with my own, revelling in its warmth, in the texture of the soft, firm flesh at her throat, in the smell of her hair. So I found that soft flesh with my mouth, my tongue (revelling, too, in the salty tang of un-washed skin) and at last my teeth; and when I forced my jaw down, piercing her, she trembled and let go a soft cry of shock and bliss that spoke for us both.

I stepped behind her and held her in my arms like a lover—for this was surely a more intimate act than that of uniting mere flesh—and drew from her, aided by lips and tongue, divine nectar, the sweetest wine I have ever drunk. Yes, it was sweet, and utterly intoxicating, so much so that I was completely lost to myself, more swept away than I have ever been either by the act of love or by drink. I pressed closer to her, closer, and with my chest against her back, my hands beneath her breasts, felt the furious rhythm of her heart as it gradually slowed, slowed, slowed. . . .

The sound of the blood in her veins was the gentle rushing of the sea. And on that tide were borne her thoughts, sailing past like bobbing bits of flotsam that I could pluck at will. Here was an appreciation of my hand-someness, and a desire to wrap her sturdy legs about mine; here a murderous thought towards her husband, drunken and asleep upstairs, and of the extra coin she might pocket should she offer me her services. . . .

Her mind was entirely mine to control, to utilise as I wished, as was her body. Yet I cared for none of it save her hot pulsing blood. I drank and drank of it, wishing for that moment never to end, for to be candid, it was as deeply pleasurable as the moment of sexual release.

But end it finally did; the ocean of her thoughts went still and placid, motionless. And then there was naught but darkness. I pulled back at once from the presence of Death and watched with revulsion and dismay as her body dropped heavily to the floor. I shall never forget her face in death: chalk-white, grey rosebud mouth open in faint sensual surprise, eyes wide and vacant.

At the sound of her corpse thudding against the ground, a door down the corridor opened, and a man—huge and slovenly, with matted dark hair and beard and a stained white nightshirt—appeared, calling: "Ana?"

My reaction was pure instinct; I held totally still. (I almost wrote the words, *and dared not breathe*—but in fact, I did not breathe at all.)

And as the man moved slowly through the doorway with the deliberate snail-paced movements of a mortal, I espied beside the woman Arminius, wearing as always his dark robes and gentle smile.

As Arkady had, he spoke to me without moving his lips. *He will see you soon, Abraham, unless you act. Remember the aura: Withdraw it tightly into the centre of your being.*

Oddly, his advice made perfectly understandable good sense to me. With a sensation of drawing in, as one might inhale air, I retracted at once from the dead woman my glittering indigo aura, with which I had pierced hers. I could feel the withdrawal of that power into the inner core of my being; there I kept it and turned to face the man, prepared to similarly dispose of him should the need arise (though, in fact, my appetite had been more than assuaged, and the thought was unappealing).

But *he did not see me, or Arminius*—only poor Ana, on

whose behalf he released a sharp cry. He ran to her side and knelt down, frantic, shouting her name. I stood right beside him, but never once did he exhibit any awareness of my presence.

I was—like Arminius before me, whose feet were planted next to the shrieking man's head—entirely invisible.

Now move, Arminius instructed, *by sending the aura ahead of you. Visualize it in the direction you wish to go.*

Again, I followed his command, mentally placing the glittering dark blue energy at the doorway.

And in the single beat of a heart, I was there: standing at the entrance; and with my will gusting like the winter wind, I shoved the door open to make my escape.

I crossed the threshold—and to my amazement stood not outside in the cold street but in front of Arminius' hearth, where Archangel the wolf lay stretched out on the warm stone, his silver-white fur orange with fireglow.

Arminius stood beside me. "You are like your mother, Abraham; blessed with a strong will. This has a great advantage: a strong-willed soul can more easily control the aura.

"And it has two disadvantages: You are insensitive to many things; and you are also very sceptical . . . one might almost say, stubborn. Forgive me if I have used drastic measures to convince you of the reality of certain things; but if you cannot believe in the aura, you will never learn to control it. Succeed at that, and you will be able to enter and leave Vlad's domain safely. Otherwise, your survival is left to chance."

His charge that I was stubborn bothered not a bit. In fact, I giggled, under the sway of giddy euphoria, utterly unconcerned that I had just killed a human being. Like a child, I held my hands, my arms out against the dark backdrop of the earthen walls, and saw that I was once again in my own, Bram's, body. Yet it still glowed—this time with a much brighter blue, edged with violet and occasional bursts of red and orange.

Like a child, too, I played with simple delight as Arminius showed me how to control the colours in order to move without making a sound, without exuding a scent. It all seemed remarkably easy, and so obvious that I could not believe I had never considered that the human body had its own electrical and magnetic field.

In the midst of my play, I turned round to find my companions suddenly gone and the door open.

It was an invitation: I walked towards it and gazed past the threshold to see feeble sunlight and a stretch of rolling green landscape.

I stepped into that place and time—into the dawn, where the waking sun filled the eastern sky with the rose-orange glow of tiger lilies. The grass was alive and green, sparkling with heavy dew, the air clean and cool, heavy with mist that left fat droplets on my coat and boots.

And in my hands rested a single sharp stake, made of wood and half as long as my arm, and a mallet; at my waist, sheathed, a long-bladed knife. In my mind, Arminius' voice spoke as though it were my own thought: *Do you understand what these are for, Abraham?*

I understood. I walked alongside the grassy lawn on a gravel path, which led past tidy rows of headstones: the plain grey quartz markers of commoners, the ornate marble memorials for the upper class. It took me to a wrought-iron fence with great black spikes; within lay a grey stone mausoleum.

I knew what I was here for and of a sudden remembered the control Arminius had taught me. I held the hand that bore the stake up against the pink-orange sky and spread my fingers. They were my hands, human hands. No longer could I see the blue glow so clearly, but a faint trace of it remained (or perhaps I simply fancied it). Using my imagination, I retracted it deep into the core of my being and realised that my breathing no longer made any sound. I moved, stepping from gravel inside the mausoleum's stone entryway, but my boot-heels made not the slightest noise. In the early morning stillness, I heard only the soft calls of birds.

So I pushed open the heavy metal door and stepped inside the dim airless tomb. It smelled sadly of dust, mildew, decaying lilies; no light shone here except the bleak first rays of the sun that fell inside the open doorway. Even that illumination faded as I walked down a long, narrow corridor with an arched ceiling—empty and silent, save for the soft insistent dripping of water, accompanied by increasing dankness. The effect was claustrophobic, like entering a close tunnel. I could not resist comparing it, in my mind, to the process of birth: In a way, I was being born anew. But something far more sinister than a mother's arms awaited me at the end of this dark passage.

At last the corridor opened onto a vast silent chamber, illuminated by feeble sunlight filtering through arched stained-glass windows and staining the air, the stone, my skin watercolour washes of red, blue, green. Here, arranged in equidistant, orderly rows, sealed coffins rested upon stone catafalques, each set beneath a marble plaque set into the wall.

Instinct led me to a far corner, where the newest casket, its finish glossy and undulled by the procession of years, lay surrounded by garlands and vases of white flowers: velvety lilies, their edges browned, curling, and roses, their blooms open and raining dried petals upon the stone. The atmosphere of desolation was increased by the ring of cold, extinguished candles encircling the site.

This coffin was smaller, gleaming white, not yet sealed with strong iron bands designed to spare mourners the stench of decay; the very sight of it brought memories of my little Jan and constricted my throat. I blinked back tears and, trembling with emotion, raised the lid.

There upon pink satin reclined a girl no more than twelve years of age but already possessing the exquisite beauty of womanhood. The light streaming through the glass cast ribbons of colour—amber, violet, red—across her pale drawn face, with the red falling upon a luxurious cascade of shining copper curls, causing them to glow like fire. Yes, she was beautiful, with skin like fine porcelain beneath a scattering of childish freckles, and full primrose lips; and there was a grace and dignity in her repose to equal any gentlewoman's, as she clutched a single dying lily in her small fine hands.

Too beautiful. I had never seen her before and could only surmise that she had been a victim of Vlad's, Zsuzsanna's, or Arkady's—or one of their hapless spawn who had somehow escaped the stake and knife. Even so, my heart went out to her. That is a metaphor, I know, but I knew then that it was based in fact. I physically felt my emotions, my will surge towards her in a rush. I should have realised my error then and been more cautious; but instead I let go a sigh of pure sorrow, stricken that anything so virginal, so lovely, should be dead, and leaned forward to plant a respectful kiss upon her ivory forehead.

As I did so, she opened her eyes. Sea-green eyes, flecked with amber, slanting and feline, unmistakably feminine. They drew me towards them like a siren's sweet song. . . .

I struggled, flailing mentally like a drowning man in

that beautiful green sea while she rose, smiling, letting go the single flower in her grasp to reach for me.

But then I recalled what Arminius had taught me. I recoiled both physically and psychically and concentrated on protecting the energy surrounding my heart.

My resolve returned at once. She was halfway to sitting when I pressed the point of the stake between her flat childish breasts, indenting the white lace that covered her unbeating little heart. Wielding the stake in my left hand, I raised the mallet overhead in my right and brought it down.

But at the last instant before the hammer found its mark, I quailed at the sight of her sweet sea eyes, at the fiery auburn curls, at the soft porcelain skin. Such an innocent beauty—a mere child. The horror of what I was doing struck me full force, like the blow of the mallet.

Bile rose in the back of my throat. Nauseated, tears stinging my eyes, I sank to my knees just as the metal hammer's head struck the wooden stake, and grasped the coffin's edge with my fingers.

Thus was my aim clumsy and the blow softened; the stake pierced her chest, but at an angle some thirty degrees to the right, missing the heart. And the poor child—oh, how she rose, clutching the edge of her little white casket, her cold small hand atop mine for an instant—and then she recoiled with a shriek high and thin and totally inhuman. The pink rose-petal lips parted, revealing small sharp teeth with unnaturally elongated canines, and in her desperate agony she leaned towards me, snarling and snapping like a rabid pup, fangs whistling through the air.

I cried out, too, in despair at her agony, at my failure. I was utterly vulnerable at that moment and knew she would have bitten me—but something held her back. I glanced down at my own chest and was relieved to see there a large golden crucifix.

So she continued to writhe and wail, struggling to climb out of the coffin, to flee from her torment, but my presence at her side entrapped her.

Release her, a voice commanded—firm and calm, yet edged with indignant anger. *She has suffered enough! Release her at once!*

I glanced up to see Arminius standing at my side, all trace of the grinning idiot gone; he instead shone with the same determined glory, the same magnificent authority I had seen in the Impaler upon his throne. I stared awestruck at his commanding dark eyes, at his aura of physical strength, at his long white hair and beard that blazed like a white-hot flame: the Son of Man in Revelation, with feet of brass and hair like white wool.

Harden your heart, Abraham. Pity her now, and she is doomed to suffer. Strike again. Strike!

The sight gave courage. Again I retracted my aura and found the action brought renewed calm, renewed strength. I rose on trembling legs and, eschewing fear, thrust out my hand and righted the stake, ignoring the girl's flailing limbs, her champing teeth now flecked with foam, the once-lovely face now contorted into a hellish Medusan rictus. The cross protected; she could only recoil from my touch.

And I struck—this time, a mighty blow that rang echoing throughout the shadowed chamber. The girl gave out a high shrill cry as the stake pierced through cartilage and muscle until it reached the spine.

I swallowed all pity and fear and watched with a fierce determination, ready to strike again if need be. But she released a single shudder, then fell eternally still—and upon her face I watched a transformation subtle yet as stunning as the one Arkady had undergone when he returned to his true mortal state. The unearthly loveliness fled like the snuffing of a lamp and was replaced by a pale, purely human beauty—a beauty that to me was far dearer. For she lay before me a sweet mortal child, her features plain and pinched, her skin the dull waxen grey of a corpse, her lips bloodless and slightly parted, her eyes clouded, sightless.

I closed those unseeing eyes and bent down to give her cool forehead a kiss; hot tears spilled onto the lens of my spectacles and dripped upon her skin, for I could now dare mourn her.

It is not yet finished, Arminius said. *The knife.*

Reluctant, I unsheathed the blade and held it against the grey-white skin of her throat. But the sight of that innocent face held me back.

Harden your heart, Abraham. It must be done to grant her rest; for the regenerative powers of the vampire are great.

I again retracted my aura, which pity had caused to go out to the child again. Hardened my heart and did the task. Must I write of it here? That terrible final chore, of the brutal effect of that knife against her tender flesh, upon her frail bones, as I struggled to separate head from body?

So it was done, quickly and bloodlessly, and I discovered within my coat a clove of garlic, which I gently put inside that tender little mouth.

And when I stepped from that chamber into the long, dark corridor again, I found that it led not to a dew-soaked spring morning in a graveyard but to the warm hearthstones in front of the fire.

This was Arminius' cottage, at night. A quick glance at my hands confirmed that I was indeed myself, free of all strange unearthly glows and glimmers, completely mortal and dressed once more in the wool homespun undershirt.

Beside me Arminius sat cross-legged, his white-furred companion's chin resting on his knee. They seemed entirely normal—except for a faint aura of sparkling gold limning them both. While my body seemed returned to its usual state, I can only say that my mind felt quite like the room itself—which appeared to contract and expand, seeming one minute peculiarly small, the next, vast as a great cathedral. I sat in front of the fire myself, my thoughts racing as I tried to make sense of these impossible new experiences.

Arminius looked up from stroking the animal's head, his dark eyes filled not with humour or amusement but with sad compassion. "You are a determined man, Abraham. With training, you shall achieve even more strength of will. In time, you will no longer require my help."

"These . . . events," I said slowly. "Are they real?"

"You are no vampire, my friend. But you must know the vampire's mind if you are to defeat him."

"Then I did not kill the woman?"

"You cannot kill what never existed."

I nodded with relief. "And the little girl?"

"She was quite real. You have provided her with the truest help any man can: Now her soul is freed to ascend to the next level. Your father, Vlad, and Zsuzsanna have all enlisted human assistance in order to avoid creating others like themselves; but mortal aid of the sort you have just provided was not always available. So the vampire plague is now sprinkled throughout the continent."

The revelation filled me with alarm. "What can be done?"

And before the question issued entirely from my lips, I was no longer seated in front of the warm reassuring glow of Arminius' hearth but was standing in an alleyway between two tall brick buildings. A nearby streetlamp cast a sliver of light over my boot-tops, revealing cobblestones lightly dusted with snow.

The night was clear, bright with stars and moon, so bone-chilling it stung my nose, my cheeks, and turned my warm breath to mist. The rapidity of the sudden shift of scene made me slightly dizzy (as did the noxious smell of rotting garbage, festering somewhere nearby); I leaned against the nearest cold wall and tried to orient myself.

This was a large city; for though the position of the moon and the deep blackness of the sky indicated a late hour, the wide avenue beyond the alley was not silent but singing with the click of horses' hooves and the creak of carriage wheels. The alley, however, was long and narrow and dark, somewhat sheltered from public view.

I thought myself alone. But as surprise passed and my senses and attention slowly returned, I detected to my left, at the alley's walled-off end, a feminine voice, drunken and raucous and giggling. I turned—careful first to retract my aura as Arminius so often warned me to do—and spied, standing in a feeble pane of light, the source of the noise.

A woman, white-skinned and voluptuously plump, with a round, plain face and ornate hair an unnatural shade of hennaed red—almost as red as her bright crimson gown, cinched impossibly tight at the waist, and so low-cut her full breasts seemed on the verge of spilling out. She stood against the brick wall, unmindful of the cold, her red cape pulled open and held back teasingly by red-gloved hands upon her hips to better reveal her wares.

"Come on, then," she said in German with full scarlet-painted lips, fluttering eyelids thickly lined with kohl. And she tossed her head, clumsily seductive, at her companion, who stood hidden by shadow.

Apparently, her words were not enough, for the dark

figure did not move; not until she grinned and revealed her secret—grabbing the folds at the front of her skirt and slowly parting them to reveal a petticoat beneath . . . then parting those folds as well to reveal black stockings and white thighs, and the golden-brown triangle at the top of her legs.

"Come on," she urged, with inebriated vehemence that verged on angry impatience. "Come on. . . ."

Her suitor stepped forward into the ribbon of light. I could see only his back but knew he was white-haired, rotund, well dressed. He moved swiftly to unfasten his trousers and with an abrupt, savage motion, impaled her—at which she let go a startled, then pleased cry—and pressed her fast to the wall. She spread her pale legs wide, the red skirt spilling down on either side of her, a bloody cascade, and wrapped them as best she could about his thick middle.

My cheeks warmed with embarrassment and titillation; I could not understand why Arminius should have deposited me in this time and place simply to witness such an illicit encounter. But again, I forced myself to attend to my own mental protection, imagining again that I was surrounded by my own blue and violet glow, taking care that it was thickest around my heart.

At once the sense of lust eased, and my eyes perceived —not *saw*, I must be careful to note, for it was a sense beyond that of mere sight, but *perceived*—a darkly glittering glow about the harlot's customer. A veil of indigo, much as I had perceived myself when I had taken on the vampire's form, and the realisation made me study the man more closely.

I could not see his face, but of a sudden I recognised his form, his portly bearing, his white hair, though I had never before seen him standing—only lying dead on the floor of a moving train. This was the man Arkady had killed and begged me to mutilate in the same fashion I had the twelve-year-old girl. But I, in my self-righteous anger, had refused; and here, now, was the result.

He was thrusting vigorously, swiftly, unrestrainedly, pounding the woman against the wall with such force that her guttural cries, in the same rhythm as his movement, grew shrill with as much pain as pleasure. . . .

Oh oh oh oh oh . . .

I looked about me and saw that I had no weapons this time—no stake, no knife, no hammer—nothing but my medical bag and the large crucifix over my heart. The latter I clasped in my right hand and, lifting it up so that my enemy might see, began walking towards him.

Up to that moment, I think he did not sense my presence. But at the instant I lifted the cross and held it aloft, he swivelled his neck about with preternatural ease and glanced over his shoulder to see me approach.

This galvanised him. While I was still many steps away, with a quick violent motion, he seized the woman's neck in his teeth. There was no time to hypnotise, to entice, to lull into dreamy cooperation. He was determined to feed, and this he did rapidly and efficiently, tearing brutally through the skin.

She screamed in startled agony, writhing, flailing as the blood sprayed forth, spattering her white face and bosom, disappearing against the red of her lips, her bodice, her hair. He thrust his hips once more, so powerfully that I heard the muffled crack of bones breaking. She wailed again—a long, piercing sound that faded to a moan as she hung, legs dangling, helpless, while he drank quickly, greedily, throat working, white hair dappled with her dark blood.

And then I was upon him, cross lifted high. "Leave her! Leave!"

He turned his blood-smeared face towards mine, the long white mustache dripping crimson, and growled like a wolf warning another to stay away from his catch. But I felt no fear—only self-recrimination that I had not moved quickly enough to spare the woman his bite. I thrust the cross into the midst of the bloody fray, between him and his victim.

He gave a feral yelp of rage and surrender and pulled away. I stepped in closer, closer, forcing him farther back until at last the poor woman was freed.

She slid down the wall to land sitting upon the snowy cobblestones with an unceremonious thump, black-stockinged legs spread in a V atop scarlet skirts. Her head lolled forward, causing hennaed ringlets to spill down and mingle with the ribbon of blood that trickled down between her breasts; I might have thought her dead save for the soft moan that escaped her lips.

At last I stood between the vampire and his prey. For the space of three heartbeats, no more, he stood his ground an arm's length from me, growling and champing his blood-stained teeth in rage—a demonic version now of a jowly Papa Noel, with death and hellfire in his blue eyes. This was the first time I had ever witnessed the transformation from mortal to vampire (rather than the reverse), and to see what had most certainly been a kindly grandfather transformed into such a mindless, murderous beast was chilling.

Still I did not fear him, but knew he was no more than a defeated predator posturing vainly to keep his fresh kill from an interloper. I concentrated on maintaining my imaginary protective shield as I held fast the cross. My confidence in that weapon after my experience with the red-haired child had only increased. I could feel the power coursing down the length of my arm—and was fascinated to find that it did not

issue from the relic itself, but rather *from me;* and that realisation only increased my determination.

"Go!" I said to the snarling creature before me. "You
cannot have her. In the name of God, go!"

And with a boldness that surprised me, I lunged towards him with the cross. This at last convinced him all was
lost; he spun about and dashed down the alleyway with a
speed and agility unlikely for one of his girth.

I turned my attentions at once to his victim and knelt
beside her, taking a wad of bandages from my bag to stanch
the flow from her lacerated neck. She was still alive, though
pale with shock and barely conscious; happily, the vampire
had not damaged her esophagus or trachea or severed the
carotid artery, only badly torn the skin at the base of her
neck. But I had heard the crunch of bone and feared damage
to the spine.

So I pressed the cotton firmly against her wound and
taped it in place, covered her legs with skirts and cloak to
protect her from the cold, then gently probed her back for
damage and repeatedly asked her questions to which, amazingly, she was able to whisper replies. To my relief, the only
injury appeared to be cracked ribs.

I gathered her up and staggered out into the street;
from there, a hailed carriage took us both to hospital.

I swore to myself during that fateful ride, as I held in
my arms the scarlet woman—no longer a harlot in my eyes,
but a pale shivering innocent who laboured pitifully to draw
each shallow breath—that if she died, her blood would not
rest upon the head of her attacker, but on mine.

⁂

And at the break of dawn when I emerged wearily
through the hospital doors to step back onto the street, I

found myself transported magically once again to the alleyway, the sunlight glittering prismatically on cobblestones and piles of rotting garbage veiled with snow. Upon the wall of russet brick was a small dark brown stain, the level of my chest—a silent witness to last night's vicious attack.

My black bag was unusually heavy in my hand, and I held it knowing that whatever weapon I required, it would provide. I knew, also, what I had been brought here to do. My senses—especially that mysterious sixth one, which permitted perception of the aura and an inexplicable capacity for *knowing*—were growing keener with each experience, beginning with the staking of the young girl. Even the rescue of the unfortunate prostitute had had some effect on my abilities, so that when I stepped into the alley and gazed up at the unwashed brick buildings on either side, I saw that the one on my left possessed a barely perceptible trace of the malevolent indigo aura I had come to associate with the vampire.

Snow squeaking softly beneath my boots, I walked from the alleyway to the main thoroughfare, which, compared with the bustle of the night before, was quiet in the frosty dawn. This was the street of a large city, in a section tainted by sadness, squalour, decay, and the stink from a nearby paper mill.

The building that demanded my attention—an inelegant box of brick, its cracked, yellowed windows covered with an opaque film of dirt—stood in front of a sidewalk covered with refuse and footprints in soot-blackened snow; and there were other human and canine detrita. At the building's entrance, a woman's scarlet glove lay in the charcoal slush.

I knelt to retrieve it with an odd sense of reverence, and

swore to its owner that I would avenge her, free her from the evil that awaited her upon death.

And while I crouched brooding with glove in hand upon the stoop, I sensed a stranger's approach—human, yes, but hungry. An upwards glance revealed a mousy young woman standing on the street, shivering with cold and exhaustion, yet pathetically attempting a seductive air. Her clothes were worn, the skirts patched, and instead of a cloak she wore only a wool shawl. This she draped open so that it might expose her flat bony bosom.

"Would you like some company, good Herr?" she asked, her voice and eyes dreamy from laudanum; then she coughed, the desperate, phlegm-filled hacking of a consumptive. Yet even the poppy's brew could not mask her despair; her troubled gaze so reminded me of Gerda's that I could not meet it.

Instead, I paused and tried to imagine her aura. Almost immediately a faint yellow-green glow surrounded her—except for an ominous grey shadow over her lungs.

I was tempted to stop and open my bag, to offer her medical help. But a condition as advanced as hers required far more treatment than I could offer at the moment, and I knew I had little time to accomplish my objective.

Her appearance and notice of me reminded me to attend to my own aura; I withdrew it at once, centring it over my heart, and watched as her insincerely lecherous gaze turned to one of genuine astonishment. She gasped, then turned to look about her, as though searching for me; I knew then that I was quite invisible to her.

I rose quickly and pulled upon the building's front door; the wood was warped, causing it to stick and come open only after considerable effort. (The sight of the door opening made the young lady give a startled yelp; she picked up her skirts and ran away down the street.)

I stepped inside, into a tiny foyer that led to a narrow corridor of separate flats and a stairwell, from whence the indigo aura seemed to emanate. I bounded up the stairs, trying to ignore the overpowering smell of urine and vomitus (on which I almost slipped). My destination and the source of the indigo glow lay on the third level, behind a sticky, splintering wooden door with a loose, rusted knob.

Taking care to remain soundless and within the boundaries of my aura, I used a small fine scalpel and hammer from my bag to pry open the lock. The knob was already so worn that my task was not difficult; soon the door was open, and I walked stealthily into my prey's den, a two-room flat.

At once a sensation of pure evil overtook me, the same sensation I had experienced in Vlad's lair; this was combined with purely natural disgust at the filth surrounding me. The outer room was devoid of furnishing, with rotting wooden floors that had long ago lost their finish and windows too dirty to permit much sunlight to filter through them. Strewn across the floor were empty bottles of liquor and laudanum, and in one corner was a filthy mattress spotted with brown, upon which a rat stood, busily chewing straw. At my entry he took no notice but continued oblivious; this I took as a good omen.

Even so, I focussed on protecting my heart until the sense of revulsion eased, then opened my bag to replace the scalpel and retrieve the other needed weapons: stake and knife. The knife I sheathed at my waist; the stake and mallet I carried in my hands. Leaving the bag on the floor behind me, I headed for the inner sanctum.

Here, as I expected, was a plain pine coffin, surrounded by the glittering indigo aura.

I did not hesitate, as I had the previous time, but moved to it at once and pulled open the lid. There lay Papa Noel, with neatly trimmed hair and mustache of silvery white, and round nose and cheeks faintly flushed with the blood of prostitutes.

My confidence flickered only an instant as I considered his grieving wife, his grandchildren, and his other victims whom I had not saved. Only a flicker of emotion and sympathy, no more—but at once, he opened his eyes, small and blue above his apple cheeks, and narrowed them at me malevolently.

He might have risen then, but I came to myself at once and leaned forward so that the cross dangled between us, mere inches from his face. He bared his fangs and hissed in a threatening display, but I knew it was no more than the bravado of a trapped animal. And in that moment of confidence, I actually saw my own bright blue glow surge forth, settling atop the malignant indigo mist like fog on smoke, forcing it down, down, upon my victim.

And with a swift singular movement, I placed the stake upon his breast—against the fine wool gentlemen's vest, adorned with a golden watch fob—and struck a mighty, ringing blow.

My foe bucked and screamed, but the stake had pierced him solidly. Soon he was foe no more, but a man whose death I mourned as I performed the decapitation that would free him. (I almost wrote *desecration;* yet while the grisly act of beheading a corpse might seem so to be, in this case it was an act of mercy, and the look of peace upon his once-hellish visage was worth any degree of revulsion.) I placed a clove of garlic in his mouth and closed the lid, leaving him to his perpetual rest.

And when I retrieved my bag and stepped through the

doorway that led into the stinking corridor, I was not the slightest bit surprised to find myself once again standing in front of the hearth, with Arminius and Archangel seated at my side. It was still night, though I could not have judged how much time had passed—to me, it seemed a century, no less. But the room now seemed entirely normal; my perspective had returned, and the strange sense of giddy euphoria had gone. For the first time since I had drunk the vile-tasting tea, I felt entirely myself—enough so to know that I had been drugged.

Arminius was gazing into the fire as he stroked his dozing companion's head, speaking to me as though I had not been gone, as though our conversation had never been interrupted. "I think you are ready now, Abraham, to deal with the vampires alone—"

I interrupted at once, my tone indignant, demanding. "What did you do to me? How on earth did I go to all those places, commit all those acts? They were all imaginary, weren't they?"

"Only the first. The other two were quite real," he said sombrely, without any trace of his usual merriment. "I am sorry that such a desperate measure was necessary. True, it was dangerous, risky, but as I said, you are far from psychically sensitive, my friend. There was no time to draw out your abilities by a safer method; that would have taken precious years. Fortunately, your mind and heart were strong enough to bear it. And now that the channels are open, they cannot be so easily closed."

"Opening my abilities?"

He gave a slow, solemn nod. "To permit you to hunt the vampire. As I say, the method was successful. You are ready now."

I turned towards the shuttered windows, beyond which

lay the night. "Then I shall leave for the castle in the morning."

To my surprise, he shook his head. "No, Abraham. When I said 'the vampire,' I was speaking generally. You have the strength now to destroy young vampires of limited ability—but you are far from ready to take on the oldest and strongest of them all."

"Then what must I do?" I demanded. "Drink more of your potent brews? My poor son—"

"I understand your desire. But you will never be strong enough to destroy Vlad as he is now."

His statement stunned me to disappointed silence; before I could open my mouth to protest, to question, he continued. "As I said, the covenant is a two-edged sword. Vlad gains power and extended life for each eldest son he corrupts to evil. But *if an eldest son was to commit acts of good,* by destroying Vlad's monstrous vampire offspring, Vlad would be weakened. Each soul set free from the vampire's bite *on behalf of good rather than evil* drains him and strengthens you."

My jaw dropped slightly as I stared at him, aghast. "What are you saying? That this is to be my life now—frequenting graveyards at night, committing gruesome acts?"

His face was kind but implacable, blunt but harbouring no judgement; he held my gaze intently as he replied, "Only if you wish to redeem your father and all your ancestors. Only if you wish to save your unborn children and all future generations from this curse."

Let it end with me. Dear Bram. . . .

Exhaustion and the weight of his words overwhelmed me. My legs trembled, buckled, and I sank to my knees on the hearthstones, my capacity for reason crushed, obliterated by such a heavy burden. I would gladly have succumbed to unconsciousness there in front of the hissing fire, but Arminius lifted me with a grip surprisingly strong and carried me to my bed.

I slept and dreamt again of Arkady and my ancestors, their arms outstretched as they pleaded for my help. . . .

❧19❧

The Diary of
Abraham Van Helsing, Cont'd.

22 DECEMBER. Arminius was correct. Though I never again partook of his strange brew, my keener perceptions and ability to sense and control auras have remained and in fact been strengthened through further exercises under his direction.

Days and nights bleed together. It seems I have spent a lifetime under Arminius' tutelage, but it has been only weeks. I am in a perpetual state of exhaustion similiar to what I experienced in medical school, but my grisly studies are now of an altogether different breed of cadaver.

Upon occasion I find myself mysteriously transported to cities and towns across Europe, both eastern and western; this I know is due to Arminius' intervention.

Most times, however, I resort to more mundane means of travel and spend many hours in trains and carriages in search of Vlad's malignant spawn. I have visited towns and cities in Hungary, Roumania, Austria, Germany, but I know little of them beyond their nighttime streets and dawn mausoleums. And with the rescue of each potential victim from the vampire's maw, with the release of each trapped, tormented soul, I feel my own powers grow.

I have written Mama and Gerda to explain my absence, but there was no way to put such words on paper and make them sound sane. I pray my mother understands. Coward that I am, I could not relay little Jan's true condition; I told them a far kinder lie, that the child was dead. I could not also break to Mama the news about Arkady and Stefan. That I shall save until I see her face-to-face—if ever that time comes again.

And what of my poor wife? So long as Zsuzsanna exists, Gerda remains in danger because of the marks left on her throat. I cannot rest until my darling is freed, and our child avenged. . . .

The Diary of
Abraham Van Helsing

9 JANUARY 1872. No respite. Stronger still. Though the task grows in some ways easier, the grimness of it pervades my soul. In the hour before dawn—the hour before I strike—the dark burden so oppresses me, I sink to my knees, silently crying out:

Father, take this cup from me. . . .

But once stake and hammer are wielded, I and my victim release a final sigh, grateful for rest.

Justus et pius. I am harsh but just.

When finally I sleep—at odd hours parenthesised by

sunrise and dusk—dreams of my family haunt me. Stefan, Gerda, Arkady—and most of all, little Jan. They cry out to me from their individual purgatories; they beg for help I cannot yet give.

Soon, my child. Soon.

·‡·   ·‡·   ·‡·

The Diary of Abraham Van Helsing

23 JANUARY. After a month traversing eastern Europe, I returned to Arminius' den for respite and further study. He has brought to my attention an ancient manuscript known as the *Goetia,* or *The Lesser Key of Solomon,* a guide to the summoning of demons. "Understand this," he says, "and you will understand how pacts are forged, and how Vlad remains in communication with dark powers." It is a fascinating and frightening subject.

But I cannot remain.

I dreamt again last night of little Jan—as the mortal child he once was, with guileless, loving eyes and his grandmother's sweet, even temper. But surrounding him was the bleak grey stone of Vlad's castle; and as the image coalesced in more detail, I realised he was held fast in Zsuzsanna's lovely, treacherous grasp, struggling to break free, holding out his plump little arms towards me:

Papa, come! Please, Papa. . . .

He smiled at first—the scared, tentative little half-grin he sometimes gave when fighting tears. But the more he reached for me, the more the vampiress tightened her grip, forcing down his little arms and pinning them until the poor boy could not move, could do nothing but break into help-less sobs.

Oh, Papa, come!

And in my dream I wept in anguished frustration as the woman leaned her head down to cruelly bite his neck, her long hair loose and spilling over him like a blue-black veil. The barrier hid him so I could not see; but I could hear his feeble wail as she pierced him.

The detail grew sharper once more. I saw they stood together on the stairs, beneath the portrait of the Impaler, wavering with candleglow. And as I watched, the green-eyed image in the portrait stirred, moved, and turned its haughty gaze on me.

Mocking laughter.

And then a hysterical scream:

Papa, come!

He is only a child; he cannot speak with the eloquence of an adult, yet his frantic tone conveyed to me a wealth of heart-rending information.

His torment grows daily, and no one but I can free him. I *must* go to him. His trapped soul has cried out in its anguish and touched mine.

I woke, weeping and convinced. The dream was simple and swift but possessed of such emotional power that Jan's image haunts me during my waking hours.

After a near-sleepless night, I spoke of it darkly to Ar-minius this morning, over a breakfast of gruel with sheep's milk.

He did not reply for some time, which is his custom; and when he did, his tone was careful, his dark eyes averted.

"It is a common thing for a vampire to haunt the dreams of a loved one."

"Perhaps," I said, defensive. I sensed his disapproval, even though I could see no overt sign of it in his bland expression, hear no sign in his voice. "But that does not mean he needs me any less. I am strong now. Strong enough to defeat Vlad and put my child to rest."

He pushed himself back from the table, his eyes focussed on the oats in his bowl, and released a long, low sigh. There was no recrimination in it, yet I sensed a coming disagreement and tensed for an argument.

Again there came a pause. At last he lifted his gentle gaze and answered, "Abraham. You are strong, true; but not yet strong enough to defeat Vlad."

"But I am!" The helpless rage that had filled me in the dream overcame me again. I struck the table with my fist, causing the milk in my cup to slosh over the side. "For the past two months, I have done nothing except rid Europe of the scourge of the undead! And none of them—none of them—could overpower me. None could escape. Two months of my life, gone! How much longer must I wait? How much longer?"

He fixed on me a look of infinite understanding, infinite pity, and parted his lips to say one word.

"Years."

At that I jerked to my feet, incensed, raving. I screamed as I flung my terra-cotta bowl against the mantel and took angry satisfaction in seeing it break into shards. Milk and oats flew through the air, spattering onto the mantel, the hearth, and poor Archangel, who leapt up growling.

"You are asking me to let my son remain in that—that *hell,* with those two demons. You are asking me to surrender his memory, to surrender my wife, to surrender my very life, and replace it for years to come with purgatory for us all! I am strong enough, I tell you! Strong enough, and I can bear no more. Vlad *must* be destroyed, and *now!*"

At the calm compassion in his soft brown eyes, at the quizzicalness in Archangel's white ones, I gulped in a breath. And when I released it, I was startled and ashamed to find it accompanied by ragged sobs, torn from my very core.

I collapsed back into my chair and covered my face, struggling to regain control. A warm hand touched my shoulder; the act of comfort only brought more tears.

"Abraham," Arminius said. His tone was gentle as a mother's, yet stern as a general's. "There is no other way. Can you not see that Vlad manipulates you even at this distance? He has grown weaker and fears for himself. So he has made your own son attempt to betray you—to draw you to him."

His last words rekindled my ire; had he not said them, I might have listened, might have been convinced. But his insult to my child made me even more determined. I rose again and glared down at him with tear-blurred sight. "Jan would never betray me! He is only an innocent child, and my *son.*"

He studied me in silence for a time. And then I believe he sensed my resolve, for he sighed in weary defeat. "You have free will, Abraham. Evil compels; goodness, by its very nature, cannot. I will not hold you here if you wish to go. But mark this well: I might not be here when you return."

When you return, he said, not *if.* He was that entirely certain I would fail and come back begging for his help. The thought again rankled, and in my emotional, exhausted state, I made no effort to control my temper.

Instead, I went straightaway to my cot and gathered up

my belongings. And just as I had so long ago stormed from my house in Amsterdam, slamming the door on Mama and Stefan, so I now slammed the door on Arminius without another word.

⊰20⊱

The Diary of
Abraham Van Helsing, Cont'd.

With my cloak and my bagful of medicine and weapons, I strode out to the neighbouring barn, which housed sheep, a few chickens, and the two horses that had drawn my carriage. I fitted only one with reins and threw a blanket over her back in lieu of a saddle. The carriage I did not need. Though the last week had grown unseasonably warm and melted most of the snow, the mountain passes were still treacherous and icy. My chances were better upon a single mount.

Thus I rode—foolishly, without provisions or water—until daylight waned. To my confusion, a journey that I remembered as taking no more than a handful of hours now took an entire morning and afternoon and part of the evening as well. By the time I reached Isten Szek—God's seat, the magnificently high snow-capped peak in the Borgo Pass—it was washed with the rose-orange tint of sunset.

Still I rode. And when, some hours later, I arrived upon Vlad's family estate, night had fallen utterly. Taking care to remain undetected, I went not to the castle but to the family home I had seen in a dream (or was it more properly a vision?), the night Arminius rescued me from an icy death.

There it stood in the moonlight, upon a slope of dead grass peeking through half-melted snow. Beyond to the north the forbidding stone turrets of Vlad's dwelling jutted into the heavens, their predatory blackness blotting out stars and light and indigo sky.

I entered the home of my ancestors with a deep sense of awe and obligation, with a sense of their presence. This was indeed a house haunted by restless, whispering ghosts. For when I at last managed to light lamps and tapers, their portraits stared beseechingly at me from the walls—pleading for help, for release from torment.

How could I refuse them? For my own son was among their unhappy ranks.

With lamp and bag in my hands, I found my way up the stairs to the little chamber I knew was waiting: The nursery, with dried-out braids of garlic framing the window, and its poignantly empty cradle. Here I took my rest for the night, on the floor beneath a Byzantine wall icon of Saint George the dragonslayer. I lit the votive candle and whispered the prayer I remembered from my mother's diary:

Saint George, deliver us. . . .

But I could not help feeling I prayed only to myself.

⁙ ⁙ ⁙

And on a morning bright and blue and bitter cold, I went to the castle. I took great care to prepare myself mentally, adjusting my aura so that not even the Devil himself could hear my breath, my step, or smell the scent of my warm living blood. I crossed the short distance between home and castle on horseback, trying not to remember the single short word Arminius had spoken, the word that had sparked my ire and frustration:

Years.

I was convinced of my ability to destroy Vlad, still angered at the mere thought of the accursed existence that word doomed me to.

As I rode, I marvelled at the view that had been earlier hidden by the night. In the distance stood the wintry white peaks of the Carpathians, sparkling in the sun as they spiralled high into the heavens: an awesome sight for one accustomed to the flat broad expanses of Dutch polders. This was not the drab colourless landscape it had seemed the night before; the soft hills and steeper mountains were bright with evergreen. Indeed, there were trees everywhere, more than I had ever seen in one place: gigantic pines in the forest, and orchard after orchard of bare-limbed fruit trees surrounding the estates. In spring, the area must be fragrant with bloom.

Overall, it was a scene as cheerfully blue and white as the Swiss Alps—until one looked to the northern sky and saw the huge sinister grey towers of Vlad's castle overshadowing the estate.

Soon I arrived at the castle's main entrance. The looming structure sat on a great three-sided cliff, so that on all but its front face was a sheer dizzying drop down to thick evergreen forest; beyond those wilds lay the steepest mountains in the Carpathian chain. The building was indeed a fortress, impenetrable from all sides save one.

Once I gained entry, I did not hesitate but found my way quickly to the terrible throne chamber. It was empty, devoid of any sign of the violent struggle that had once taken place. The corpse of the aged woman, Arkady's body, Stefan's, had all been removed. No trace of their final agony remained, save for the large dark brown stain upon the stone where my brother had died.

I did not linger at the sight, nor permit myself the luxury of sorrow at the memory it evoked. My brother would be better served by my hardening my heart and completing the task at hand; the time for mourning would come later.

So I stepped quickly, lightly, soundlessly through the great chamber, to the door that led to the much smaller room within—the room from whence Zsuzsanna and little Jan had emerged. It lay half ajar, as though in invitation.

I entered without fear, without hesitation, without thought other than attention to maintaining my protection and silence.

But had I not been so prepared, the sight that greeted me would surely have filled me with unease. Against the windowless room's far wall stood an altar draped in cerements of black, upon which a single candle burned. Before that candle, carefully arranged, sat the golden chalice and a round medallion on which was etched a five-pointed star.

The malignance, the evil that issued forth from that altar provoked from me an involuntary shudder. For it was surrounded by an aura the likes of which I had never seen: one of such utter darkness that it did not glow but rather seemed to emit a hunger, an unalloyed darkness that consumed all that came near it—all light and life and love.

And before that altar lay two coffins: both polished ebony but of different size, the larger being draped with a banner bearing the emblem of the winged dragon. From each issued the unmistakable blue-black glow I had learned to associate with the vampire; but the smaller's aura was feeble compared with that of the larger, which radiated a dark streaming brilliance to match the glory of the setting sun.

I stood some time before those coffins as I contemplated Arminius' warning. Should I yield and make no attempt to destroy Vlad now, instead limiting my attack to the safer, less cunning target of Jan? Or should I surrender to instinct and risk the danger, in hopes that Vlad's second death would free my little boy from his monstrous existence, without his suffering any further pain?

Reason could find no hold in this father's heart.

Softly, I placed my bag upon the ground and retrieved from it the stake and mallet. With my mind set upon the cross shielding my heart, and the stake held aloft in one hand like a spear, the mallet in the other, I lifted the coffin lid.

Inside lay Vlad—completely white-haired, with skin pallid and drawn so tight over sharp features that he had lost his illusion of handsomeness. His eyebrows had grown wild and bushy, his ears faintly pointed at the tips. His normally ruby lips had faded to pink and were slightly parted to reveal the darkly yellowed fangs of an ancient predator. He looked altogether like the monster he truly was.

And upon his chest, sweetly aslumber, lay my son.

I quailed, tempted to lower the stake, to let it drop to the stone, to surrender. But the memory of Stefan and Arkady, of the dream where Jan begged for my help, bade me hold it fast. Summoning all my protection, all my courage, all my resolve, and banishing all sympathy and familial love, I placed the tip of the stake—as tall as he, poor child!— above my sleeping son's heart.

Such a perfect, handsome boy, with his golden curls and the smooth, plump, impossibly soft and unblemished skin of childhood! With pale, blue-veined, gold-fringed lids that hid his grandmother's eyes, and his beautiful mother's fine features—

Papa, come! Oh, Papa. . . .

I cannot write of the horror of that moment when I lifted the hammer above my head and brought it down in a mighty, ringing blow. Oh yes, it was swift and merciful, but there are no words, no words that can relay a father's anguish at such a deed. I am Abraham, and he was my Isaac; but this time, God did not rescue, did not provide a substitute sacrifice.

The weapon plunged deep into my poor child's body— but no farther, for my strength was not enough to also pierce the heart of him who lived by the stake and so richly deserved to die by it.

Jan screamed, a cry high and shrill and utterly inhuman, as he opened eyes afire with terror and rage.

It was not my son's voice, not my son's eyes; this was merely his shell controlled by a malevolent force. Yet I grieved for him just the same. Despite my precautions, despite my efforts to steel myself, I could withhold my emotions no longer but let forth a loud sob while my little boy writhed, thrashing limbs, champing teeth.

But of a sudden he fell still, and the evil glamour veiling his features parted to reveal a sweetly mortal face, like storm clouds scattered by the wind to reveal the sun's bright rays. He entered peacefully into eternity with his blue eyes open wide, and I watched as the darkness in them gave way to the guileless, loving expression I had known.

His peace gave me strength. I raised the mallet to strike again—a blow that would echo throughout Hell.

A force, burning cold, clamped down upon my wrist: Vlad's hand. Startled, I looked beyond Jan's eyes to see a second pair—this one ancient and crafty and compelling.

Come to us, Stefan. . . .

I felt his dark aura surge forth and attempt to engulf mine. The grip on my wrist tightened until I thought it would crush bone; the mallet dropped from my hand and struck the floor with the bright clang of metal against stone.

Instinctively I sent a rush of energy to protect my heart and leaned lower towards my attacker, which caused the cross to dangle low over his face. He disengaged as though my flesh scalded like vitriol, and leapt from the casket. The act sent me tumbling backwards and poor Jan's staked body spilling out onto the floor in front of me.

I fumbled for my bag, then crawled towards his little corpse and crouched over it protectively, desperate to wield the blade and complete the act that would bring his young soul freedom. All the while Vlad stood before us, stretching out his arms, his voice soothing, beautiful, the voice of my true father:

"Stefan. My child, look at me."

I disobeyed, refusing to meet that magnetic green gaze, instead keeping my attention fixed on the task at hand. But ere I could retrieve the knife, a fiendish shriek came from the smaller coffin as the lid was flung back.

Zsuzsanna sprang forth like the ills of the world escaping Pandora's box, jet hair now gilt with silver at the temples. Her appearance, though still formidable, had lost its freshness, like a rose that has begun to drop its petals. Her frame had lost its womanly curves and grown thinner, bonier, while her features had, like Vlad's, taken on a taut severity. Shadows had begun to gather beneath her sculpted cheeks, her eyes—eyes that had lost their soft brown-gold colour and now blazed hellish red, like the eyes of an animal catching the lamp-light at night.

She was still beautiful, yes—a beautiful monster.

At the sight of Jan lying on his side, little arms flung forward, hanging limply above the cruel stake that emerged from his chest, she howled again, a sound that chillingly evoked Gerda's keening. And as I knelt behind my son, reaching for the knife that would free him, she struck the air in a sweeping gesture—with a fury directed at me.

I thought it an empty, frustrated gesture, as the cross held her at bay. But in the next instant, I was pummelled by a blast of wind that lifted me from my knees and slammed me backwards against the stone wall.

I struck it with a force that cracked ribs and skull. The sharp blow to my head knocked all thought from it as I slid, stunned, to the floor and pitched forward onto my elbows. But the worse pain was in my chest, when I attempted to take even a shallow breath. I closed my eyes and fought to gather myself, to find the strength to rise to my feet, even to my knees, while Zsuzsanna screamed:

"Murderer! You've killed my child! And now you'll pay in kind!"

Her words cut through my disorientation; and despite it, they provoked such anger in me that I opened my eyes and whispered, though I yearned to shout: "He was never yours. Never! Just as your life is not your own but stolen from others."

But she was too lost in rage to hear my words; instead, she shouted out past me, at the doorway, "Kill him! Kill him —he has murdered the child!"

I followed her gaze to see the peasant woman—but not as I had ever before seen her. Though she wore the same dress, her face had taken on the unearthly beauty and youth of the vampiress, and the reddish cast to her long, dark hair now gleamed as though infused with the brilliance of the setting sun. At her mistress' order, she raised an arm to strike from a distance, as Zsuzsanna did once more.

I knew I could not survive another blow, much less two from either side. But before the fiendish women could strike again, I heard a roar like that of a mighty storm and another rushing of wind.

"Harm him and die!" Vlad thundered at the women, hurling Zsuzsanna herself at the opposite wall. Despite his frailer appearance, his strength was far greater than hers; she struck the stone with an ear-splitting crack. But it was not the sound of immortal bone breaking, for she slid down to the floor in a heap of black and white, revealing a long, jagged fracture—a lightning-bolt in stone—behind her.

The blow would certainly have killed a man at once. But Zsuzsanna was merely stunned and fell forward, propping her upper torso up with her arms, skirts and legs sprawled behind her upon the floor, dark hair spilling down over her livid face.

"I swear to you," she hissed at me, lips contorted downwards to reveal a razor-keen row of lower teeth, chin tucked to reveal a face consumed by large blazing eyes, "there will be payment for this! I shall relish every moment of your torment, your suffering, your corruption. And the day your soul joins your father's in Hell, I shall rejoice!"

"Silence!" Vlad commanded, with a rage that outshone hers as the sun outshines a single candle flame. "What is the one thing I demand above all others, Zsuzsa? That you should never harm him, never speak ill of him, never bring him sorrow! And what have you done? What have you done? *His son* is lost to us and for that we must now pay!"

She turned her face from him, sullenly mute.

As he shouted, I pushed myself onto shaking knees and crawled back to my child, only steps from where the Impaler stood. Beside my black bag, Jan still lay on his side, pale and silent in death, untouched by the force that had torn me from him. Had it not been for Arkady and all the past and future generations who looked to me for rescue, I would have surrendered gladly to the monsters—if only I could complete the task that would give my little son rest.

And in the time it took me to draw a single pained breath, Vlad's tone abruptly changed, grew warm, loving, beautiful to the ears, like the sweet high sound of a nightingale on a quiet starlit eve. "Abraham," he said softly, for the first time acknowledging the man I had become rather than the babe who had escaped him, "your child is not truly dead. I alone have the means to revive him. And I will, should you do one small thing: Come to me now. Perform the ritual with me, and you and your child will be free to return to your home."

He spoke with Arkady's voice; and the sound of it so moved me that I forgot myself and glanced up from my child's body to the Impaler's countenance and saw it shift, transforming itself to that of the father I had never known.

I struggled to maintain the protective glow around my heart; blinked, and saw behind the illusion the Impaler's malignant, skeletal features. With one hand, I fumbled in my bag without looking and drew out the sheathed blade.

"Enough of suffering," he said, and I stared into Arkady's soft, compassionate eyes once more. "Dear Bram, enough! Must you give up everything? Your own life, your wife's, your son's? No! Cast aside the cross and hand me the boy. I shall restore him to you; restore also the happy life you once knew. I ask but one small ritual, one brief exchange, and all can become as it once was; take the boy home to his mother, and let the joy of that reunion restore her as well. You have sacrificed enough . . . Look at him, Bram! Look at what you have done to your own blood, how cruelly you have mutilated his innocent little body! What sickness bids a father to so defile his own flesh? Do you wish him to remain thus—or become again a happy, living child?

"Cast aside the cross; grant me this one small thing. And the grim darkness your life threatens to become will turn to day, and you can once more rest in the love of your wife and son."

His words pierced me more thoroughly than any blade could; I gazed down at Jan's tiny corpse and fought back a wave of grief so powerful I feared it would wash away the last remnants of my defense. I felt myself surrounded by the inky darkness of Vlad's aura, felt my own glow engulfed, consumed.

I closed my eyes; unshed tears burned behind the lids. And with a desperation beyond any I have ever experienced before or since, a desperation that transcended time and place and physical frailty and rent the veil separating earth from Heaven, I cried out mentally—no, I *prayed,* to Arminius and Arkady and the generations dead and to come:

Help me!

Whether the dead and absent heard me, or whether my genuine prayer summoned help from within my own soul, I know not; but an act of emotional alchemy followed. The dross of my despair was transmuted into the gold of a determined will. Physically, I was dangerously weak and dizzy; the agony provoked by drawing a breath had only increased, and with it came a sense of heaviness in my lungs. I worried they had been punctured, and that I would collapse ere I dragged myself from the castle.

Nevertheless I found the strength to gather Jan's body into my arms and rise, unsteady and gasping, to my feet. The poor boy was heavier in death than ever he had been in life.

"Bram," Vlad wheedled, coaxing, still affecting Arkady's voice and visage; yet I glimpsed the decadent monster behind the facade. "Come, bring him to me."

I disobeyed, staggering instead to the doorway, past the peasant vampiress (who dared not touch me, nor meet her master's eyes) and into the throne chamber. Vlad followed alongside, still sweetly soothing:

"You are a stubborn man—but weak and tired. Surrender your suffering, Bram. Surrender your burden. . . ."

I made it past the implements of torture, past the bloodstains, past the throne, on sheer will alone. And when at last I emerged into the long, narrow corridor that led down to the stairs, I leaned heavily against the cool wall. The large stake protruding from Jan's small body scraped against the stone, leaving a shiny trail to mark our passage.

My pain increased, as did my light-headedness; but to allow myself the luxury of unconsciousness would mean failure. As I staggered down the stairs, I suddenly saw Arkady waiting upon the landing, his arms spread in welcome:

Abraham, my son, you are tired! Give me your burden. . . .

For a fleeting instant, I felt a surge of hope, thinking that Arkady had somehow been spared and had come to aid our escape. But then I blinked and saw behind his smiling countenance Vlad's malevolent features. Again I prayed to Arminius and my ancestors; again I found strength.

Grimacing with pain, I shifted my son's weight to my left arm and with my right hand held aloft the crucifix that hung over my heart. Pain and necessity eclipsed all fear; I approached my nemesis boldly, ready to touch the relic to his flesh if need be.

Indeed, I came close to doing so; I was less than an arm's length from him, close enough to smell his foetid breath before he stepped aside.

Thus did I progress raggedly through the castle—growing weaker, dizzier, yet more determined with each step. And at last I arrived at the open door that led to the day beyond. With a sense of triumph, I stepped into a pane of bright sunlight.

Before me, the door slammed shut, pushed by a sudden gust of wind; a heavy black iron bolt slid through the lock.

Vlad's voice behind me, faintly harsher now, commanding:

"Put down your burden, Abraham. Surrender to the inevitable and rest."

With a burst of energy that exhausted all my reserves, I moved to the door and, with my son still in my arms, leaned my forehead against the cool wood. I tried to shift Jan's weight to my left arm to that I might unbolt the door; but weakness and pain overcame me. Brow still pressed against the wood, I slid to my knees and gasped.

The Impaler approached, smiling, no longer bothering to maintain Arkady's appearance. There was no need; I was too physically weak to struggle. I tried to raise a hand, to lift the cross, but my arms were as heavy as the stone that surrounded us. Only one thought gave me hope: Perhaps I was dying. And if that was so, then my death would purchase Vlad's destruction.

The Impaler was right to sense my craving for peace, for silence, for rest. How pleasant, to surrender all emotion, all joy, all suffering, all love, all hatred. All striving . . . I need only close my eyes and yield to the void.

This I did. But a light shone in the midst of that darkness; and as I watched, an image coalesced.

It was Arminius, with shining white hair and beard. Strangely, his features looked precisely as they always had; but I realised for the first time how much they resembled Arkady's—as if this were my father, somehow still immortal but redeemed.

Get up, Abraham. Get up and save your son. Save us all.
The very thought of movement made me sigh with weariness—which brought a sharp, fresh surge of pain. That pain bade me open my eyes, which by chance were directed downwards to the pale still corpse of my son.

Vlad stood beside us now, his feet planted beside little Jan's head, his hands reaching out to grasp my child.

I clutched the black iron handle of the door and pulled myself up, then unbolted the door and flung it open.

Bright sunlight streamed in, caressing my face with its warmth, spilling over me, my child, the Impaler's crouching body.

Vlad gave a low cry that was a wordless curse and re-coiled instinctively. I took advantage of his hesitation to seal the doorway with a bit of the Host, then lift my son and stagger outside into the blue brilliant day.

⪪21⪫

The Diary of
Abraham Van Helsing, Cont'd.

How I managed to climb upon the horse with Jan's body and ride the long, torturous distance back to Arminius' cottage without fainting and falling off onto the icy ground, I cannot say. I only know that when I arrived there, I was as close to death as I have ever been; had my little son's soul not required my further help, perhaps I might have succumbed.

It was early twilight when we arrived at Arminius' sheltered glade. I dismounted and laid my child's body beneath an ancient fragrant evergreen. The dying coral rays of the sun streamed down upon us as I performed the grisly deed that put him to rest; only then did I enter the cottage to seek Arminius' help with the burial.

But the rooms were empty, the charred ashes in the fireplace cold and dark. I called for Arminius, then in my desperation for Archangel; the only reply was the echo of my own frantic voice.

I was too ill and exhausted to do more than build a fire and fall fast asleep by the hearth. In the morning when I woke, I made a pyre with logs from the woodpile and set my little boy's remains atop it. As it blazed, I watched the dark smoke carry Jan's soul heavenwards.

⁘ ⁘ ⁘

I sit once more before the fireplace, writing it all down. No detail must escape my memory, for I am sure this record shall be of use to me in the future.

I will remain here a few days to regain my strength and hope for Arminius' return. If he does not come, I intend to take with me the *Goetia* and certain other texts I have found, and carry them back to Holland. I know I am meant to return home; but my life there will not, cannot be the same.

Staring into the fire, I need no magical intervention to see a vision of my own future in the flames. I see two paths divergent, as though I stand at a fork on a fogbound forest road:

The one path is the future now denied me, the life of a man loving and loved, surrounded by children and a wife who grows contentedly old by his side. A lifetime of laughter and arguments, of tears and ten thousand good-morning and bedtime kisses, ten thousand stories recounted by candle-light, ten thousand slammed doors and ten thousand unwilling apologies. A lifetime of watching my children grow to proud adulthood and raise families of their own. Grandchildren, a life well lived, a gentle death, and interment at my Gerda's side: All this might have been mine.

But for the sake of those I love and those I never knew and never shall, I cannot be that man. I see too clearly now the fate that lies before me:

A life alone, eschewing love lest I bring forth another heir to be broken and destroyed. Ten thousand days spent in cold silent graveyards murdering those long dead, ten thousand nights on squalid streets, in villages and cities where I come and go a stranger.

Ten thousand nights so the day might come when I am the stronger and can complete the task I was born to do.

I go willingly down this road, never before trod by human foot, so that the other path might be safe for those who travel it; so that the dreams of other men might be sweet.

And for my own lost family, whose blood cries out to me as it drips from the Impaler's hands:

Justus et pius.

I will be avenged.

⊰ EPILOGUE ⊱

The Diary of
Mary Tsepesh Van Helsing

13 FEBRUARY 1872. Bram has returned at last.

Writing those words should bring joy. After all, my heart's greatest fear never materialised; the child for whom so much was risked, so much gladly sacrificed, is safe, and here with me once more.

But at what price? At what price?

Gerda shares my room now—I am too fearful to let her spend the night unattended. Many nights, in the heavy hours before dawn, I am wakened by bright, tinkling laughter and sit upright in bed, heart pounding because the voice does not belong to my daughter-in-law, but to Arkady's sister. Sometimes, the voice turns petulant, then shouts in anger.

I know with whom Zsuzsanna fights: Him. *He* still walks the earth, and many an hour in the darkness, I have lain weeping silently, listening in vain for news of those beloved by me.

Little more than a fortnight ago, Gerda emerged from her self-imposed silence to shriek again, in Zsuzsanna's voice,

leaping from her bed to stand like a distraught ghost in her
white night-gown, elbows akimbo, hands clutching skull,
dark eyes two fathomless voids in that pale, pale face. *Mur-*
derer! You've killed my child . . . ! And now you will pay in
kind. . . .

And then she collapsed to her knees, sobbing, cupped
hands to eyes as she moaned, "Jan . . . Jan . . . my sweet
little Dutch boy . . ."

I listened with a horror, a grief beyond the reach of
tears. For some time I could only lie stunned and sweating,
wrapped in linens and wool, feet pressed against the now-
cold brick bedwarmer as a burning chill ascended my spine.
But the question that consumed me became painfully tangi-
ble, so much so that it pounded in my ears until I could not
bear to remain in bed, but rose and padded in woolen socks
across the cold floor to ask it of her:

"Dear God, who has killed Jan? Gerda, I must
know . . ."

She did not hear me. I put a hand beneath her chin and
lifted her face towards me: but the eyes were blank, the
lips faintly moving, but producing no sound. She had retreated again to vacancy, to muteness, unable to answer my
question.

I already knew my grandson to be dead; I wanted now
to know the name of his murderer. For I had received only
days before a terse letter from my eldest son saying that his
only child had been killed, and offering no details—not even
mentioning Stefan's death. And in the midst of my weeping
over the death of my grandchild, I found myself besieged by
a mother's hope: If Bram had not mentioned Stefan's death,
then perhaps he, at least, was still alive, and Gerda mistaken. . . .

But in the meantime my grief was mixed with fury. I

was certain that Vlad was directly responsible for the loss of our little angel, and this added kindling to the fire of my hatred.

"*Who* has killed him? Who? *Speak!*" I commanded, this time with such vehemence that Gerda's dark, empty eyes flickered, and the moving lips produced a faint, low whisper before they fell silent again:

"Abraham . . ."

I staggered backwards from her and sat upon my bed.

Of course Bram had not harmed his own child; that I did not doubt, even at that horrible moment. But Zsuzsanna apparently thinks my son a murderer. And if the poor child had died by the time Abraham wrote to me, then why had Zsuzsanna waited so long to mourn him?

The only answer is too horrible to contemplate.

Yet, I see it reflected in Bram's eyes. Only five days before, I received a letter announcing his imminent arrival, post-marked from Hungary.

Two nights ago I sat alone in my room (alone, though Gerda slept quietly nearby), staring into the dying fire and grieving as I had the night—so long ago, it seems—Arkady returned to me.

Two swift knocks, soft yet insistent, at my bedroom door. The sound made me at once raise a hand to my startled heart: for I had heard no footfall in the corridor, on the stairs. Yet the cadence was unmistakable; I released a cry and hurried at once to fling open the door.

There stood Abraham, as he had so many months before the dark night of the past had descended on us.

This was my son—and yet it was not he, but a stranger. In the instant before I threw my arms round him, I drew back, fearful. This was indeed the same man who had come to my door only months before; for these were the same bright blue eyes behind thick spectacles, the same wavy, copper-gold hair.

And yet this man was not the same. There was an air about him that was new, an air of great power and mystery and sorrow. The bright blue eyes were tinged with hardness, such hardness as I had never seen in him before, nor thought him capable of.

"Moeder," he said, and his speech was different, too, possessed of authority and a weariness deeper than any which can be borne by mere mortals.

Undead, I thought in a moment of dizzying horror, for there was an aura of the unearthly, the esoteric about him. *Undead, or tainted like poor Gerda . . .*

But no; his haggard features revealed no immortal glamour, only shadows and lines and the burden of a responsibility that had aged him far beyond his years. Stricken at the sight, I touched fingertips to his face—warm, still warm —and saw it soften ever so slightly.

I took his hand, as comfortingly warm as his cheek. "Bram," I said, my own voice trembling as I searched his eyes to find therein even one small spark of hope. I had meant to welcome him properly, but had languished in uncertainty too long. "You told us of Jan, but your letter did not mention Stefan or Arkady. . . ."

He briefly averted his eyes and drew in a breath—a small, hitching sigh, but that instant's hesitation revealed the horrid truth more than any words could. I pressed both hands to my heart and wailed a mere second before he answered softly, "Dead. Both dead. But Vlad still lives."

How shall I ever mourn them all?

Arkady, my darling, would that I burned in Hell in your stead! Yet can there be greater torment than mine: to live knowing that your pure soul suffers unjustly while the monster still walks the earth, revelling in the blood of innocents? Knowing that your death and damnation have failed to free our child from a life in the Impaler's shadow?

And how shall I mourn the loss of the one now called Abraham? He has returned and lives here with us in this house, but much of the night and the day he is either absent or closeted in his study, poring over strange manuscripts. He speaks little, and will not talk of Transylvania at all. When he does speak, he does so absently, with his gaze focused elsewhere—on the shades of his brother, or his father, or his son, in this house full of ghosts both living and dead.

Bram is here, but he is not with us. My son is lost to me, as surely as if Vlad had plucked him from my arms the day he was born. . . .

start, then, with the momen
but begins. I write the
from me the same day as
same day as my life.
monster: Vlad, known
to others as Dracul, wa
moment of my death,
this for you, dear son,
day as your brave moth
my life. For you are the
known to some as Tsepesh,
son of the Devil. Let me
th, for it is then this wa
son, dear Stefan, taken from
taken from me the same
heir of an immortal monste
clus; known to others as
then, with the moment of
gins. I write this for you, de
same day as your brave